Dark Queen

Book 1

Book 1

Published by Krystal Lee Enterprises (KLE Publishing)
Copyright © 2025 by K. Lee All rights reserved. Please send comments and questions:

Krystal Lee Enterprises
770-240-0089 Ext. 1
sales@KLEPub.com

To Reach the Author:
Email: me@authorklee.com or me@drkrystallee.com

Web: www.AuthorKLee.com
Social Handle: AuthorKLee on all pages
FB, IG, Tiktok, Twitter (X), Pinterest, LinkedIn, YouTube

ISBN: **979-8-89987-907-4**

I want to give special thanks to the wonderful people who helped inspire this novel. To my Lord and Savior, Yashua the Christ, thank you! To you, the reader, enjoy a great story.

To my husband, Keane, honey I love you. My children, mommy loves. Jacob, thanks for being a faithful friend and brother.

Wendy, my favorite editor and auntie. I love you and I am so grateful for you!

To my family and friends, you are all in my heart. Shalom.

Book 1

Your New Partner

It was a sunny day, and nothing seemed to be wrong about the day, in the air, or about Charity's life. She was a pretty girl with long curly hair and big, beautiful, brown eyes. Wearing a cute pair of jeans, white tennis shoes, and a blue jean jacket, she walked up to the school doors. Entering, she felt like a princess—not because everyone's eyes were on her, but because anyone who was someone knew her.

She didn't mind standing alone and didn't draw her power from the crowd, though she liked the attention. She went to her locker and was unfazed by the day. Inside her locker were a group of friends. She had Freda, Johnny, and Rachel posted with different emojis. Since they were children, the four of them have been as thick as thieves.

It's halfway through the year, and Charity is excited about going to high school next year. Eighth grade is supposed to be a milestone because it marks the transition between middle and high school. This is when everyone gets to decide who they will become, at least for the immediate future. How serious is middle school, really, to the point that anyone can figure out their lives anyway?

Charity is tapped on the shoulder by Freda and a friend of hers, Carla. The two of them are always together. They act like twins and are close enough to finish each other's sentences. Freda asks, "Hey, girl. So, how was last night?"

Charity closes her locker and replies, "It was boring. The ending was so predictable. If you two think of signing me up for another werewolf or vampire dramedy, count me out."

"Are you even a girl in middle school? No one cares about the movie; it is all about the actors. Asher could have said one word the entire movie, and I still would have watched the entire thing," says Carla.

With a smirk, Freda says, "Right. He is so good-looking with his shirt off. I don't know what else to do with him, but I do like a good chest when I see one." She starts laughing and kidding around. Charity is not really into small talk. She rolls her eyes and says, "If that is all a movie has to do to keep you two involved, don't make any more recommendations for me, hound dogs."

Carla and Freda laugh as the three girls head down the hallway, "What? This is what we are supposed to do. This is middle school, and in about 6 months, we won't be here. You gotta live it up, Charity, and stop being so uptight."

Charity flips her hair and says, "You can speak for yourselves. I ain't trying to be a teen mom because some kid with a nice chest told me I was pretty. Baby, I know that already. Plus, he can't do a dang thing for me that I won't do for myself. You girls can be so predictable. It's pathetic."

"Woo. That was too deep. Nobody said anything about sex, Charity. Chill out. Besides, is it really all that bad? Everybody leaving this school is practically not a virgin. You are like the last one standing," says Freda.

"Speak for yourself. I am still good. Yes, I play around, but I haven't done anything worthy of calling my mother," replies Carla.

"You girls are gross and are going to end up with a disease. There is no way I am going to let any boy ruin my virtue. So he can talk about me on social media or share rumors in the locker room. I'm good. I can't be around them long anyhow; they give me the ick with their hot breath and sweaty armpits. You two can have all of that," replies Charity.

They enter the lunchroom and sit at their table. Moments later, Rachel and Johnny come to the table. The cafeteria is lit with different groups locked into their own worlds. The geeks are doing what they do. The nerds are talking math. The Bible thumpers, or goodie two-shoes, are tucked in the corner reading their Bibles. This is probably the smallest group at school because most students don't practice their religion at school. Only the brave bring their Bibles and risk being criticized or made fun of for their faith.

It's not a big deal what you believe in at this school. There are Christians, Muslims, Jews, Buddhists, Atheists, and tree huggers who believe in everything. Politics and faith really haven't made it into most conversations; they are still kids. The biggest question is about body parts, sex, cussing out teachers among your peers, or what you did last weekend. Crushes in the school are a dime a dozen, but there are only a few good-looking boys who claim most of the girls' hearts. Johnny is one of them.

Johnny is a blond-haired boy with a Spanish background. Looking at him, you would assume he was a white male, but looking at his last name, you would quickly realize he was of Spanish descent. Johnny Alvarez was slightly muscular, taller than most of the boys, and already had a teenager's voice. He was held back a year, so he was really a 9th grader already.

It's rumored that he dated girls in high school, and he wasn't shy about exploring sex and other topics with girls. Charity stayed clear of him in any other capacity than friendship. He was a big flirt but knew when to turn it off with Charity. She would joke and laugh until she felt things weren't funny. The others would eventually follow suit because her eyes and heavy controlling spirit had a way of making everyone agree with her.

Charity wasn't the type of girl who had to have everything her way, although she believed her way was the best way. She was a brat if anyone asked, and she owned the term. She wasn't evil, no, but she was selfish and tried to pretend she didn't see it. She had secrets, but she knew how to keep them.

It is strange to know of a teenage girl who could hold water; she was one of them. She couldn't explain it, but she could look at people and sense things about them. Sometimes, she would see a vision, and other times it would be a knowing she couldn't explain. She wasn't religious and not overly spiritual, so she just called the premonitions good luck. She trusted the voice in her head most of the time, although she wasn't sure of where it would take her.

The bell rings, and the cafeteria breaks up the cliques as each student finds their path, like ants marching to class, they appeared to any onlooker. The hallways from up above always looked like an orchestrated band maneuver during period exchange. Having seven classes doesn't bother Charity; she likes the break in scenery. She is not the smartest in class, but she has the most sass that gets her by when she doesn't know the answers.

Finding a lab partner is not hard because she is popular, but not everyone is smart enough to cut it. There is a girl in the class named Zoe who is somewhat of a Bible thumper and nerd. She is very smart, pretty, smells good, and dresses well. Charity isn't superficial, but all of these things do help; she figures the two of them should pair up and work together. "Hey, you want to be my partner?" says

Charity.

Zoe points to herself and says, "Me?" while her eyes shuffle from side to side. Charity nods yes to confirm her intentions. "Oh, I was going to pick Samantha to be my partner. We always work together."

Charity, not saying another word, turns to Samantha, "Hey Sam, you are going to work with Derek, is that cool?" Samantha was beyond thrilled because she had the biggest crush on him. She smiles and says, "Yeah, I can work with him."

Charity looks at Derek and says, "Derek, go work with Sam." He was going to say something to her, "But I already have–" and Charity puts up her index finger and replies, "Shhhh. Trust me, you will get a better grade, and I think Sam is thirsty for you. What are you gonna do?" He takes back his words and walks over to Sam. Charity looks at Zoe, "Looks like I am your new partner."

"Well, played. So why me?" replies Zoe.

"Because you are smart and have some fashion sense. I want a good grade. You think you can do that?"

"This is a team project, Charity, don't you mean do we want a good grade?"

"Yeah, yeah, I know. But we both can't be the brains. You can be the brains, and I will be your support. Cool?" After careful consideration, Zoe agrees.

If she is honest, she hates working with brainiacs because they start arguing about details and fighting for control. It is far better to have a brain and a person with style to best the grade.

The two of them start working together, and the day flies by; day one of their project is complete. At the sound of the bell, Charity says, "Do you need anything else from me?"

"Not now. But if that changes, I will let you know at lunch," replies Zoe. Zoe had no intention of asking for anything else. She liked to sit with the Bible crew, and she knew that Charity had nothing to do with their table. She had no intentions of making friends with her, just getting the work done. She didn't want to come across as a kid looking to become popular by latching onto Charity. She thought it looked thirsty and came off like another teen movie.

Charity completed class that day and put on her popping pink lip gloss as she left the double doors. She thought the powder-pink color was perfect and made for her. She liked how it looked as the sun touched her lips when she emerged from the school exit doors. When Charity puts her headphones in, she blots out the world around her. The world becomes a secondary world outside her inner thoughts.

She walks past many students who want to give their salutations. She sees her mom, and she speaks very little. The two of them are close, but they both need a moment to warm up to each other before having a conversation. Her mom is on her phone and looking distant, so she doesn't seem to mind the silence that fills the space.

The drive for the first ten minutes is silent as her mother navigates down the road and through the lights. They lived only fifteen minutes from the school, which was a wonderful happenstance. Her mom, Jezebel, finally looks up from her phone. "Honey, take those things out for a second. Tell me, how was your day?"

Charity obliges her mother and removes one earpiece from her ear, "It was great, mother."

"Don't mother me. I'm just asking you about your day."

"I think it gets old to tell you the same thing every day. There are the same people at school, Mom, and nothing is new under the sun."

"Well, I like to ask how my baby is doing. I don't know when the weather might change for you, and I don't want to miss it."

"Whatever that means. I am good. My day was good. You gotta work tonight?"

"Yeah. I got a few things to do. Will you be alright to be home by yourself?"

"Of course. I am used to it."

"Don't say it like that. You make me feel like

I neglect you."

"You don't. It's just the way it is, and I am cool with it."

"I will be back after dinner time, so go ahead and make yourself something. I might just pick up something at the meeting, and I don't want you to wait to eat."

Charity replies, "Sure," as they pull up in the driveway. "You coming in?"

"No, I gotta get going. I already unlocked the door and turned off the alarm. Turn it on when I leave to safe mode."

"Roger, that." Charity enters the quaint brick home. It is the smallest house in a very nice neighborhood. Her mother never told her how she got it, and Charity is somewhat unclear about what her mother does outside of the numerous meetings she attends. She was a little girl when she last attended an event, and she was fine with never returning. She made a fuss, and it was unanimous that she didn't need to come back anytime soon.

She was raised for a little while by her grandmother until she was old enough to take care of herself and not set the house on fire. Funny to think 12 and a half years ago, she was a newborn, and now, she is practically a lady taking care of herself. She didn't have any siblings, so she learned to become self-reliant. Her mother and grandmother were a big voice in her life, and they made sure she knew that men, fathers, and boys didn't have a place in their picture.

She is beyond thrilled for her thirteenth birthday and the loads of fun she will have as she welcomes her transition into her teen years. Her mom usually goes all out for her birthday, and she had pictured this year to be no different. She looks at the portrait of her mom hanging in the hallway and sees why she was born beautiful. Her mother is gorgeous, shapely, with long curly hair. She has the kind of hair that requires a little water, and it coils up to a tight curl that women would pay for.

Charity wonders what life would have been like if her mom had a husband or a man around the house. Maybe she wouldn't be so lonely sometimes, and the echo on the floors as she walked wouldn't seem so loud. Her mother was gorgeous. She often said she wouldn't ruin her body to have another baby. One was enough, and she was born perfect.

Charity lives in a bubble, and she doesn't know the depths of how large the bubble is. Much of this credit is due to her mother, who has carefully crafted the perfect plan to walk Charity into a life that she could only imagine. Her mother saw something in her when she was young that made her dangerous and unpredictable. No matter how much she tried to hide Charity from the other side of her existence, there was something in her veins that would not die.

It was like her father found a way to pierce through the veil she threw over Charity to keep him from her. He was a persistent man, but Jezebel was crafty and devised new maneuvers to maintain just enough distance to keep them disconnected. What Charity didn't know was that the loneliness she felt was created. Her days weren't meant to be alone, but shared with a father who prayed for her nightly. Unaware, she had a family that didn't rest on any day without saying a prayer of protection over her life and future.

It was these prayers that kept the light over Charity, and this light held back the darkness from closing in on her life. This light, this covering, was due to fall in a few months when she turned thirteen. This birthday party was going to be different from all the others, because this would be the first time in her life that her choices would have to be her own. Neither her mother nor her father could stand in the gap for her like they had in times past. It is now time for her to decide what her future will look like on her terms.

She is cooking in the kitchen, and the latest pop song is playing. She stops mid-maneuver as she sees a fair-skinned man with curly hair inside her mind's eye because she knew he wasn't there with her in the kitchen! He had a gentleness about him, and the music she heard in her ears served as a background track to what he wanted to say. He looked her in the eyes as if he knew her, and she was connected to him, although she didn't recognize him.

"Charity. Baby girl, I know you don't know

me, and it is not because I haven't tried. I want to tell you so much, but I cannot. I don't want to scare you, but there is something happening that you need to be warned about."

"Warned about? Who are you?"

"You don't know me, but I was sent, and I just wanted to give you this message. Be careful. Don't trust everything you hear or see. If you can, make your own food and pour your own drinks. Those you think you can trust, you can't. I can't tell you more than that now. I gotta go, but believe me like you have in the past."

The vision cut off, like a TV episode ending abruptly and fading to black. She was quiet, the house was silent, until she heard a beep from the air fryer that nearly sent her phone flying into the air from her being startled. She took a deep breath, grabbed a plate from the cabinet with slightly shaky hands as she tried to process or forget the vision. She knew the voice, although she didn't recall his face. How did this man know her, she thought.

It was hard to move on from the vision, so she ate in silence as she pieced the words back together in her memory. She didn't want to forget something she needed. Something about this vision was different from what she had experienced before. There was a burning in her belly, like a silent alarm was triggered, and she knew it was serious. She ate cautiously as her stomach performed somersaults, trying to determine whether it was hungry or full with each bite.

Her Mother and Her Meeting

Jezebel sits at a table filled with women who are moderately dressed. Her mother is dressed in a white gown-like dress, wearing a gold turban with a snake brooch, holding the patterned fabric together in a fashionable way. She wore gold sandals, bangles, anklets, and hoop earrings. Her skin had a glow like gold dust sprinkled over her, landing in all the right places. She had only a few curls that escaped from under the hat she wore. There was something almost regal to her face and demeanor.

She didn't speak; she only stared at the women at another table who were talking. Something about her movements seems to make the room hush and wait for her next word. She carried a weight that even a stranger could sense being close to her. She opened her mouth to speak, and the women, men, and all others stopped talking to await her escaping breath.

"I know why I am here, but do all of you?" The question didn't require a response. Those looking on did so with quick glances and then shifted their eyes downward. Carol had a way of not letting people look her in the eye. She didn't want anyone to think of using a charm or spell to reach her soul. She knew what was at the bottom of her soul, and she intended to protect it. She was born into this life and intended to preserve her lineage beyond every generation.

"This is the season that we must move quickly, and like every year, we have to have the numbers, the power, to achieve greater heights. Are you all comfortable?" Again, no one responds; she doesn't move, but her eyes seem to hover over the crowd. "I see you all in your fancy houses and cars. The things are nice, but don't let the distractions we use on others work on us. We have an assignment, and we cannot fail. Do you understand that?"

The insidious group replies, "Yes, Lady Mother."

"This meeting is not a social hour. We are here to plan, to strategize on the direction of this coven. You all know my heart on this matter. I know what I am doing, but I also know when the darkness is dawning. There is a shift happening here, and I want my daughter to stand in my place. But I also understand that every person here has the same ambitions. So I know you won't make this easy on her."

The lady shifts in her chair as she moves her delicate arms and shifts the fabric in her dress. "I didn't get to this seat because it was given to me; I got here because I earned it. My daughter is prepared to earn it too. We know what this will require, and she has been committed since her youth to birth the brightest light, to be the sacrifice for the greatest victory. We all want the same things, ladies and gentlemen, to create a world where we are supreme and our use of power, influence, and divination will allow us to lord over all of our subjects."

The room falls even more still. They are awaiting the announcement, "So, now, Jezebel, will rise and be your queen. She will align her household to be the ascending crown for generations to come. She is committed to your growth and dissension into deeper levels of darkness to pull off the move of the century."

She continues, "Money is just paper, houses are merely buildings, but what you really want is power and freedom. We understand how to harness this power and utilize it to our advantage. If you stand with us, everyone in this room will become a general over 200 witches and no less. We can take this city, and it will take us only a generation to do it. Are you interested now?"

The room grows quiet as minds ponder the requests that are soon to follow. Every person in the room had their own agenda for joining the table of the Crown, and no two were the same. They all want to have a lineage that would rise no matter the tide. They each knew the witch at the bottom was the first dead witch, and their goal was to rise to the top or descend to the lowest level undetected to achieve their goals. The risk for the most exposed —the pawns who were disposable —wouldn't weather this storm; they were in the line of fire and greater danger. Conversion to the light, love, change, un-derstanding, and worst, realizing their shame are all possible.

That night, the room extended their oath and commitment to see Jezebel ascend to the throne, knowing they had every intention of taking her place should the moment avail itself. Jezebel, already aware of the disloyalty among witches and thieves, devised a plan that wouldn't fail. She knew the secrets, the weakness of every witch present. She had no depths she wouldn't go to lie, betray, expose, or sacrifice to have what she wants. Her true desire is not for legacy, but for her. She wants beauty, status, power, respect, and everything else she can get with it.

The meeting is adjourned, but Carol calls her daughter to sit. Jezebel knew what would come next, and she loathed the occasion. "Are you certain you are prepared for this?"

"Mom, I have been waiting to do this my whole life. I know my role. I know my legacy and my oath."

"Does Charity? Do you think he will stop now? He has pulled me for years and waxed me sore. If it weren't for the others, I might not be here. She has to be on our side," inquires her mother.

"She will. She just needs to hear us out. She needs to be the right age because we cannot touch her, and you know this. Nothing we ever tried to do would work, and her birthday changes all of that. This is what we have been waiting for," replies Jezebel.

With a powerful laugh, she says, "What about you? Are you committed to this?"

"I am," says Jezebel comfortably.

"Don't waste my time, Jezebel. You are not the only witch I can use to get this done." For the first time, she sits back in her chair after she speaks. Her energy appears to be fading somewhat. A woman who seemed to have all power is shrinking back.

Jezebel leans forward and assures her mother, "I know, Mother, don't threaten me. You don't have to. We are on the same page, and I know my role. Soon, Charity will, too. She doesn't have to understand it, or believe, for this to work."

After she watches her daughter's eyes, she is satisfied with what she sees. She nods and says, "Good. We are depending on you. Don't embarrass me, like you did before. We don't have time for you to pick another screw up."

Leaning her head down, Jezebel flicks her hair and responds calmly, though she wants to snap back and says, "Mom, that was a long time ago, and it worked to our favor."

"It nearly killed me, Jezebel," Carol retorts.

"I will never put you at risk again. You have my word," replied Jezebel.

"As good as a witch's word is," she replies unmoved.

With a firm face, Jezebel replies, "It is enough."

Back at home

Charity lies on her bed, wrapped up in her covers. She likes to feel the blankets snuggled up against her skin; it helps her not to feel alone. Something about the night seemed colder than normal. The sky felt darker, and as she looked at the moon, it seemed to shine brighter. She lay there awake for an hour before drifting to sleep.

A Hunt
For Love

Jezebel gets inside and looks around the dark house. The house still feels like him sometimes, no matter what she tries to do to erase him. He keeps coming back. She places a bowl of oil near every door in the house, thinking it would push away his spirit. Every time she tries to bind him, he finds a new way to get in. He is exhausting, and the work she has to do —she knows —he is to blame.

Her mom was never a loving mother to her. She was always the lady in the white dress who slithered around igniting orders that would set lives ablaze. No matter how much Jezebel wanted to defy her and prove she could be her own person, she had to crawl back to her mother.

Charity's father is a classic example of why she is fit to rule, she feels. Even at a young age, when she had every reason to fail because of her choices, things turned in her favor to be better and better. She believed this circumstance would be no differ-ent.

Jezebel was a lot like Charity when she was younger. Strong, beautiful, confident, and bold. She had a desire to be somebody, not in a magical sense, but in a real sense. She wanted to be a lawyer, doctor, or something important. Her mother never allowed her to see the light that could be within her. She kept pointing to the darkness; she wanted to rise to the surface. She banked on Jezebel walking in her stead, and she never considered what she wanted for her life.

Carol needed Jezebel to be the last light she would have before she ascended. Carol, although she looked young, was nearly 120 years old. She was growing tired of her circle, and if Jezebel had done everything right years ago, she would have already gotten the body she longed to have. Jezebel fought her mother over what she wanted for her life, and all of her relationships ended prematurely because of her mother.

She was forced to play a game that felt like Russian roulette with her romantic life. Her mother would select the man and test him to see if he could hang around or prove useful. When he failed, he would be dismissed, and she never saw him again. She was a pawn in her mother's hands. She was a vessel that she used like an offering to get what she wanted, no matter the expense. She never felt bonded to her mother, so she secretly longed for a baby of her own, so she could become something she had never been —a mother.

Jezebel grew tired of entertaining the men

of her mother's choosing. She wanted to feel love like the other girls did. She wanted to be special and picked because of who she was, and not whatever demented plan or concocted game her mother drew up to gain power. She wanted what she saw in the movies and longed to feel love. It never occurred to her that the essence or root of love is a God-of-heaven concept. She saw love as an expression that anyone could have and share. Even the most vile of people, she thought, could experience love.

The hunger for love must have been on her face because she had men throwing themselves at her left and right. Contrary to popular opinion, and what her looks, clothes, and forever license say, she is forty years old. She doesn't look a day over thirty, and on her best day, twenty-eight. She didn't want her beauty to be wasted on men who didn't deserve what she could bring to the table. She was gorgeous, but also thoughtful, headstrong, and powerful, and she wanted to share that — herself — with someone else.

She couldn't tell her mother her plans; she knew that she would disapprove. She had to find a way to hide this from her by first hiding it from herself. Carol had a way of reading people, and Jezebel knew she stood no chance if she looked her in the eyes to deny her heart's intention. So she averted her eyes. She would look at the floor or purposefully get distracted to keep her secret.

One day, she was running errands, working for a flower shop where she sold herbs and crystals.

I know, a bit of a cliche, but the money is good on social media. She doesn't sell rocks, but she creates jewelry and engraves symbols in the stones to help people achieve what they want out of life. She thought it was roughly harmless since it wasn't a beacon or portal but merely a trinket that flirted with the occult.

She doesn't actually have customers come into the store because most shop online. She considered herself a white witch at the time because she participated in nothing dark. She was a white witch when she was in her late teens and early twenties. When he walked in, Curtis, the air seemed to leave the room. Her mind felt foggy, and her voice shook a little bit when she spoke, "Can I help you?"

He looked her in her eyes, and his warm brown eyes disarmed her. He replied to her with a smile and a voice that brought air back into the room, "I was looking for something to give to my mother. Her birthday is coming up, and I wanted to do something nice for her. I hear that you make jewelry?"

Her voice is full-bodied as she speaks, "I do make jewelry, with all kinds of designs. Do you know what she likes?"

He smiles and gently replies, "She likes gold. Nothing flashy. Something simple. She is a simple lady."

"Okay, I can give you something simple. When were you wanting something made by?"

"I was thinking in a few days. She is planning to head out of town, and I want to have it to give to her before then."

"Oh, I see," replies Jezebel with hesitation.

"Is that a problem?" He asked in a boyish tone leaking with boyish charm. He was used to asking the right questions accompanied by the right tone to get his way. Jezebel was warmed by him but tried to remain steadfast.

"Well, I am booked for the next few days, and I don't think I can get this done in that time. I would hate to slow you up."

"I really was hoping you would say yes. I heard you were the best, and I need something that is…special. My mom is picky, and for what I need, I really do need your help."

"I can try, but can't make any promises," Jezebel replies in more of a matter-of-fact tone. She was professional when it came to her business and the promises she made. She knew her workload was a lot and had no idea what her mom had planned for her time.

"Why don't I take you to dinner and show you why I need this. I am sure that after you see what I show you, you will jump at the chance to help me. Can you meet me tonight at, say, 7:00?"

"I don't know. I have a lot to do."

"Just tell whoever you need a few more days, and all will be well. This won't take you long, right? You are a professional. We can get a bite to eat, maybe go dancing. Just have a good time."

She ponders the thought, and she is on the verge of saying no. Then, he touches her hand and urges her to come with him, and the only answer she could formulate to come out of her mouth is, "Yes. Okay. I will make it work."

He is excited but still reserved as he says, "You will have a good time with me." Something about his words and his touch made her know he wasn't lying. His aura and smile lingered in the air as he left. She wanted him to stay, although she was unsure of what he would do. She didn't expect him to sit around and watch her work, but she also wanted to be in his presence longer. She thought about him for several more seconds before the weight of what to tell her mother crept into her mind.

She was a young adult, but her mother kept a tight leash on her time. She was grateful for the flower shop because it allowed her a place to breathe. She went back to work with a smile on her face, floating in and out of her thoughts of what their date might be like together. She wanted the day to hurry along, and it did. She phoned her mom and thought carefully about her words. She knew her mom could smell a lie from a mile away, so she told her the truth at 6:30pm.

"Mom, I still have a lot of work to do. Can I stay at the shop until about 9?"

"Nine? I really wanted you to meet someone for me this evening."

"I can do it tomorrow, I just have to get a few pieces made, and I fear I would get behind and won't have a clear schedule this weekend either. I've been going to a lot of meetings and not having much time."

"That's fair. I know I have been putting a lot of pressure on you lately. I have plans for you. But what I am planning, we will need some money first, anyhow. Let me work on what I gotta do, and I will come get you at 9."

"I drove, so I can get back. It's really not a problem, Mom." There was a slight hesitation on the line. The silence made fear creep up in Jezebel's gut. Not missing a beat, Carol replies, "Is there something you want to tell me?"

"No, Mom, of course not." She was nervous, and the only thing keeping her calm was Curtis's face. His face felt like warm sunshine, and she just had to see it again. She prayed that her longing didn't appear through the phone, and it looked as if it hadn't because her mother agreed to butt out of her life for an evening.

She wondered, is this what love could feel like? Feeling this swooning feeling that makes you feel like you are gently moving around in water. The shift of the water isn't abrasive, rough, or jarring. Jezebel was feeling something that she had never felt before. Could it be hope?

Coming to the shop, she didn't have many options for what to wear. She could wear what she wore to work. Or b, wear what she kept in a closet for a rainy day. She never knew when she had to hop to something with no time to spare, so she kept a black dress that might be over the top for the circumstance, but what other choice did she have? To show up in the same thing he saw her wearing mere hours ago didn't seem like the right play.

As she put on the dress, something zinged through her body, and she wanted the feeling to remain. She wanted this euphoric feeling of butterflies swarming in a beautiful dance to keep playing to the music only she could hear in her soul. She wanted to believe this was a date, although it was more like a bargaining chip for him to get something from her; for today, she was alright with it. She wanted to treat today like a fairytale in case the vision was never meant to reappear.

She drove to the venue, and the ride was uneventful. She hit a pothole that nearly sent her into the opposite lane of traffic, but all the hairs are still on her head, and she is wide awake now, if she thought of drifting to sleep. Nothing like a near-death experience to wake you up as the moon chases the stars in the sky. I don't know why the night sky seemed to grow darker than night, and paint the perfect landscape for the light of the street lights to kiss the moon.

She pulled into the parking lot and parked. She thought on whether she should come in right away, or make him wait a while since he did want something from her. This whole time, she was thinking about her feelings and emotions, and not planning as much as she does for his next move. What will he tell her at the dinner table that will help her understand the necessity for his rush order?

Jezebel pondered this as she exited the car and entered the restaurant. The low-lit space was perfect for her to tuck away in a corner, hoping not to be seen by her mother. She hid her face behind a menu and gave no second thought to his recognizing her in the dimly lit section. She flipped the page of her menu and saw the bright yellow hand that waved its way into her heart earlier that day.

She watched enough movies to have an idea of what love at first sight could look like, and she thought this time was surely as close as she had ever come to the real thing. He smiled and said, "I pray I didn't keep you waiting too long?"

Jezebel, taking in the cologne he was wearing, intoxicated replies, "No, not at all. I was curious, so I read a bit ahead. I trust you don't mind?"

"Not at all." He takes a seat and leans close to her. "I am sorry, but I must ask, can you stand up for me?" Not knowing the reason, Jezebel looked slightly puzzled but not offended.

She replies, "Excuse me?"

"I just have a hunch, and I need to see if I am correct. Stand up real quick, this will only take a moment." Jezebel, on cue, stands up, and she could feel his eyes eating up the dress she was wearing. She had never second-guessed her outfit before, but in a moment, he had her mind racing. He replies, "Can you turn for me?"

"Are you serious? All this for a piece of jewelry?" Without a word, he simply replies, "Shh-hh. Trust me." She turns to his behest and sits down without another care. He pauses for a moment and says, "What a lovely black dress. You look to be a size 5, size 7 in shoes, gorgeous brown eyes, and gold eye shadow is subtle and elegant. Your blush, powder brown with a bronze highlighter, makes your skin look flawless. You, you are fit to be a queen!"

Understanding Curtis's smooth, sultry tone, she admires his observations and is not offended. He continues, "You, without a shadow of a doubt, are the finest woman in here. Even in low light, you shine. I didn't mean to change our conversation, but I could not ignore your beauty or downplay how you have captivated me."

She is a bit surprised —not by his words, but by his boldness and debonair presence. He was a gentleman, his words soft, feeling like a satin sheet rubbing across your chin. You can't help but smile and welcome the snuggle you want to feel; the warmth and allure cannot be explained. How could Jezebel be so captivated when he hadn't done anything outside of the ordinary? What had her so charged to get to know this mystery man asking her for a favor?

She gently pulled her head out of the clouds as she replied, "You have a way with words. Do you tell all the ladies that?"

His boyish charm went into overdrive as he joked and flirted with the idea of him being a Playboy. "No, no. That's not my thing. I am best in small doses, so one woman is good enough for me. I am an intense person and very picky. I like the best, which is why I came to you."

"Really?"

"Yes, I have been looking to have a special piece created for my mom for her birthday. It's this weekend, and I need a bit more than jewelry if you follow what I'm saying?"

"You want enchantment?"

"I need her to love it, and for it to solve a problem I am having," he replies.

"You are in trouble?"

"Not exactly. You see, I am a very wealthy man, but right now, my wealth is held by my mother. My great-grandfather and family were some wealthy French people who came to this country to build. They wanted a legacy, but they had to make partnerships."

The waiter came over and apologized for disrupting their conversation. "I'm sorry to bother you two. But if I didn't come over here right now, my boss was going to give me the evil eye. I am new, and I am supposed to greet a table within 5 minutes. I've been waiting for a break in your conversation so I didn't disturb you. "

Curtis replies, "No, not at all. Thanks for coming…"

"Oh, Natalie. Sorry, my name is Natalie, and welcome to Alabaster," replied the waiter.

"Thank you, Natalie. I will have a brandy, top shelf, and the lady would have–do you mind if I order something for you?"

"No, I usually don't drink, though," Jezebel replies.

"She will have an amaretto sour to start. Thank you." The server thanks him for the order and whisks away. Not missing a beat, "You will love the drink. It is light and tastes more like candy than anything. My sister loves those things. She reminds me of you."

"She does?"

"Yeah, she's short, sweet, and observes more than she speaks. She is pretty and smart, like you."

"That's how you see me?"

"Until you prove me wrong," he replies. Jezebel doesn't say anything else. She is normally a watcher, and today, she is paying special attention.

Curtis, in an attempt to recapture the moment, says, "I was speaking about my roots. My family is predominantly French and African American by marriage. We have some other stuff, but that isn't important now."

He looks at her more seriously than before and says, "What I wanted to talk to you about is my mother. She is a holy roller, and she loves God. I respect that, but I am not a believer in what she's got going on. She is a really wealthy lady, I mean loaded, and she has a check with my name on it that is to be passed down to me from her side of the family. I am not wishing her dead, I just need her to be agreeable."

Inquisitively, she says, "So you know what I do?"

"I have heard some things, but I am not sure of the depth. However, if you can create a charm or something similar, it may make her more receptive to my suggestions. I want to do some things for myself, and I need my money to do it. I am not stealing or seeking to harm anybody, but I have a mind. I got plans, and I intend on doing them all. Can you help me–will you help me?"

She pauses to think as the waiter comes back with their drinks. She appreciates the break in tension and struggle. She is excited to have a break. She thinks nothing about this seems unusual compared to what most people ask her for. They all come to her wanting money, power, or love. He was no different, but something about his eyes —his intensity —captivated her.

She couldn't resist him; she got her drink and said, "Should we have a toast real quick?"

"What shall we toast to?" replied Curtis.

"New beginnings, and a future of our choosing," replied Jezebel as she sips her drink and feels the coolness running down her throat. This magic, she wants to last, and she starts to envision what he could offer her if he were to inherit money. With a clearer head, she replies, "So if I help you get what you want, what do you plan on giving to me? I have goals and plans I want to see come to pass, too."

"Okay. So you are a businesswoman. Don't you have a flat fee for your pieces?"

"Depends on what you want to accomplish. But I will say it is relative. How much money do you stand to gain?"

He smiles and replies, "You know I won't tell. But I will tell you this, it's more than a million. I need you to do what you do, and don't tell me what that will be; I will just let you know when it is done," he says with a smile.

"I expect my money in full and a bonus after. I want $10,000," Jezebel says with a warm smile.

"Wow, that is a steep price, don't you think, for a necklace or something?"

"You want it to work, don't you? Ten thousand is a drop in a bucket if you stand to make more than a million. Don't you think one percent is the least you can do to thank me? That, of course, is a deposit. I think five percent would be an ideal figure to settle on. If you are good with that, we can shake on it."

Jezebel reaches her hand out, and Curtis gently kisses the top of her hand. "It's a deal, beautiful. I am at your disposal. Just tell me what you need." Jezebel smiles because, for the first time, she feels like she is in the driver's seat of her life. Fifty thousand dollars can change her life and give her a chance at a life of her choosing. But what would she do? Where would she choose to live if her mother couldn't control her anymore?

The excitement about the change of scenery was enough for her to meditate on for the rest of the dinner in between glimpses of Curtis's smiles, laughs, and good conversation. She couldn't help but recognize that he was attractive, smart, seemingly kind, and a go-getter. He was the type of man she would choose, if she had a choice about that, too. Just maybe when this is all over, more could be between the two of them, she thought.

The night wasn't an all-nighter because Jezebel knew she had to get home and get to work. She needed to do some research on what this piece needed to have to do the trick. She knew the hedge that was around the mother, so a simple spell wouldn't do. She needed something deep, someone close enough, to disrupt or distract her. But who?

Clearly, she wasn't close enough to her son for him to have an incredible impact. She also needed him to be untouched to be sure she got her money. She would only touch Curtis if he turned his back on her, but for now, they are partners of sorts. She went home to find the right cluster of spells because she couldn't add just one. Her mother asked about her evening, and she didn't divulge any details beyond the fact that she had made progress and had lots of work to do.

Her mother allowed her to work in peace as she busied herself with the next scheme to get money. Her mother was good at what she did, but she started to leave the little things to her daughter. Local requests for love, small money, and family problems, she no longer dealt with. She wanted the big bucks, so she chased larger fish and those who had political seats who were in desperate need of a favor from the dark side.

Her mother had a lot of secrets, and they were intentional. She told Jezebel enough to make her suitable for her ambitions. Carol had been shamefully grooming her since her birth for a sinister plan she was unaware of at the time. Her grip was tight, not because she cared about Jezebel's future, but her own preservation. She was approaching 120 and knew her body was on the way down.

She looked great on the outside because she knew enough magic to keep her looking 60 years old, a good-looking and desirable 60-year-old, of course. She had no intention of ending her life at the ripe age of 120, she wanted to keep living, even if that meant snatching bodies and transferring her spirit to someone else.

But for a great triumph like this, not just anybody would do. Carol was specific, picky, and she wanted a body that would be built and empowered like how she was to continue another 120 years. She wanted the beauty, the power, and for the body to have the bloodline of her choosing. She wanted to be completely consumed in the body she would take. For a spell like this, she needed a willing participant with enough light, or the spell would be short-lived, and she would die.

She wasn't trying to get a body all ready for her to only get another twenty or thirty years; she wanted another full lifetime to live her days how she wanted. When she was younger, she didn't have the power or the wealth she stands to make as her spells and contracts mature. They are all banking on her being dead, but she has already outsmarted them and has been using Jezebel's body as her own for years.

While Jezebel is worried about Carol controlling her life, she is unaware that Carol plans to take over her life, and day by day, she plots how she will achieve the most power in her transfer. The difference between a witch and a white witch is that a white witch is blind to the hell they bring. They believe there is still good in the world, and that makes them perfect targets for witches who have been sold out, to possess them and use them for their will.

Carol cares for herself and her desires; she is not a blind witch, but sold out to her agenda. Her pregnancy with Jezebel was planned. She selected the man she thought would be a good match for carrying out her objectives. She selected a man from Louisiana, a Creole man, African American, French, and Native American. This cluster of people is known for their roots in voodoo, beauty, and spiritual know-how. She wanted this girl to be a dark queen, one fit to carry on her legacy and be her incarnation.

The plot thickens as the two women hunt for the love they both hope to find. Jezebel wants to find the love of her life, but stumbles upon a chance at freedom. Carol wants another chance at life and to enjoy the men she likes, the food, the travel, and to live her years collecting on blood oaths that will have her living lavishly until her next embodiment of an unexpected soul.

A Mother
On A Mission

The ladies are on a mission, and long nights for Jezebel are becoming the norm as she pours herself over books. Carol watches from a distance, and she likes her progress. She could have quickly done the job, but she wants the body to have source memory so that she wouldn't have to teach it.

The more intuition she built in Jezebel, the more she could pull on the power from both her, her mothers, her grandmother, and Jezebel's father. Jezebel, with her book, she could connect with their source powers, but she struggled to strengthen her bonds. Her mother had no intentions of teaching her, but she would master the gift when she took over.

The week seemed to fly by as Curtis waited for his prize piece of jewelry that would release a butt load of wealth into his hands. He was excited, almost salivating at what all he would do with the money. He wanted to travel, buy some toys, and enjoy some money before he got serious. Paying the down payment for what Jezebel wanted was pennies he could afford with the petty cash he got. He was due to acquire nearly 50 million when he got control of the family trust.

He phoned Jezebel and asked about the piece. She told him, "You can come and get it. I think it will work out great." Without a slight hesitation, he drove to the shop and looked over the piece. It was a sapphire, beautifully adorned in his mother's favorite color, pink. He picked it up and asked, "How did you know?"

"I do my research. Do you like it?" He continues to look at the ring, but before he could touch it she says, "Wait! Don't touch it. It is enchanted. Whoever touches this ring will have an experience; they won't die, but it will send visions and dreams, tormenting the soul until they find the source. I doubt she would ever assume a ring from her dear son would be the culprit for her pain or brain fog."

"So, it won't kill her, right?"

"No, a season saint like your mother will be fine. She will pray to soothe her condition and symptoms, and that will buy us time. It could buy us years."

"And if it doesn't work?"

"I will have to implement plan B, and that you may not like. So I won't tell you, but just know your mother will be in good hands and you will have your money."

"Woe, you are not going to kidnap her and hold her for ransom, are you?"

"No, we use magic, not meat heads. Get out of her, take your ring, and call me when you get your money," replied Jezebel.

"You will be my first call. Thank you, beautiful." He takes the box and heads out the door. He is grinning as if the sun is shining differently on his face. No matter the weather, it is the perfect day in his heart. He drives his car to his unexpected mother and presents her with a gift in an elaborate attempt to impress. She sees the pink sapphire encased in rose gold and loves it.

The dual-purpose engraved lettering on the inside of the ring makes her feel the piece was specially made for her —and it was. She touches the ring, removing it from the box. She tries it on several fingers, but she can't get it to fit. The ring is too small to fit past her knuckles. She pouts about the misunderstanding, and Curtis offers to get the ring resized.

"No, no. I don't want you going through that kind of trouble," she tells her son. "Maybe my fingers are a little bit swollen. I changed my medicine, and in a few weeks, I will be able to sort it all out and wear it. I got a cruise coming up, and it will be perfect on my finger!" Curtis hesitantly agrees to allow her to keep it. He knows this means his plan will be months away instead of days or weeks.

There was another problem: he had already

spent the rest of his petty cash last night visiting a favorite dancer. She was cunning and knew how to stroke his ego strongly enough to make him feel like a boss, even though he was on borrowed time. He didn't want to wait months for the ring to have a chance to get his money; he needed to speed up the time, but what could he do to make that happen now?

He needed a favor; he had to go to Jezebel and get her to go with plan B, or at least give him something else to try. He wondered what that would cost him since he didn't have money until his next deposit. It is laughable to hear of a rich, broke man, but at the moment, it was the truth. He went back to the shop a few days later and saw Jezebel busy working.

"Hey, beautiful," he said as he entered the store with his cologne, making the announcement of his arrival. Jezebel looks up from her piece and replies, "Back soon. It worked in a day?"

"No, unfortunately not. The ring was too small. Her hands are swollen because she is on meds that cause the swelling as a side effect. There is nothing we can do about that until she transitions to medicine in a few weeks. But you know I can't wait that long. I need some money now."

"Okay, what were you thinking of doing?"

"You mention plan B."

"Plan B is very risky, and I didn't want to do

it, unless you were sure the ring wouldn't work."

"I am sure it would take too long."

"Alright, give me until tomorrow to put it in play. But it will cost you some more money. You paid for one spell, not two."

"Look, I think we both could stand to make a lot of money when this happens. What if I doubled your money?"

"That sounds cool, but what if you burn me? I can't assume you are going to pay me without me having to chase you."

"You think I would do you dirty? Aren't you the one with magic whom I should fear?"

"That is true, but what is my collateral?"

"I got a house. I could quickly deed it to you. It would be a deposit towards my balance."

"I want the house and the full balance."

"Really? That is like quadrupling the cost?"

"How bad do you want your money?"

"You are a hard bargain."

"I just know what I want."

"Deal. When will I see it happen?"

"Tonight."

"Tonight?"

"Yeah, you give me the deed, and it will be done tonight." Jezebel came across some books, but she also let her intuition take over to show her how to make a spell that will bind, monitor, and manipulate the day visions of a person. It will bring them to temporary insanity, to where his mother would be placed under supervision, and in a mental condition like this, she would have to release her authority over the trust to her son, the next of kin.

She had it all planned out. This tasty baked cookie would be irresistible. Eye-catching, pretty, and baked to perfection. She waited for her deed that would come to her before she closed for the day. She gave him a time in the morning to pick up the cookie, and he was shocked that something so unassuming would be the source to transform both of their lives.

He carefully brought the cookie home to his mother, but she was sleeping. He left her a cute note and told her to have a sweet treat on him. He thanked her for all she did for him and shared how much he loved her. The letter had to be sweet and enticing like the cookie. He had to go out because he was meeting up with a lady friend, who he knew would give him some. He was the biggest hoe, and he and money were the last thing his mother planned on combining.

She knew he would be the ruin of the family

unchecked, so she had always planned to give the money to her daughter to care for. Her daughter was not a practicing Christian, didn't believe in God as of late, and she was more into being open to what the universe would tell her to believe for the moment than God. She called it freedom, but her mother saw it as hell in disguise.

Her daughter was smart, funny, and full of life. She enjoyed working and bossing people around, especially her baby brother. She came to check on her mother because they were going to head out for dessert. She was a sucker for her sweet tooth. Seeing the package on the table with a single cookie, she thought to eat the cookie and replace it with something from the restaurant.

She knew her brother was a suck-up, and the letter he wrote was enough for her to suck her cheek and sink her teeth deep into the succulent cookie. It tasted just as good as it looked. She thought it was small, so her plans for dessert were not canceled. She came to her mother's room and knocked.

Courtney was wearing a comfortable suit and a light colored blouse. She is the type of lady who wears a suit to any event, so she is always ready to close a deal. She recently launched a software company that uses AI to help banks operate more fluidly and comply with new laws. If she didn't inherit a dime, she planned on being very wealthy either way. Her eyes weren't on the trust because she trusted in her own degree, education, and special gifts. She was nothing like her brother.

Her mother answered the door, stumbling a bit as she walked. "Man, I needed that nap. It was a long day at church, and I had to lay this body down," replied Cassandra, her mother.

"I understand. I remember when we had to be in church for fifty-eleven hours. Sleep couldn't come fast enough." Courtney and her mother share a laugh before Cassandra goes into the bathroom to freshen up. In the bathroom, Cassandra calls out to her, "So where are we going anyway?"

"It's a surprise, Mom. I cannot tell you. But you will love it. Your big-headed son left you a cookie that I ate."

"Now, why would you do that if he left it for me?"

"Because where we are going is better than that little bite-sized cookie he tried to give you. Ooh! Do you mind if I wear that pink sapphire he got for you? I feel like my hands look plain," she says as she looks down at her bare fingers. She starts rummaging through her mother's things to find it.

"Alright now, I want what your brother got for me. I don't want him thinking I don't like it."

"But for real, you like it that much?"

"I mean, it is the thought that counts. At least it is not a common blue sapphire; I would be less impressed. Pink is my favorite color, so there was some thought to it."

"If you say so. With all the money he blows on strippers, he could have given you a huge diamond rock that would really shut the streets down."

"I don't complain about what you two do with your money. It is none of my business. You invest it, but he will have to figure out his life at some point. He will come around. I am still praying about him and believing for it."

"You keep that hope alive, Mom, but I see my brother for what he is. A mooch, and sex fiend."

"Easy. We all got a past, Courtney. There ain't nothing too hard for God," she replies with a smile filled with hope.

"I don't believe that, but if I did, I think my brother would give him a run for his money."

"Girl, hush. Don't talk like that. You know we don't do that. We don't disrespect God even if we don't serve him."

"I told you, religion is for poor people and those who don't have a good head on their shoulders. I am not either."

"We are blessed, but Yahweh gave us that, and you remember that. I don't take a day for granted. Money comes and things come and go, but favor from God is irreplaceable. Keep living and you will find out real quick that money ain't everything."

"Let's go eat. I am hungry," replies Courtney making light of her mother's statement. The two head out of the house and go to a nice, brightly lit restaurant with jazz music playing. The view is breathtaking as they look out at the lake and enjoy desserts and lemonade. Courtney's drink is spiked, and they talk about her plans. Courtney seemed to have her whole life figured out, except for when she would get married and have children. Her grandmother feared she would never have children the way she was headed.

Cassandra was silent and smiled on cue when she talked about her plans with big eyes and language her mother knew nothing about. She was not tech-savvy, but old-school. She still wrote checks if she could because she liked paper. What she never told her children was that if her daughter didn't need her money, she would likely give her money to her eldest grandchild to manage because she didn't trust her son in the least bit.

The plan seemed like a good one, except neither of her children appeared to want or be in a position to have a child. The night carried on, and the pair had an almost uneventful drive home. On the road growing dark as the sun tucks away, it was harder for Courtney to see the street lights. She didn't speak about the daze at first because she thought she could have dirty headlights.

She turned on the washers and blades to clear the path, but she saw a flying bird heading to the window seal and pushed on the brakes. Her and her mother jerked forward at the stop, and Cassandra looked at her daughter, "Courtney. Are you okay to drive?"

In a snap and slightly frustrated tone, she replied, "Mom, of course I am sober. I only had one lemon drop, and that wasn't strong, but a high-priced, watered-down drink. It ain't do anything. You didn't just see that bird?"

"What bird, Courtney?"

"I just saw a bird heading straight for the window, and I panicked, so I put my foot on the brakes. I saw it switch directions just before hitting the window." Courtney was confident in her reply. Cassandra wondered if the bird flew in their direction, and she missed it by looking out the window. She's never seen Courtney make a bad judgment call while driving; she was super safe because she wasn't trying to tear up her 5 Series BMW coup.

The two think it is just a misunderstanding, similar to seeing and hearing the windshield wipers scrub the window. Cassandra said nothing because Courtney can get pushy when she thinks she is right. They arrive at the front yard, and the ladies exit the vehicle. Courtney thinks to walk her mother to the door, and as she unlocks her door, Courtney ducks down and puts her hands over her head. She is looking up at the sky as if something is swarming over her head or that she is a target of a bird poop dropping, maybe her mother doesn't see.

Cassandra is unaware of the silent battle Courtney is facing on the front porch. She enters her house, and Courtney thinks of staying briefly. She mentions that she is tired and will head home, but Cassandra suggests that she stay a while longer and take a nap on the couch. She agrees because at this point she has a roaring headache and wonders if she didn't eat enough before drinking, or her sugar dropped, and she doesn't know it.

She enters the living room and takes a large step to the right. Cassandra, looking on, says, "Did you see a spider web or something?"

"I'm not sure what it was. I think my sleepiness is playing tricks on me. I am just going to lie down and see how I feel when I get up," replies Courtney.

"Okay, if you need something, I am here." Cassandra shuts off the parlor doors and allows Courtney to rest in peace. She's not certain if she was drunk, but she knew that Courtney was in no condition to drive. She took a moment and said a silent prayer, "Father, thank you for getting us home safely and for us having a good time. Please keep my son safe. I know he's out there doing no good, and he needs your mercy. Thanks for keeping us all, Father."

Her prayers were always short and sweet. She and her God go way back, and she knows through the power of her own testimony what God can do. Growing up in a Creole family in Louisiana, you see and hear things that make you believe in God. She saw a ghost walking in her first home when she was a child. Uncertain of what to do, she called on "Jesus," and she didn't see that ghost anymore.

From that moment forward, she promised herself that she would always call on the name of Jesus and make an intention to include him in her life. She didn't have parents who went to church. She was the first and the only in her family to embrace her faith and walk with God in every aspect of her life since she was a young girl, about twelve.

Although Courtney tried to rest on the couch, she couldn't get comfortable. She tried closing her eyes, and when she did, it felt like her heart was going to beat out of her chest. When she thought to stand, it felt like the ceiling was swirling. She felt sick if she lay down, and she felt worse as she stood up. She didn't know what to do about the pain, so she asked her mother to call the hospital for her.

Cassandra looked at her and replied, "You sure you don't want me to just drive you there?"

"Mom, I don't know how I feel, and I don't want whatever this is to get worse. I think I'd better just sit here and let them come to me. I don't feel like anything is wrong, but I also don't feel right."

"You think you could have gotten food poisoning from the restaurant, or eaten something spoiled?" Courtney asked herself the question, "Why do black mothers think they can solve everything with no medical degree?" Courtney was in pain and didn't feel like explaining her symptoms or the source of her pain, because if she was honest, she didn't know where it was either.

As she sat on the couch, lying down made

her discomfort worse, so she was forced to remain awake. She started to scratch her right arm, although she didn't recall being bitten by a mosquito. Her mother offered to put rubbing alcohol on it in case it was a bite to relieve the itch. Although the solution worked for a little while, it did not fully go away, but seemed to get worse.

The Hornet's Nest

Still half asleep, she answers the phone. "Hello, Curtis. Did you mean to call me? It's 3 am?"

"Yes, I am not sure what to do, Jezebel. You said this wasn't going to hurt anybody. Now, my mom and sister are at the hospital. "

"No, I said no one will die, Curtis. Of course, when people get sick and don't know why, they go to the hospital. Try to get some rest, I am sure everything will be fine."

Curtis, a bit annoyed or scared, replies, "Are you stupid or still asleep? I can't do this. Just stop whatever this is."

"It doesn't work like that. Once it begins, it can't be reversed."

"What did you do?"

"What you asked me to do. Look, I am tired, and I have to go."

"Please, please, don't leave me. Don't leave me like this. I am–I am scared, and I really don't want to be alone. Can you just stay with me?" His breath lingers on the phone as he awaits a response from Jezebel. She is not quick to answer him, but weighs her commitment and involvement in this situation. She agrees hesitantly to stay up with him and do what she can to ease his fears.

"Thank you. This is, this is really intense, you know? I don't know why I thought this was gonna be like in the movies, when people take a pill and fall in love, or say, "Yes, I will do this or that." Almost like hypnosis. I–I just wasn't expecting all of this."

"This is magic; we don't always know how these things will turn out. We bank on the results of what we want to happen." She takes a deep breath and then says, "Just take a deep breath. It's okay to feel the way you do." He starts to relax and lets the comforting words ease his troubled spirit. The anxiety is not entirely gone, nor is his guilt. He is being patient as he unscrambles his thoughts, but it isn't easy.

"Thank you for doing this for me. I really needed to talk to someone to clear my head. This is helping."

Jezebel replies tenderly, "Yeah, of course. Try to relax and be natural. Let me know what happens in the next hour. I am sure your mother will call and give you an update that won't put you on edge."

He nods his head and agrees to wait for the

call. He wants to take a drink but fears he will miss the call, so he turns on the tv to try to escape, as he sits and waits. There are several hospitals within a fifteen-minute radius, and with his fragile frame of mind, he preferred the unknown silence. He sat there for nearly an hour, drifting off to sleep, when he got a call from an unknown number.

He answers the phone, "Hello?"

On the other end is his mother, "Curtis, I am at the hospital with your sister. I am sorry I didn't see earlier that my phone had no reception." Trying to play it cool, he replies without thinking and exposes his fear, "Where are you?"

"I just told you, I'm at the hospital with your sister, Curtis. We think she might have gotten food poisoning. I think we ruled out an allergic reaction at this point. She has to feel like a pincushion right about now. They are going to start her morphine drip soon to help her cope with the pain she feels."

"Man, it's that bad?"

"Yeah, for her it is. They haven't said anything terrible that makes me alarmed. I just hate hospitals, I think. Prayerfully, we will be heading home soon."

"Okay, Mom. Just keep me posted on what I should do to help."

"As of right now, just don't worry. We are gonna be fine. I just didn't want you to panic coming home and not seeing me there." The two continue a friendly conversation filled with stress, concern, and uncertainty. They both want to be strong for the other, and it feels like a knife through the belly to hear the pain in his mother's voice. He was grateful that she wasn't the one in pain, but he was struggling with being the person who caused the hospital visit.

Sitting in the dark room for the next several hours was taxing. They held her until the early morning for observation, and his mother stayed with her. He couldn't take the silence in the house, and as soon as the light showed, he got in his car and started driving around. Not needing to go anywhere but to clear his head. He's sober and wants to make a stop at the shop that sent him on this vile goose chase.

He's there, but she isn't. He decides to park and take a nap to wait for her opening time, which looks to be in two hours. He sets his alarm and drifts off to sleep as his eyes are beyond heavy.

The alarm went off thirty minutes prior, but he didn't hear a thing. He was awakened instead by a tap on his window. Alarmed, he snatched himself and looked out the window in a panic to see who or what was at the door. His dream was filled with death, and to wake up and feel that the nightmare continued was a harsh reality.

When he opened his eyes, it was the pretty witch, Jezebel, looking on with concern. He rolled down his window, and she said, "I saw you here when I arrived, but I needed a minute to get things organized for you to come in. Do you want to come in for a second?" He nods his head in agreement, and she helps him open his door and walks him into her shop.

He wasn't certain why his legs felt like jello as he tried to gather his feet underneath him to get out of the car and to a place where he could sit down. "I am sorry to show up like this. I know I paid you for a job, and all of this is extra."

"Right now, let's focus on what's going on and how I can help. I will keep track of the bill." Jezebel looks on at him, and he looks like a puppy, lost, sad, and alone. She feels her heart go out to him. Without another word, he buries his head into her breast. A bit caught off guard, she shifts him to her shoulder.

She isn't a virgin, but this was awkward. This was not like the other times; this was someone coming into her space that her mother did not send to touch her. This was someone who wanted love or understanding from her. She felt empowered in that moment to offer him something he needed: support. Often, people come into her shop with vengeance. She has hardly ever seen someone come back with remorse.

He lay on her shoulder and did not say anything. The warmth of her arms wrapping around his waist helped him sink further into her embrace. He was putty in her hands. In that moment, his life was going a mile a minute, and he didn't know how to make it stop or even slow down. He needed something —something familiar—that could help him relax and not cry. He needed a distraction, a beautiful distraction.

His body, understanding the cue, tightened his grip around Jezebel, and his face moved in to look his beautiful distraction in her dancing brown eyes. They gazed at each other—Curtis with a slight tinge of fear —kissed her, not knowing if she would respond by slapping him or by welcoming his empty emotion. He had no deep thought about what he was doing; his body was on autopilot to feel better, and at the moment, this seemed like a good idea.

To his surprise, the lips he touched embraced him back. A moment he thought would be quickly shut down, was able to progress, and then, in the early morning sun, they exchanged physical intimacies designed for marriage and true love. For what they needed or wanted, the moment felt real, timeless, and as if they had something that would last. Lying in each other's arms seemed to make time stand still, and they both forgot about their immediate responsibilities as they rested.

However, nothing lasts forever. Curtis's phone rings—it is his mother. She leaves him a message that they are on their way home, and he doesn't want to be too far behind them. He didn't know what to say, but believed the right words would come when he needed them most. He left the shop feeling lighter, but not whole. He was searching, and he wasn't too sure what it was for.

Jezebel was at the shop cleaning up the mess

they had made in their round of passion. She had hoped nobody would see or hear everything that happened, and for a very small second, she didn't care. She felt free there in the shop more than she had ever felt. What if her life could become this? What if she could have this freedom always? Could this be something that could last between Curtis and Jezebel?

She set the store up that day with a smile and aspirations for her life to be different. Her mother looked on from a secret cam and Carol watched the events that unfolded that day. She thought to turn away, but saw Jezebel's experience as her experience. She was fond of Curtis, and she wanted to see him naked. That beautiful body would soon be hers, and she might even like the romance she would step into when she switched places with her daughter.

Curtis didn't seem like a bad casualty in her plot for a second chance at life. She was disappointed in how Jezebel worked to keep this from her. She wanted some resemblance to what having a daughter should feel like. She had been so focused on using her as a double for herself that she never thought about what she wanted as a mother.

Did she want a daughter who told her everything? Did she want to know dreams or things she wanted for her life? Maybe she could pick one to accomplish as she finished out her years on earth?

It was the least she could do, given her plan. Jezebel set up her office and got to work, but her mind kept drifting, and she kept checking her phone throughout the day, hoping he would call. He was home, hiding in his room, hoping that the worst was over. His mother was running around the house for his sister like a nurse for those few days as her body recovered from whatever rattled her stomach. But as they thought she would become normal, something else began to change more and more each day.

Out of the clear blue, Courtney would start running, ducking, or pointing to objects that no one could see but her. Her response to what she was seeing was evident, so her brother and mother started to think that she might be seeing ghosts, or something. Cassandra considered getting her looked at by the church, but she refused to go. Courtney didn't want to see a shrink either. It wasn't until weeks later that Cassandra, with a heavy heart, checked her into a center to help her sleep and find the root cause of her seeing these manifestations.

The family found it bizarre, but not Curtis. This freaked him out. He thought about Jezebel from the shop, but knew trying to call her again wouldn't lead to anything he wanted to deal with. That morning, he didn't remember anything he had told her. He could have promised to marry her if it led to sex, and him feeling better. He was a liar, and lying to women wasn't anything new for him.

But he hadn't felt fear like he did after seeing his sister slowly lose her mind. He was next in line to manage the trust, surely now, but to what expense? His mom wasn't her cheery self anymore either. She seemed worried and stressed.

She went to the center all the time to keep her company and assure her that her family wasn't dropping her off there and leaving her. She needed drugs to sleep and drugs to wake up. She needed drugs to function, and with the heavy use of drugs, Cassandra knew even more that her legacy was in limbo.

Jezebel had hoped that she would hear something from Curtis that week, but she didn't. The next week went by, and nothing. She called and texted him, but he ignored them all. He didn't call her, text, or even send a Dear John letter. Nothing, radio silence.

He ghosted her, and this time, having sex with a man felt like she was being used. She slept with him for her, and so the feelings she had now, she had to take ownership of them because she caused them. What she did to numb her feelings, like she did with other past sexual encounters, wasn't working this time. She felt every stab of rejection, and she had to do something about it.

She knew she had to go looking for him because he must have an excuse for disappearing like he did. Maybe he became the caregiver and had no time, which made sense, and Jezebel could live with. She got in her car and skipped opening her shop. She wanted to drive by his home and see if he had been locked in, if he was sad, alone, and in need of a shoulder again.

She didn't see his car, but she wanted to call him even though something deep within her told her not to call. He didn't answer, but she couldn't give up. She parked across the street and committed to waiting all day, as long as it took to get answers for what was going on.

The house was quiet for two hours, but then the garage door opened, and an older woman drove out of the driveway. She assumed that must have been his mother. She didn't see the sister, so she questioned where she could be at the moment. Did they all live together? She wasn't sure, but she had a hunch she would get her answer that day.

It was about thirty minutes later that another car pulled up, and this time it was a beautiful young woman driving. There was someone in the passenger seat, but she couldn't make out his face. The girl got out of the front seat, wearing tight leggings, heels, and a rhinestone shirt. The girl was curvy, and she tiptoed to the passenger side of the car and opened the door.

Out the door came an inebriated Curtis, who must have had an eventful night. At the time, Jezebel wasn't sure of who this woman was. She helped him get out of the car and reached into his pocket to grab his keys. Curtis would grumble out words, but none that were coherent. Jezebel called his phone to see if he or the woman would answer it; neither picked up the phone.

She considered that this woman had to have been with him last night, because she didn't linger looking at the phone. She thought that if the woman had picked him up or were a family member, maybe they would be curious about what happened to him since he couldn't speak. Things weren't adding up for her. When the lady searched for the keys to the front door, she opened it quickly, suggesting she had either been there before or lived there too. Jezebel was paying close attention to where and how she left him.

She plopped him down on the couch, and he grabbed her by the wrist. He said words again that were incomprehensible, and the lady gave him a light tap to signal he needed to get some rest. The woman didn't give him a goodbye kiss, but called a ride and left shortly after arriving. She might have just given him a lift or wanted to be nice. Jezebel didn't think much of the woman, but she did knock at the door and check whether it was locked.

The door was locked, so she knocked. Moments later, he arrived at the door, and the little color he had on his face seemed to grow paler by the moment. Jezebel spoke first, "Hey, sorry to come here like this. I waited for you to call or text me back, and you never did." Curtis wiped his hand over his face and moved back away from the door. He permitted Jezebel to come inside, and she responded by walking in.

Curtis struggled to get his words together, and his breath smelled like lingering alcohol. He tried to kiss Jezebel, but she dodged him. "You need to go take a shower and brush your teeth." He nodded in agreement, and she hoped the water covering his body would help his drunkenness wear off. After the shower, his words were less slurred, and he started to resemble his usual self. He was very mellow and less smiley than normal.

Jezebel looked at him and saw that he came out of the bathroom with nothing under the towel. When he would move, parts of his body would be exposed, and she couldn't help but peek. He could sense the longing in her eyes, so he sat next to her on the couch. He lay his head on her shoulder, and she relaxed, smelling the familiar fragrance that had danced in her memory for the past few weeks.

She wasn't sure what came over her; was she bewitched by him to long for a man she had little experience with? When he turned to kiss her, he felt the way she thought he would. Comforting, warm, and inviting. He whispered words to her and said things only she would remember. She wanted his words to be sincere, that he had been thinking of her and wanted to call. When they had finished, he suggested they eat some food, and Jezebel cooked.

Was this how a relationship would blossom between the two of them? Would they be able to connect and find hope or love in each other? For the moments that they lay on the couch together, and as she cooked him breakfast, it felt like a home, a place where Jezebel could see herself. She had to go soon. She knew her mom would be snooping around or give her a call like she did around 1 or 2 o'clock, and that awkward echo in the shop needed to be in the background.

The two gave a goodbye kiss as she left him

on the couch to sleep off the night and early morning surprise. The period is still hazy for Curtis, but Jezebel didn't mind catching him up to speed when he sobered up later in the day. She got in her car with a smile on her face and excitement in her heart for what could become.

It wasn't five minutes later that Curtis heard a knock at the door. He didn't want to budge, so he tried to sleep through it, but the knocks grew louder. He felt like he started to hear the noise in his head magnified by a loudspeaker. His chest jumped as the vibration of the knock turned into a kick. He calls out, "Hey, you forgot something?"

There was no answer, so he knew he had to get up to stop the kicking. He gets up and swings the door open. "Who the hell are you?" A lady with a white dress, gold hat, and gold shoes walked past him without a greeting. Curtis closes the door behind the woman and goes back to his spot on the couch. Trying to gather his thoughts, he says, "Can I help you? Or are you looking for someone?"

"My name doesn't matter, but the woman who just left your house is my daughter."

"So you are the lady who called me and told me about the shop?"

"Yes. I need you to keep up whatever this is for a little while longer. She likes you, and that is good. So I am going to need you to play bait just a bit longer," says Carol.

"I really don't feel comfortable doing this. She nearly killed my sister."

"If you want me to help your uncle, you will do it. You will still get your money, and I will get what I want."

"What about the house?"

"Let her keep it as a gift. She doesn't suspect I know a thing. So let's keep it that way."

"Alright, but I want more now."

"You are just like a man, never satisfied," mutters Carol.

"This is more than you said it would be. I need some assurances," says a frightened but stern Curtis.

"Like what?"

"I need to know that when I am done with this, my life can be normal. You have to keep her away from me. Her popping up on my doorstep isn't working for me, given what I've got going on. She could have seen something she didn't need to if she looked closer."

"I know that the woman who dropped you off is your stripper girlfriend. That's your business, and has nothing to do with our arrangement. I will help your uncle and will ensure that she has nothing to do with you when you are finished. Are we good?"

"Yeah. We are good." She picks up and takes off out of the front door. Sometimes it feels like the woman floats as she walks because her movements are smooth and silent to the ear. Curtis thinks to himself that the woman vanished in how quickly she moved, or perhaps from how sleepy he was. He tries to go back to sleep, but he is awake enough to need coffee. He calls his uncle and he picks up.

"My boy, how are you?"

"Good, for the most part. Look, you need to hurry up with this lady. She and her daughter are giving me the creeps."

"Don't worry, once I learn what she is teaching me, I will show you how to have money and power. Money is good, but you want power."

"I trust you, Uncle. Whatever you say."

"How's your mom?"

"She is good. She went to check on my sister."

His uncle breathes in and replies, "Yeah…I'm sorry about that. I really am. Did they ever find out what was wrong with her?"

"No. She doesn't have a medical condition, but her body is going through motions as if she does. When her body is acting right, her mind is slipping. So it is a balancing act."

"Well, soon enough, Son, I will set her free." His uncle reassures him of his mounting power, which is nearly perfected. Curtis's uncle lives on a Native American reservation. He comes from his father's side of the family, rich with history, who know ancient secrets, and have connections to chiefs and occult practices. His family was one group that deepened their rights all the way to Washington. They are committed to preserving their land physically and spiritually.

Curtis' uncle warned that this partnership could become challenging, but with his skills, he could reverse enchantments or find a root to make his issues non-existent. Only his uncle wasn't fully aware of what else Carol had or knew that he didn't. She, too, had connections to families with deep occult roots. Jezebel's father came from a family of gypsies that knew how to hide in plain sight. They were good at accumulating wealth before abandoning a town.

There is more to be said about Jezebel's father, but all she knows is what Carol told her, that he left her and her mother when he could make more money elsewhere. He was the man who left her bitter in spirit and is partly responsible for the monster she became, though she would never admit it. He was her second attempt at love and the nail in the coffin for her seeing men as nothing more than commodities.

To admit a man had a hand in determining her future would give respect and power to a group she cared very little for. Her abandonment issues started with never knowing her father, and this ongoing cycle of bad relationships her mother and grandmother curated, void of love and fulfilled promises, has created a legacy of women willing to serve the devil if it meant not getting hurt and gaining power. Curtis quickly realized he was in over his head when his uncle introduced him to Carol, but as a man trying to intimidate a bear, he couldn't show his fear. This woman might know a lot, but she isn't God. So he felt there would be a way for him to get what he wanted and escape the relationship unscathed.

The time during which he and Jezebel grew closer lasted over several months. He made sure to wash his tracks and be more mindful of the late-night hour he was out. Not out of respect for the relationship, but so he wouldn't get caught and pay a penalty he knew nothing about. Jezebel was starting to glow from the outside, confirming that she was happy. Her radiance was coveted by her mother, and made her more of a body for Carol to have sooner rather than later.

She was waiting for the solstice to come, but with the brightness of her light, her daughter's joy was making her think she would be too far gone to complete the spell. But when the good news hits, her phone rings. "Okay. I think we need to cut this off now. Jezebel is talking about marriage, and I ain't ready for nothing like that. I know you wanted me to play a part, but if I keep playing this game, we will be married!"

Carol breathes out. "Okay, I understand. We still had a bit further to go, but I can imagine how persuasive my daughter can be. Just let her down easily, and everything will work out. I will expedite my plans and make this work how I need it to. I trust you or she will let me know when whatever this is, is over?"

"Yes. And remember your promise to me."

"I got it. You will get what you want." The two hang up the phone. Carol retorts through pierced lips, "Why are little brats so impatient. She is going to screw up my plans, and I won't allow it." Carol plots in her mind how to expedite her plans and observe the days heightened for dark arts. She didn't want her precious body to be damaged, so she thought to keep Jezebel in good spirits. Maybe she could isolate her, or work her through heartbreak to preserve the light a few days longer.

Jezebel went to Curtis' house after his mom left, and he was home alone. He came to the door with a somber look on his face. Curious, Jezebel reacted to his continence and asked, "Hey, what's going on?

He replied, "Nothing. I just got a lot on my mind." She nodded in understanding and asked. "So, when are we going to get this lump sum payment? It has been months already?"

"My mom has been at the hospital. She doesn't do anything but visit and take care of my sister. It is shocking, but my mom is more frugal than she has ever been. Whatever we had planned, it looks like it has failed."

Curtis was exhausted, and his real frustration was peeking through during their gathering. She tried to make him smile and take his problems lightly, but he wouldn't. He was deep in thought and perhaps struggled with his resolve to disassociate from Jezebel. She was a sweet girl, and he knew how much she liked him. He regretted sleeping with her, but if he was honest, he enjoyed it.

He didn't give much thought to what a future could be between the two of them, because he feared her mother, and anything he thought he might feel, seeing her face in his dreams, was scary enough. She had already butted her head into several of his dreams, and he had no intentions of having a wet dream from Jezebel's mother. He did have a moral code of not sleeping with a mother and daughter.

"I am just frustrated right now," he said as she reached for him and he pulled away. His distance didn't faze her because lately, she had to do more work to stay in his presence. He was shutting down, and as far as she knew, she wanted to save him from getting low. "Maybe I can help? I could do a healing spell for your sister and see about getting her released?"

"No disrespect, but I am not really keen on using magic to do anything else. I need something practical."

"You're right. Maybe your mom can learn

about me? Maybe she would be excited if you looked like you were moving on with your life and not a trust fund baby–a really handsome trust fund baby, of course." She moves in to kiss him, and he playfully moves his head away.

She reaches for him, and he allows her to grab his face. "Doesn't that sound like a good idea? What mother doesn't want her nearly twenty-seven-year-old son to have a baby when the money is there? Trust me, this will work."

Curtis thought about it and knew it would work, but did he want to be trapped with a wife, let alone a baby, just to get a check? What if he changed his mind or something went sideways? They would have direct access to his mother. He wanted his money, but he didn't want to involve both sides of his parents in what he had going on. He loved his mother too much to sacrifice her life to his scheme.

"No. There has to be another way. Let's think of something else."

"You are being difficult. I just don't understand why you won't cooperate. Is it me, or do you have something else you would rather be doing? I didn't want to ask this, but do you wish that I weren't here? You have been pushing me away for weeks!"

He corrects his posture and tries to save the situation. "Come here, no, that is not what I mean. I have just been under stress with my plans, ours, and–"

"Wait, did you just say our plans? Do you think you can see a future with us, Curtis?" He knew the answer to this question before she asked; he had to lie, "Yes, yes, of course I do. It's just a busy time and things are not set up how I want, that's all."

"If money is really the problem, I can make money anywhere. Maybe we need to get away and have a little time alone so you can get out of this house, and out of how you feel?"

"Wow, I mean I hadn't thought about–"

"Well, if we are going to be a couple, we need to start making plans as a couple. Not just you making your plans and me making mine. We need to plan something together."

"I–I don't know when I would have a break in my schedule to do something like this–"

"Come on, Curtis, grow up. You don't work, and you likely are chasing ideas to see where you land. Why don't we get away and make a real plan for how we can live as a couple? We can let the stress go and just start to enjoy each other again. I am making good money now, and I know what I am do-ing. I am way better than I was even when you met me a few months back."

"I can't ask you to leave your shop."

"Oh, please. I've been meaning to get away for years. I want to get out on my own and get from under my mom. I know how you feel because I, too, feel smothered. I don't like that everything I have done with my life so far seems orchestrated by her, except you and us. What we have is something I am building for myself."

"Let me think about it. My mom isn't all that stable with my sister, and for me to leave, I just wonder who would care for her, you know?"

"I get it. You love your mom, and I pray some day you can love and care for me like that." Jezebel snuggles up to Curtis, and his eyes tell the story of his emotions. He is looking off, calculating his next move and how he needs to tread softly. She is going off the deep end, and he doesn't know if he will have a bungee rope to reel her back in.

The two of them sat there for a little while, and before it got awkward, Jezebel looked up to him in her big brown eyes and kissed him. He hated the thought of a future, but the next hour played with his body. He longed for her physically, though his heart was a cloud of confusion beyond that.

Jezebel soaked up every moment of love she felt budding from her heart. She had never felt like this before, and she wanted to be drunk in this euphoric feeling. She felt as if anything was possible in this moment for her. She wanted to be a wife and mother, something she hadn't thought about seriously until late. She could see Curtis shaping up to be the man she wanted—more than a client with benefits, but the man she could build a family and life with.

She was head over heels for him, and she knew it. She knew when he walked into her shop, if he said and did the right things, he was a shoe into her bedroom and affection. When she wasn't around him, she thought about him all day long. Her heart felt heavy when he was away. The sex they had was beautiful, passionate, and created a desire hotter than fire in her bones. Could this be love, she thought?

Does love feel like an unquenchable fire? A strong desire that seems to blind you to the plans you should achieve, or that pushes you to go beyond your comfort zone. She had come to his house more frequently than she had ever even visited friends. He was consuming a lot of her time, and it was no wonder that she felt enamored with his presence.

She wouldn't say she was obsessed with him, but she began to plan far beyond her day-to-day life for Curtis to be by her side. She wanted a pampered lifestyle in which she could be wealthy and work only as necessary. She didn't want to work for a living or exchange white magic to keep a roof over her head, nor make her mom happy. She felt like a white rabbit; everyone wanted to pull her out of the hat to get what they wanted. Then she was put away in a cage to await the next show.

She wanted more than an act; she wanted the real thing. To be happy, in love, and build something that was hers. She wanted to be proud of what she created, and right now, her creation could be anything. She wasn't sure of what she would do. She always thought of going to school. Maybe she could take some courses and see what intrigued her.

She was good at debating and also with her thoughts and ideas. Maybe she could be a lawyer —a dang good one — who could demand top pay. She was good with numbers; maybe she could be an accountant or a high-stakes real estate broker. She knew a lot about liens, deeds, and trusts. She wanted to use more than just her body for what she wanted out of life; she wanted to use her brains, and maybe her heart could play a role in getting her to the top.

Back at

Charity is back at school, and she is walking the hallways with her friends. Zoe comes up to her, and she turns briefly, "Oh, hey. How's things going?"

Zoe looks on and sees the judgment of her friends, "Good. I just wanted to speak to you when you had a moment."

"I am about to head to lunch; you are welcome to come to my table if you like."

"Okay, no problem," replies Zoe. "See you." Zoe walks away, and her friends can't hold water.

"Eww, why did you invite her to our table? Do you really think she wants something more than to be seen with you, or us?" replied Freda.

"Be cool. We have a project we are working on together for class. She is putting the work in to get me an "A," and an "A" will do my "C+" average some good. She can sit at the dang table. Please don't act like we are really in high school. We are so beyond that," replied Charity as she closed her locker to head to lunch.

The lunchroom is buzzing with pre-teens from every sect. Those who are trying to find a place to fit in and those who love their position. Charity and her crew bring their lunch to school and only grab drinks from the lunch line. Zoe grabbed her tray and hesitantly sat at their table. The lunchroom did notice her switching sides and leaving the Bible crew. Some of her normal friends wave to her, and she holds up a hand gesture to let them know she will be there soon.

If Zoe were honest, she did like the attention, although she felt like she was sitting in a swarm of snakes. With a carrot stick in hand, Charity turns to Zoe with her perfectly pink lip gloss and says, "So, how are things going?"

Zoe was a little taken off guard because she wasn't sure when the conversation should start. She was in her world, and she was very mindful of that fact. "Oh, yeah. I got everything I think put together. But I wanted to add some points you might have, so it doesn't sound like I wrote it all. Anything you want to say in your words?"

"Well, I guess you can teach me and put what you think makes sense. I feel like people should have a right to choose how they live their lives. I don't think parents should be able to tell us what to do, but I do think they should, like, coach you — you know? We don't know everything about life, but we do know a lot. I mean, we watch tv and live lives like everyone else."

"Okay, so you think people should have their own free will. Do you feel like you agree with abortion or the death penalty?"

"Woe, Zoe. That's in the presentation?"

"The topic was how do we feel about the death penalty and if we think it should remain a law enforced by cities. I feel like the death penalty is like humans playing God. Kind of like how a mother plays God if she kills an unborn child. I agree that parents shouldn't make all the decisions, especially for who lives and dies, when they are being selfish. Too often, babies are dying because of someone else's inconvenience or selfish desires."

"Maybe I should have read the assignment more. I might have more to share on this than I am saying now. You want to hang out this week at my house and talk more? Lunch is almost over. I see your friends need you to come over."

"It's cool. I don't think my sitting away for one lunch period will make a difference for our group. I can stay," replies Zoe.

"Well, let's talk about something else—not this project. I want to enjoy my lunch and not have to think of death or dead babies."

"Fair," replies Zoe with an impressed expression.

"So, what about last night's episode of Hungry Vampire?" replies Freda, ready to jump in.

"I don't care about your shirtless tv crushes either. I want to eat in peace." Charity dismisses their plan to discuss boys and lust. Today, John isn't at the table. He is sitting next to his latest victim and talking whatever she wants to hear. She has been laughing the entire lunch period, which caught Rachel's eye.

She's always liked John, but the two of them didn't hit it off in the romantic sense. She was willing, but he isn't the single type. Rachel isn't the single type either, if she is honest, but she hates to see him make baiting girls seem so easy. She often thinks, "Who does he think he is? He is fine, but not that fine where he can just chew up women like toilet tissue and wipe his shit on us."

She regrets sleeping with him, but appreciates that he keeps it a secret from everyone in the group. She would be so embarrassed to look like this, googly-eyed girl he is talking to, knowing the lies behind the sweet but devilish smile. Knowing the empty promise of his touch beneath tables, under sheets.

While Zoe sat at the table, she and Charity kicked up other random conversations that Freda and Rachel tried to get in on, but for some reason or another, found the exit. Either Charity told them, "Wait, you are not on topic," or she dismissed their comment as "lame." It hurt their feelings how she was switching up on them and acting like she was really into these adult topics that they never discussed.

It never occurred to them that she might be genuinely interested in the news and other trending topics on social media that weren't dance videos or challenges. She seemed like Zoe's bright light, better than all of them. They could never tell her they didn't like her because they knew, from their parents, how important she was.

The normal life of Charity was anything but a fairytale. She was hand-picked to have her friends, and if she only knew about the target on her back that encircled her, she might have planned talking more to Zoe that day than the clacking ducks sitting to her left and her right all this time. The lunch bell rang, and everyone rose to head to their classes. Zoe left the table with no response from the girls, and Charity looked at them as Zoe walked away with judging eyes.

"What's up? Why were you two being so rude?" inquires Charity.

"Sorry, not sorry, to disappoint you, Charity, we don't like her. She is trying to steal our friend away." Freda made the comment confidently, with a slight wink.

"I can tell you this, and I ain't joking. I don't like her. It is just something about her that makes me feel like she is competing with us. Who does she think she is to come up here and almost demand we be quiet?" replies Rachel.

"Girls, don't get catty. She is just trying to be friendly. Nothing like what you guys are doing. Just be cool and stop being bitches. I hate when ya'll get in your feelings."

"Really? Bitches? Since when do you curse like that?" asked Freda.

Charity responds matter-of-factly, "When the word fits. Stop being jealous, there's no reason for it, and you look stupid."

"Look, I gotta get to class. See you later," says Rachel as she looks for a moment to escape the conversation. Yes, she was being a bitch, but she didn't like how Charity called her out on it. It is different when she calls herself a bitch, it is empowering, but hearing it this way made her feel it differently. She was silent the rest of the day until she got home. She knew she didn't like Charity, and the more she was burdened to hang out with her, the more she hated her.

Arriving home, she found her mom burning sage and smoking weed. It was the norm around her house; her mom stayed high and made it seem like she could connect more with the spirit realm around them when she smoked. Seeing Rachel's face, she replied almost instantly, "Was it her again?"

"I am really starting to hate this girl? How much longer do we have to pretend to like her?"

"Long enough for us to get what we need. But, we are nearly there." Rachel's mom exhales a puff of smoke.

"Mom, can you point that in a different direction? I want to protect my organs for as long as possible."

"Child, smoking weed won't kill you. Besides, we die daily no matter what we do, so what difference does it make?"

"You sound crazy, Mom," replies Rachel.

"But remember, I am your mother. You are not mine. As long as you respect that, we won't have problems. So are you doing what I told you?"

"Yeah. I keep trying to encourage her to break rules, be a bitch, or talk about guys and stuff like that, but she isn't interested. She cuts me off before I can get a word in."

"It's cool. She will have an interest in something, then we just need to exploit that."

"This girl is a goody two-shoes. It's like she isn't into boys, drinking, drugs, she doesn't even wear short skirts without some kind of conviction."

"She will break, and when she does, we need to be there to harness the light. We need to take back what should have been ours anyway. Before Carol had the top spot, it was our great-grandmother, and I am determined to get it back."

"Does it really matter, Mom? I mean, that

was a long time ago."

"It will always matter. Our power is locked in the past, don't you see that? We could be running this city, living like Carol or Jezebel, but instead, we are near the bottom of the drip. I want more power. If you don't, give me yours and I will make sure I eat for the both of us."

"I never said I didn't want power. I just don't care who replaces them. I want to see them gone. If it were up to me, I would like to see them all disappear, then we could have whatever we want, and the others could have more."

"Let me tell you how this works. You don't eliminate your enemy to help others; you strategically place people, so you can move all the pawns to work your will. Death is easy, but holding your hand on someone's throat to watch them squirm and be able to get them to do what you want, that is real power. To have the ability to take life but instead of killing it, to suspend it, holding your grips around their neck and them on the shortest leash, is power."

"So you want a pitbull on a leash, Mom?"

"I want a fleet of wolves to pull my sleigh. I don't mind if Carol, Jezebel, or their little prize Charity all pull my slay. I just want their power to be subject to my will. Once they see that I can lead better than Jezebel and Carol combined, I am a shoo-in with the district. They know what I am capable of and how committed I am."

"Whatever you say, mother, that could get Charity on a plate and make John pay, is what I want to do."

"Now, I told you not to play around with that boy. Now you see how being a dumb teenager can cost you everything."

"I didn't know he was going to use me like that."

"Every one of us has an agenda; there are no friends. Don't trust Freda either. She will burn you the first chance she gets, too, just like John. These little witches want power, and they are like runts of the litter. Neither of their parents is of our caliber, although they have tried. If they didn't have pretty faces, both of them would be trash and bottom feeders, I almost guarantee it."

"Hmm, I really liked Freda's mom."

"Yeah, and she was a dumb pet that stood no chance at staying alive. You can't help those at the bottom. You are only wasting your time, energy, and power. They can't give you what they don't have. If they are a means to an end, embrace that; if not, get out of magic."

"You sure, there is nothing I can do to get some of my power back?"

"John tapped you dry and then put a limiting spell on you. Until I figure out how to get it off, unless you want to become a Jesus freak, I can't do anything about it. My power is too weak," she says regrettably.

She inhales a puff of smoke and then says, "Carol has had her darts in my back for a long time. But she will need me, because she's not looking too good lately. She tries to hide it, but we old witches can see she is struggling to use her power."

She takes a deep inhale and says, "There are no smoke and mirrors on this level. Just saying that makes me want to vomit inside my mouth. I am the great-granddaughter of a grand empress, and here I am muddying in the dark, in mud, around maggots and fake wizards. I need another blunt." She takes the last drag from increasingly small blunt.

Her mother leaves the room and turns her music full blast as she lights another stick of hallucinations and repeats coveted whispers influenced by spirits she wants to use to wreak havoc on those who she feels have robbed her. She wants to be free to roam around and torment souls for her benefit. She has no light in her, and her plan is dark. If she were a cartoon character, her goal would be to take over the world, starting in her city without question.

She hardly makes apologies because she believes every move she makes is linked to the greater good for something she considers a good thing, her power. She is drunk on the power of the past and enjoys the momentary possessions that make her feel like she can conquer the world. She knows the limits of her power in the dark and dealing with the light, so for now she plays with her powers in the shadows, waiting for a chance to flex her muscles.

A one-night stand between John and Rachel robbed her of something she never knew she had. John pretends to be no threat and a light sorcerer, but if you were to get into his window, you would see how deep he is in the occult. He initiates more witches than all the teenagers combined. He leaves his intoxicating scent on their lips and in their hearts. He fills them with his spirits and charges them with crystals, leaving them as tokens of his affection.

All are lies, meant only to distract the girl and open her heart and mind to his sinister games. He likes to project himself into their dreams and give them wet dreams if they allow it. He flirts with demonic spirits that are jealous of him, and these spirits will torment the girls or drive them mad as they play around with their lust for him. He has a spell that will exchange the birthright of the person he sleeps with for another person he barely knows.

He is demented and evil at his core. He wants nothing more than to cunningly take everything these girls and women have to offer through sex, lies, and manipulations. There is no limit he would cross to replace his mother and all the witches as the head wizard. He is ready to perform whatever rite he must to elevate to the highest level. Carol is aware of his schemes and of all the witches under her control; he is the one gaining momentum to have an empty heart strong enough to take her as she ages. She keeps her distance, but his mother knows there is something very special about her son, too —almost as special as Charity.

Charity has a voodoo priest as a grandfather, but so does John. They both come from families who have magic on both sides; the advantage John has is that he knows his family on both sides very well. He is loyal to the arts and to new converts, seeking to grow his subjects. He has sights to make Charity another one under his reign, but there is a time for his plan, and the time is not yet.

Freda is at home with her grandmother. Her mother died years ago in a car crash. It was after this crash that she started to play with a Ouija board. At first, the random happenings scared her, but as the spirit kept talking to her, she started to feel more empowered, more safe. She tried to hear out the pastor when she was grieving her mother, but why should she if she could just talk to her mother?

In her wild pursuit of finding and reconnecting with her mother, she settled for listening to a familiar spirit who knew her mother well. Her mother was a woman who had a long battle with depression. This demon, that would whisper in her ear daily to remind her of her shortcomings, started to whisper to her daughter. This same demon that pretends to be a good friend to protect Freda and her mother doesn't reveal that he is the reason her mother threw her vehicle in front of a semi truck.

She was low, and no one could save her, she thought. Her grandmother, who prays and does right by her beliefs, is not a practicing Christian in that she attends church. She mostly drinks now to subdue her pain from losing her daughter. She blames herself for not doing more, but she cannot bring herself to forgive her actions as a mother. She has been an alcoholic for decades, and although she has disappointments with the unfaithful lover, she will not divorce alcohol to save her granddaughter.

She is unaware of how she is running with Rachel and trying to find God in all the wrong places. She is hurting, and this demon is feasting on her pain, hoping to grow it to something more grand to have a larger impact on her life's direction. He had plans for her mother, but taking her life was what she chose to do, instead of living as a dead soul. The demon felt robbed, so it turned its attention to Freda, intending that she would pay double for the trouble her mother had caused it.

In her last days, the mother began attending church. And although she was not a frequent attender, some of the messages got through, and she was able to battle the demon a few times, making him lose ground. He knew that she was almost at the edge of no return, so he spoke louder that day, crying out for her to end it, saying she couldn't make it, and for a moment, he needed her to believe him most; she took her life with a fatal mistake. It is not clear if she turned into the semi or if another witch, Rachel's mother, was at play also the entire accident was very convenient to her advancement.

She saw the spirit of Freda's mother and did nothing to save her neighbor. They lived up the street from each other for years. Freda's mom was no threat to what they were building, and they knew she was too weak to make a strong connection with them. She would be here today and gone tomorrow. So she did all she had planned to do, gave her a crystal in hopes she would keep it near for the time she would use it.

Freda's mom was a sacrifice Rachel's mom was not afraid to make if it meant she could advance in her path. Her demon connection was stronger, so she sought to use that spirit and hers to claim more lives who had an ability to serve in her kingdom in the making. She saw Freda struggling and offered her the Ouija board, knowing she couldn't resist using it. Freda could be a great blind witch, but she doubted she could be anything substantial.

Freda was dealing with a dark secret that Rachel's Mom knew about. She knew she had a love for girls. She wasn't following Rachel around because she liked her as a friend, but she had more plans to explore her interest in girls and had hopes Rachel would feel the same way. Although she talked about boys and Rachel did too, she thought the two of them felt the same way about boys.

She hoped that Rachel felt they were icky like she did. She wanted to believe the path in life she was embarking on was one she wouldn't have to do alone. She knew that Charity was too cultured to take an interest in her, but she had hoped the connection and closeness she and Rachel shared would be enough for her to see that the two of them should be together.

She thought this passionate friendship she had would be the source of love. A way to reconnect with the mother who passed, and the woman who whispered to her through the board. The board told her secrets only her mother could know. So when she was told to pursue Rachel, she assumed that was her mother's blessing to pursue Rachel and her passion for girls. When her mom was alive, she didn't dare tell her of her thoughts. She knew that on a good day, her mom would quote old biblical scriptures she had heard growing up that she too didn't live.

Her grandmother, who drank until the sun came up nightly, would say scriptures, but again, neither of them proved the power in the words they spoke. They used the bible as a weapon in her eyes, but neither was strong enough to stand up to their own problems using that same bible. She had no interest in God because she saw that God was weak. He was something put on like jewelry to avoid the disgruntled looks from those who expected you to say you were a Christian. She started saying she was a Christian so people would leave her alone, but she was far from it.

But if you looked at her life and those who called themselves Christians, I guess you wouldn't see much of a difference anyway. So in a way, she felt she blended in. There was nothing wrong with the bible as long as you didn't practice it, she felt.

So she could be Christian since no one she

felt who called themselves one followed it either. It is funny how young minds can work in that way. They can find a way to support how they want to live and assimilate into any culture.

Freda was in a dark space, and she had no one to go to who wouldn't feed her more hell in the guise of bringing good news. She was in a dark space, and it looked like the road ahead would get darker before the light would shine outside.

Back at Zoe's

Zoe would head home and often find her older brother Sean. He was a young man in his early twenties, still figuring out life and faith. He was a wild man just a few months ago when his parents had to bring him home because he got into some trouble with drinking on campus.

He had two choices: stay in school and risk expulsion, or finish out the rest of the semester from home. He chose to go home and finish the semester. He was a good son, but he just got caught up in all the freedom he had.

His parents raised him to know the word, but he didn't know it well enough for himself. He struggled with seeing the practicality in faith and real life. He saw the Bible as something helpful for a moral code, but didn't see how to implement it into his regular life.

It wasn't until he got caught drinking at a frat party that his parents knew how far away he was getting from his values and core morality. His parents knew he had to want a better life for himself, but they would do everything they could to win him back to the accountable son they had raised before he left for college a short year ago. He came home with a lot to prove, and he wanted to be the son they deserved.

He knew they gave a lot and paid a lot to get him in. He was a star athlete in school, but not to the point of getting on a major team. He did get a small scholarship at a local school, but he was currently on academic probation and at risk of losing it. He had to get his stuff together, and any more screw ups could mean he loses everything.

He came home at a great time because his parents had to go on a mission trip to Kenya. They weren't planning to go this year because he was away at college. They didn't feel comfortable with leaving Zoe with friends or family that long. With him home, however, they considered the trip.

Today, they were packing and getting things together to leave. This trip would be a bit longer than their other mission trips. They were planning to help on a building project, but at the last minute, their father was asked to run point.

The other partnered church, the head of missions director, had a hospitalization for stage three cancer concerns. His wife made the decision they weren't going, and that meant Zoe's parents could both go for this 45 day trip to ensure the final construction elements were completed and to dedicate the building. It was a bit stressful for his wife because she was unsettled in her spirit.

Zoe's father was a pastor and had been serving at his church for several years. He wasn't the senior pastor, but the assistant pastor who was very active. He was the heartbeat of the church, although he didn't preach every Sunday. He made sure the church ran flawlessly and with dignity and respect for all.

Everyone loved him except those who sought to have him displaced. His wife was an intentional target of many of the witches sent on assignment to the church. The church was a stronghold in the community that kept the dark arts from invading their block with the hell that quickly surrounded the holy grounds of their church, Holy Ground Temple.

Zoe's mother wasn't just a woman who supported her husband; she was a woman given the eyes of God, and her spirit was extremely sensitive. It was so sensitive that it scared Zoe. She knew sometimes what she was going through without her saying a word. She tried her best to hide things from her mom, but it seemed her mom would find a way to peek into her dreams sometimes.

As Zoe has grown older, her mom has influenced her thoughts less; she has noticed, so she is leaning on the power of God to walk with her as He walks with her mother. She knows that Zoe is gifted to walk with God, and she wants her daughter to receive this gift from her. The gift of prophecy and being an eagle-eyed prophet. Her mom had a lot of hatred in the church because she could see the spirits they brought and called them out. Although the leadership doubted her words, the power of God always made the visions she gave come to pass.

She was a hidden gem in the church for real, but her husband always respected her gift. She covered her husband in prayer because together they were advancing the community of God in the area, and any witch would never come within 10 ft of them without more than five supporting them in case of a hostile takeover. This simple means, in case the spirit of God were to be released and overcome their evil with good. The love of God had to be quickly screened and blocked with a comment or distractions to keep even the strongest witches focused on their mission, to divide and conquer the church.

This long-standing assignment has been ongoing for years, and the progress has been slow at best. When Zoe entered the house, her mom looked up from a box, "Hey, beautiful. How was school?"

"Good," Zoe replied.

"Just good?"

"Yeah. It was good. I got to talk to Charity about our project, and I feel she is more deep then I gave her credit for. I am impressed. Yeah, most girls don't really think about the stuff I do."

"Yeah?"

"It's challenging for us to have people who can think about stuff more than boys, sex, or drugs. Sorry, Mom."

"No, I get it. The truth is the truth. I am glad you might have found a friend," she replies warmly.

"I wouldn't say friend, but someone I can talk to for sure."

"I will take that too. You know me and your father will be leaving soon. You sure you feel good about us going?"

"I do. My brother is not the smartest in the world, but he is responsible. Plus, I can cook and practically take care of myself. What could really happen with how quiet it is around here anyway? I know I can call grandma or somebody if we really need help."

"Yeah, but I ain't gonna lie. I do feel a little odd leaving at this time."

"Come on, Mom. Sean and I are almost grown. You cannot babysit us forever. Go live your life and help dad conquer world hunger and bring peace. I think it is really cool," Zoe replies.

"I believe that." The two chat a bit more about their plans for Kenya, and the atmosphere of expectation is thick. Her mother isn't sure of what she feels, and although she knows she must go on this trip, she is praying silently in the spirit for the power and presence of God to remain in her house as she leaves.

In the coming days, she is very busy ensuring all the to-do items are completed for safe travel and entry into and exiting from countries. It is a whole process to travel anywhere with shoes, medical, visa requests, and other items to ensure they and the team coming with them will all be accommodated there in Kenya. She had many late-night conferences with a time gap, and all of them seemed filled with love and great expectation.

Sean thought it would be a quiet time filled with him attending school and enjoying food while watching tv. Something he couldn't do without his mother telling him to go to the kitchen table. She always told them to eat in the kitchen, and he thought what harm could there be to eat anywhere in the house, for real? In his dorm, there was no kitchen, so eating on his bed was the best experience. This sounded like 45 days of freedom in his heart.

Driving his parents to the airport, they both sat in the car as their mother packed their bags. The ride was filled with jokes and laughter. There were no wet eyes, though emotions suggested they would all miss each other and the bond they shared for the days ahead. When they pulled up to the airport, the father said, "Now, Son. Don't do anything stupid. You are smart and I trust you, but kids do the craziest things when you set them free. I need you to take the car out only when you need it. No joyriding.

And I would suggest you be in before dark. Nothing good happens in the dark anyhow."

"I got it, Dad. Relax," replies Sean.

"You gotta be the man of the house and protect your sister. No parties, late-night hangouts, or anything like that. If this is too much, you call us and we will come home."

"Dad, come on. I can watch my little sister. I got this."

"Oh, and don't use my baby for nothing. She is in the garage, and that is where I should find her when I get home without a scratch."

"Come on, Dad. I cannot drive it just once?"

"No. Not even once." His baby was a classic cruiser he got for a Father's Day gift from his wife. The only two people ever on the bike were him and his wife. He felt he should have something for himself, and the motorcycle was that for him. His son learned to ride bikes in college. He has been begging his dad to drive it since he got home, and every time, his dad replied with an emphatic, "No."

But we know how things go when the one who tells you "no" is not home to see you follow the "no," don't we? Will the temptation of not riding be stronger than his resolution to obey his parents? Can he really handle his sister and all of her new friends and their schemes? What would the next several weeks hold for him? I guess time will tell it all.

Zoe and Sean's parents boarded their plane and were en route to Kenya. The two of them got home, and the night was quiet. Zoe sat at her desk, looking at her computer and social pages. She noticed a friend request from Charity and searched her page before clicking accept.

Her page showed Charity in her many looks, but all featuring her pink "poppin" lip gloss that Zoe wanted to wear, that Zoe's mom said was too much for a young lady. She could only wear Vaseline and lotion. It did do the trick, but what was so wrong with lip gloss anyway? A little color couldn't be a sin, could it?

She didn't see the big deal, and she dreamed of having her own color that would speak to her freedom and life choices. She had recently turned thirteen and was fresh into teenager mode. She didn't mind her mother being overbearing in the years prior, but she felt that now that she was a teenager, she could start making some decisions on her own. I mean, how would she ever learn to be an adult if she can't think for herself?

She looked at the pictures on Charity's page and saw her mom. Her mom was beautiful. She wore her hair in bouncy, beautiful curls. She wore dresses that accentuated her stunning figure.

She was so beautiful she could have easily been a housewife on a reality tv program. She wore heels, and her face was young and fresh. Something about her eyes captivated Zoe, and she wondered what her life would be like if she had a mother like Zoe.

Would she wear lip gloss? Could she wear skirts and shirts to show her stomach? She knows she should be modest, but it is fashionable to wear somethings that require an undershirt at least. Her mom wasn't having any of that. She told her, if you raise your arms and your belly button shows, you can't buy it. She felt a bit dated with her wardrobe and admired the freedom Zoe had.

Charity liked the family structure that Zoe had. She hadn't met her brother, but she liked hearing about him. She thought, What could life be if I only had an older brother or sister? She never mentioned how lonely her days are going home to an empty house.

Her mother never mentioned dating anyone, ever. She thought her chances of having a step-sibling or a stepfather were unlikely ever to happen. So she found some comfort in getting close to Zoe over the past few weeks.

They seemed to have a lot in common, and she thought about inviting her to her birthday party that was coming up next month! She knew it would be a big thing because her mom hardly ever did anything that was chill. One day, while Zoe was over at Charity's house, she was looking at the pictures in her den and the hallways. She asked, "Whose the creepy lady?"

Charity laughed, "She's my grandmother. She would cut you eyes that would make you stop mid-sentence if she heard you call her that. She is a powerful lady in her women's club. Growing up, I was always scared of her. I tried my best to keep from being punished."

"Man, her eyes are scary, girl. I feel for you having to wake up and see them." Zoe starts to laugh and Charity joins in and says, "Yeah, she can be a little rigid, but she is cool too. A lot of the time, I was growing up, she watched me while my mom worked."

"So what about your dad? I don't see his picture," inquires Zoe innocently.

"I don't know too much about him. My mom doesn't talk about him much. She still won't tell me about him, even now when I ask. He is like a ghost. I am guessing he is the reason she chooses to be single. I don't know. Maybe he cheated on her or did something that broke her heart for her to be so mean towards men. I have never seen her even date a man once."

"Really?" replies Zoe in shock.

"If she gets a comment, she starts off really nice, like she likes him. Then she will cut him up into two sentences, like she could read his thoughts or something. It was so embarrassing; they would leave her alone and not look twice in her direction. She dresses like she does, but it isn't for attention from men."

"So why do you think?

"I think it is just because she can, almost like for power or something. My mom doesn't care about a man. So I guess she dresses like she does for herself because no one else benefits from it."

"Interesting. I don't think I ever heard that before. But I can see how that can be true. My mom would say that is a form of low self-esteem, or some kind of spiritual problem for sure."

"I don't know about that. I wasn't raised like that. All I know is that we choose how we want to live, and by our choices, we create the world we live in. Not sure of how I got that. From watching social videos and piecing my values together, or from dreams. Sometimes I have these real-like dreams, and I wake up still thinking about what I heard. It's scary."

"Who do you think is talking to you?"

"I don't know them all based on their faces or voice. Some feel familiar and others, strangers," says Charity.

"Are they trying to help you? Maybe that could help point to if it is God or the devil talking to you."

"Girl, I don't know. I told you I don't believe in all of that. I just know what I see, hear, or feel. I can believe what I see, hear, and feel–and that is real to me. Anything else in the invisible realm is hard for me to acknowledge."

"So do you believe that wind is real?"

"Yeah. You can feel it," replies Charity

"Just because you can't see it, and although you can feel it, you still want to know who sent it. What is the source of what you are seeing, feeling, or experiencing?"

"Okay, you are getting too deep for me, Zoe."

"Sorry, my mom is a prophet, so she teaches me a lot of stuff."

"So your mom is like a witch?"

"No, no, she is not a witch. She can hear from God, and he tells her stuff. She is not a witch."

"So what's the difference between her and a witch then? What witches talk to the devil?"

"In short," replies Zoe.

"Whoa. You believe that? Well, I don't know anything about either, but they sound similar. I keep my feet on the ground and my eyes open. All that stuff in the invisible realm I don't do. I don't even watch horror movies if I can avoid them," says Charity

"Alright, let's watch a movie. What do you want to see? Because what I really want to see is your mom's closet. I know we probably shouldn't."

"It's not a big deal. My mom won't be home for hours. She works a lot." The girls enter Jezebel's room, and the room is neat and cute as a pin. Nothing seems out of place, even the pillows are placed in a specified order. Zoe looks around, sees the few pieces of jewelry on her dresser, and perfumes. She doesn't squirt any of perfumes, but she smells the bottles to sense their scents. The smells were intoxicating.

Then she arrived at her walk-in closet after seeing the bathroom. Her bathroom was beautiful, covered in black, pink, and gold accents. The room might have been a bit dark if it weren't for the pink that was thrown in, which softened the goth feel. It was dark to Zoe when comparing it to her mom's room and even the living room. The blackout curtains kept out much of the light, and the chandeliers cast a seductive glow throughout the room.

Entering her closet felt like stepping into a high-end clothing store and receiving special attention. Charity joked as she said, "Fine, lady, thanks for coming to our beautiful English selective store.

We have a few special pieces we can show you today if you are interested?"

Following the role play, she replied, "Yes, darling. Show me something worth dying for. I have been all around and I have found nothing to reach my particular taste."

Charity brings out gorgeous gowns and dresses of every kind. Although they were beautiful, none of them impressed her enough to risk trying it on until she saw a black, pink, and gold dress that had a whole vibe even on the hanger. It seemed to float into her arms, and she knew she had to try it on. She replied in her accent, "Wow, darling. Now this, this is beautiful. Do tell me. Is it my size?"

"I think we can work something out if you like it. But I only have a few of these left, so if you are impressed to have it. You will need to make a move on it, and quickly. Try it on and see how you feel with the enchanted fabric, the brilliant gold trim, and vibrant pink accents to make anyone see you as the star of the show. We have a full mirror right over here."

Charity leaves the closet to allow her to change into the dress. Moments later, Zoe emerges from the closet, wearing the dress and matching shoes. She is struggling to walk in the shoes, and Charity says, "Girl, you better take those shoes off before you tear up that dress and we both end up dead."

The girls laugh and quickly Zoe takes off the

shoes. "Girl, this dress is gorgeous," Zoe says as she marvels at the body she never knew was beneath the jeans and t-shirt she wore every day without fail. She loved the fabric —how it hugged her waist and legs, making her look like she had a chest to catch the attention of a worthy guy one day.

She loved how she felt in the dress, and she could only think of how beautiful she looked. Then it happened, Charity came to her with a lipstick she said would be cute with the dress. It was a pink, silky lipstick that felt like liquid butter as it glided against her lips. The color popped with the dress and was the finishing touch.

She wanted to sit around in the dress but knew that was a bad idea. Charity senses her nerves wearing off and said, "Okay, dress up is over. You need to get out of that dress before we damage it." Zoe changed out of the dress, but she still could feel the fabric on her skin. She still wore the lipstick that made her look how she pictured. Why couldn't she wear this with her mom? She knew color on her lips would be a perfect addition to her everyday look, and Charity did something she didn't expect.

"Hey, if you want to keep the lipstick. You can take this one. She hardly ever wears it and won't miss it. She doesn't like pink."

"Really?"

"Yeah, it's cool. If she asks about it, I will tell her I took it. I usually borrow from her all the time, stuff she won't miss."

She smiled as she sat on the couch and watched the movie, feeling good about the day. Time passed quickly, and her brother was outside the house honking the car. He insisted on picking her up to make sure she didn't get into any trouble he would miss. She hugged Charity and told her "thank you" as she left with the lipstick.

She got into the car and forgot it was still on her lips. Her brother did a double-take when she entered the car, "Girl, is that lipstick on your lips? Mom will kill you."

"Sean, come on, relax. It is just lipstick. I didn't do drugs or something. This is not an emergency."

"It starts small like this before you young people spiral out of control," he jokingly replies as he laughs.

"Stop acting like a shrink. You are not a psychologist yet. So relax. I am just enjoying some freedom. And don't think I won't tell mom that you are eating in the living room and your bedroom. You know the rules about eating food, don't you?"

"You brat. You wouldn't," he replies in a slightly less joking mood than before.

"If you can keep a secret, I can too," she replies with a smirk. The two of them laugh as they drive home. They get home, and he cooks a frozen pizza because cooking dinner wasn't something either of them had planned on doing that night.

Zoe wanted to live a little and reminisce about how she looked wearing Charity's mom's dress. As she lay on her bed, she heard her phone beep. She checked it, and it was a text from Charity.

The text read, "A little gift to remember your finest moment yet." It was of Zoe wearing the dress and looking in the mirror, loving every second of it. She was so captivated by what she looked like that she didn't even notice Charity with her phone, taking photos. She gave her three pictures of the dress, and it was truly gorgeous. She thought, *'One day, I will have a wardrobe like this.'* A girl has to have dreams, she said in her heart as she lusted after the photo.

The night came to a close, and the house was quiet. The phone rang, but no one answered. They were both exhausted and dead tired as their parents called to check in. They determined to call back again when the day hours would be more aligned. They hated that their times were so far off from each other.

Zoe's mother would call several hours later and catch them in the car on the way to school. Her heart lit up at the sound of them, but they were both focused on their plans for the day. Her children spoke, but you could hear that they were distracted and focused on what they wanted to give their attention to. Sean had a project he was working on that took up a lot of his time. Zoe was excited to sit with Charity at lunch and be around her.

Her life had become busier since she became

friends with Charity. More people noticed her, and she had plenty of friends who wanted to work with her or sit with her at lunch. She no longer sat with her original crew from the Bible study but usually sat with Charity. She now had other options for sitting with the popular kids, who knew she was smart. They wanted to ensure an A for their next project, too, so she was a coveted partner.

Her life for the first time was making sense, and she was wearing her pink lipstick as much as she could. She even got a few compliments for her "breaking out of her shell." She laughed at the comments and replied, "Thanks." Freda and Rachel were talking, and Rachel's mom said she wanted to have a party for her recently passed birthday. At first, she had no intentions of inviting Charity in front of Zoe. She didn't want Charity to extend the invitation to Zoe either.

The only way to control the invite was to control where and when she was asked to attend. At lunch was definitely not the time since Zoe was like a fly on shit, as Rachel describes it. It wasn't until Zoe asked Charity, "Hey, are you busy this weekend? I was thinking we could go skating or something like that?"

Charity thinks for a moment and says, "I ain't never really gone skating before, but sure."

"Well, she can't go, because she is coming to my party," replies Rachel.

"Wait, what party? I thought you canceled

it?"

"My mom postponed it. The weather sucked on my birthday so she owes me. I asked if we could have a simple party at my house with some of my friends, if you want to come."

"Yeah, of course. Is it cool that Zoe comes with us, too?"

"I mean–" Rachel started to reply.

"You don't have to, it's cool, Charity, if it is just for close friends. I get it."

"No, I am sure she wasn't going to say that. You're cool with her coming right, Rachel?" With nowhere to hide, she replies, "Yeah, I mean, I don't know you well, but if you are cool with Charity, you're cool with me." Her skin boils as she replies because she hates to invite either one of them. It bothered her how Charity acted as if she were some kind of princess, and she was void of all understanding.

How could this girl be so her, and not know her story? If she had enough power to overcome the backlash for letting the secret out of the bag, she wouldn't hold back for a moment to *release the kraken* to see if it would take off Charity's head. She has a beastly past and an ancestry she knows nothing about. Both sides of her family have blood covenants they will have to make good on. Why couldn't she sit in the front row with popcorn and watch the best film of girl vs dragon?

She smiles through her aggravation, and lunch quickly wraps up. Freda notices Rachel's bothersome mannerisms and offers comfort as the two walk the halls. "Hey, are you good? You seem a little frustrated?"

"No, I am not good. That bitch just keeps getting everywhere. First, the lunch table. Then to Charity's house. Now my party! I don't know or like her. Why should I have to deal with her?"

"If you feel like that, just disinvite her."

"How will I do that, Freda?"

"You call her and tell her."

"I don't have her phone number."

"Babe, you have the internet. Send her a dm." Right then and there, she sends a dm to Zoe, "Hey, I am really not comfortable with you coming to my party. I would appreciate it if you didn't mention this to Charity. I get that you guys are friends, but we are not friends, and this party was supposed to be with me and my friends."

Zoe didn't get the message yet because her phone was already in her locker. She went through the day feeling on cloud nine. She got so many messages from her friends that she paid no attention to the notification. She didn't get it or read it until late in the game. She asked her brother to take her to Charity's house so she could give her the gift she bought. She felt it was only right not to tell her about the dm, and instead make up a story.

She got to her door, and Charity was beautiful like always. "Hey, Rachel will be here soon to pick me up, or my mom said she would get here and take us."

"Well, actually, I came early because I am not going, but I did get her a small gift. I wanted to give it to you."

"But why, what are you doing? Don't tell me you are still going skating, and alone?"

"No, it's cool. I just think you should go and be with your friends. I am new and I don't want to cause any problems."

"What are you talking about? She said you can come, so we are going. In fact, let's go. I will call my mom from the car and tell her I am riding with you. It's Rachel's party, but you are my friend."

She smacks her lips and says, "If I have a plus one, she will have to deal with it. She said yes, and I don't care if she changed her mind. She should have said 'no.' We're going."

Charity can be strong-willed and bossy when she wants to get something done. She practically drags Zoe to the car and meets Sean for the first time. "Hey Sean, I have heard a lot about you. I am Charity."

"Hey, so you are the girl that my sister talks

about all the time," replies Sean.

"I trust she is saying good things?"

"Yeah. So where am I going? She said she wasn't going to the party anymore. Ya'll going somewhere else?"

"No," replies Charity. "We are going to the party."

"But if she got disinvited, why would she show up to the party?"

"Wait, Rachel disinvited you? Why didn't you tell me, Zoe?"

"I just saw the message today, and she asked me not to make this weird. It is getting weird now."

"No, she should have told me. I will get this sorted. I hate it when she acts like a child. People are going to make new friends, and she can't stop that. She just needs to be the friend she is to me and not worry about everything else. I think she has control issues."

"You think so," replies Zoe in a slight sarcastic tone.

"Don't you? Why would she disinvite you? Have you two ever gotten into a fight or had some problem I don't know about?"

"No, I'm cool with Rachel, Freda, and John."

"Good, so we're good," replies Charity. "Let's go have some fun."

Sean doesn't say anything. He keeps his eyes forward and only gets quick glances of the 12 and 13-year-old girls in the back, seemingly having conversations beyond their years. He had to think to himself, *Is this why they say girls mature faster than boys?* He is a grown man and still hasn't seen so much drama, resolve, and processing in a short period. These girls are quick, and he knew it might be a little bit more demanding for him to keep his sister on the right path with whatever circle she just landed in.

He decided not to leave the party but to stay parked across the street in case he had to dip out quickly from the party. The neighborhood was quiet, but he didn't underestimate a calm beginning. He knew how quickly fights can ensue, and he was ready to deal with that if he must. He really didn't want to get into an altercation about children's problems, but this is why he was made in charge.

The party was outside, oddly enough, so he was able to see the entire event unfold from the comfort of his car. The party was full of young teenage girls walking around, playing music, and seemingly having a good time. He checked his phone and got busy doing things he loved —playing games and scrolling on social media. With the workload he had lately, he had hardly any time for any fun. He was escaping inside the space of his phone as his sister was immersed in a world she knew very little about.

The party, as soon as she entered the house, seemed different. The theme was about vampires and werewolves, which Charity told her quickly to ignore. She mentioned to Zoe that Rachel was more obsessed with boys than with bloodthirsty human monsters hunting other humans. Zoe dismissed the party and the theme as something she could survive, but she forgot about the awkward air there would be when she stood in front of Rachel. She also thought: *Did Freda or John know she had been disinvited?*

Before she could run down the list and assess how she was feeling, she was face-to-face with Rachel and Freda, whose faces told her they knew about the dm. John couldn't care less, as he was feasting on all the young girls at the party. He was a hound, and everyone knew it, but his eyes, hair, and appeal made the girls give him a chance to woo them and impress them with his seductive approach to compliments. It was surreal how he could make a woman laugh and swoon over his boyish charm and good looks.

Rachel says, "Hi Zoe. I am sorry I sent that dm to you. I didn't mean to make things weird. I was just in my feelings, but I am so glad you came anyway." Rachel knew to get ahead of the problem before it became a problem. She knew that to swipe this away, she had to fall on the sword, but at least she could angle the blade so it didn't stab her in the back.

Charity replies, "So you two are good?"

"Yeah, we are good. Right, Zoe?"

Zoe, picking up on what was being dealt, replies, "Yeah. We are good. I get it. Freda was not sold on the apology or the quick pivot. She was pissed for Rachel, her future lover, and she felt obligated to make Zoe feel uncomfortable with being subtle about it. She intentionally didn't speak to her and tried to separate her from Charity by asking her to get things or play games she had no interest in.

Zoe caught on to their games and was thinking of leaving, but as she was walking toward the door. Charity came to her side to rescue her from her great escape. "Hey, where are you going?"

"Oh, I was just going to find the bathroom," says a slightly uncomfortable and busted Zoe.

"Oh, yeah, I will go with you." That was her chance to escape, Zoe thought. Now she was stuck at this party that slowly felt like the walls were closing in on her. It was a bad idea to come, she was realizing, but now she is stuck in the middle and can't leave.

She goes to the bathroom and she looks around to see if she could fit out of the window. She can't, and she knew the idea was too desperate. She just needed to say how she felt, she thought.

When she opened the door, she was whisked away to where all the girls were gathered in the living room. Rachel's Mother lowered the music to a very low volume where it was hard to make out what was playing. She quieted the girls down for a bit to say, "As you all know, I wanted to have a little fun and bring a bit of magic to this party. What better way to have a party that fits my daughter's theme of vampires and werewolves than to have some card readings! Who wants to go first?"

The girls laugh about the ordeal, and, one by one, many of them start to come to the front. Zoe replies to Charity, "Hey, this might be where I need to exit. I don't believe in cards and things like that."

"They are just cards, Zoe. They don't bare an effect on your future. Plus, you don't have to do it if you don't want to," Charity responds.

"Yeah, but this is getting a little weird for me if I am honest."

Freda comes over, "Come on, Zoe. Charity, don't you both want to get your cards read?"

"Uh, no. Thanks, but no," replies Zoe firmly.

"I will do it only if Zoe does it," says Charity, thankful for the outcome.

Freda looks at Zoe for a reply, "Then my answer is no. I am good."

"Come on, Zoe, these cards are just cards. We shuffle them up and see what happens. My mom likes doing stuff like this to make us have a good time, just try it," replies Rachel.

Zoe is still not buying it, but Rachel starts to talk to Charity and invites her to do it herself and forget about Zoe, since she is scared. Zoe, not liking how the tables are being turned on her, says, "If you want to do this, I will sit next to you, but I am not going to do it."

"Okay, I never got my cards read. It might be fun," says Charity to play along.

Zoe replies, "I don't see how this is fun. I think we should turn the music back on and keep dancing or something. Maybe get some food?"

"You're right. I am hungry. Where is the food at?" Charity's reply got the other girls more interested in food than in reading their cards. She took the bait, and Zoe started to breathe. The atmosphere was changed, and Zoe felt grateful not to sit through a card reading she knew was devilish. The party after that was normal, considering the theme. The cupcakes were red velvet, and when you cut into the center, it looked like red blood oozed out.

This was another hard no for Zoe, eating her cupcakes. It was something weird about this house and these friends she didn't trust. She couldn't put her finger on it, but Charity also didn't eat the cupcakes. Rachel and Freda hated the power or influence Zoe had on Charity. They started asking the right questions—Who is this girl ?—and made it a point to figure it out.

All the girls got these cute baggies that didn't have blood or something dark on the outside. When they got to the car, they looked inside and found a bracelet or a necklace with a stone wrapped in wire.

The pieces were colorful and beautiful.

The necklaces were both different, and so they figured Charity's mom must have made the pieces. She had a signature style that Charity could always pick out. Many of Charity's friends would give her jewelry away as party favors or high-end gifts for the more expensive ones.

"Yeah, you should keep the gift. I think my mom made it." Zoe looked at the piece and really liked it. She thought of the outfits she could wear it with.

The drive home was filled with them talking about the event, and Sean eavesdropping a bit. He was glad that Zoe stood her ground and didn't do anything her mom would frown on. Maybe she was mature enough to handle peer pressure. Her older brother was proud of her.

After Charity left the car and went home, she saw her mom step outside and wave to the car for the first time. She walked up to the car, and she was more beautiful in person than in all of her pictures. She leaned in the car near Sean and said, "Thanks so much for taking my angel to the party. I got her text that you were taking her. And I wanted to introduce myself. You can call me Jaze or Ms. Jaze."

She put her hand into the car near him, and he took it and was going to shake it, but she gave him a kiss on the top of his hand. "Sincerely, thank you for allowing Zoe to be friends with Charity. I know, with my schedule, it can be hard for her to be home sometimes when I'm gone. I am glad she has a friend like Zoe."

"Yeah, of course. The girls are having fun, and I am here to help. But uhh, I gotta go."

"Yeah, of course. Good to meet you both. Ya'll have a good night." She walks away, and although Sean didn't want to watch her walk away, he couldn't help it. Her perfume seemed to draw him in, and he felt his awareness of her movements heighten, and that was the moment he knew: this woman was dangerous. He pulled out of the parking lot and headed for home.

He looked over and saw the necklace in his sister's hand. "Hey, where did you get that?"

"It was a party favor from the party."

"I don't think you should keep that. That party seemed a bit creepy, and anything from that party is probably bad news."

"Sean, relax, the necklace came from Charity's mom. I am sure it is fine."

"I don't trust her, and I think she has a weird vibe too."

"Is that your spidey sense kicking in?"

"You can say that. But trust me, something is up with your friend's mom."

"You were just busy looking at her booty as she walked away to see anything about her," playfully retorts Zoe.

"That's what I am saying. I tried to pull away, and I couldn't. I don't want her getting close to me ever again. Are you sure you can trust this girl? Maybe they are into some dark magic or something? That thing could be a beacon or something to the dark world."

"You play too many video games. You need to stop scaring yourself, Sean."

"You say what you want, but you'd better get rid of that thing, or I'm telling mom," replies Sean sternly. Zoe knows he ain't playing and she replies.

"Fine, scary cat. I will throw it away when I get home."

"Thank you." He breathes out relief. Just seeing the thing and being in the car with it made him nervous. He wasn't deep into spiritual warfare or things like that, but he respected it. His mom would tell him things she had seen, and he prayed he would never have to see. He was a newbie in spiritual matters and preferred that the topic remain a mystery.

They pulled into the driveway, and she threw the necklace into the garbage. They entered the house, and she kept thinking about the necklace. She didn't see how a simple necklace with a small stone could be harmful. What did her brother really know?

He played video games that were more magical than her life. She felt she was a better judge of something spiritual than he could ever be. For him to be so scary, he didn't resist the chance to play a zombie apocalypse game. How can that be okay, but a necklace means satan?

She laughed, just thinking of the hypocrisy in his logic. She cooked that night and cleaned the kitchen afterward. Her brother retreated to his room, and she took the chance of throwing out the trash to pick up the pretty necklace she had left behind. She hid it in her room, knowing a place her brother would never look, her period drawer. All the clothes she would wear during her time of the month, she put in this drawer.

Her brother knew to be sure she didn't keep the necklace, so when she went to school, he searched everything. Or at least he thought he had. She was cleared as a good listener, and the house was calm. But ever since meeting Jezebel, he kept thinking something was off about her. He wasn't sure why she kissed his hand; that was something that had never happened to him before.

Something about the gesture bothered him. He washed his hands with all kinds of soap that night, thinking to wash off her scent and whatever she could have left behind with him. He wasn't sure of how spells worked, but he didn't want to find out in a negative way. He didn't have time for matters like this with his parents being so far away.

Jezebel was calm. She watched every move Zoe made in her home, and she wanted her first meeting to have an impact —and it did. She saw her eyes light up when they met, and she had a twinkle that day she tried on her dress, too. She was longing for more than what she had, and soon, she would want more than all she had. That is how it always starts. First with curiosity, then with an uncontrollable attraction, the two are pulled together like a moth to a flame.

But who is this girl that Charity has befriended and brought into her home? Jezebel had to figure it out, and so she put a light spell on Sean's hand that was blocked fairly quickly. She got what she needed to learn more about his name and whereabouts. She felt she could do minor research and have him pegged, but this girl. She wanted to get to the root of who she was and her parents.

In most homes, she could send a monitoring spirit to enter doors and walls, but this house was covered in every room. There was a bright light that shone all around the house, and she knew whoever lived there had power–and lots of it. For hours, she was looking for anything that could help her solve the riddle behind this family. It wasn't until the lid was opened and the necklace reemerged from the trash that she had a second chance to enter the house undetected.

Entering the house, she could see the address and the location, but she couldn't leave the drawer she was placed in. She was in a drawer and briefly saw the light of day when her brother looked into it quickly, but he shut it, sensing a violation of his sister's privacy. This is where Jezebel had to remain content until the time was right to manifest in a bigger way. At least she was in the house, and she knew that would become a portal she would use later, when and if she needed it.

She refused to be dumbfounded by the tricks this girl could have up her sleeve. She made a pretty large impression on Charity in a few short weeks, and, to say the least, Charity was curious about her life. Now, Jezebel was interested to learn more about this girl who had dominated her daughter's time. She had to get into the girls' history and see what threat she would have for her plans, and the plans, most importantly, she had for Charity.

Her curiosity was also seconded by Carol, the grandmother who monitored the house, overshadowing her daughter and granddaughter. She saw the girls playing, heard the conversations, and the light Zoe had, she knew could be dangerous even though it was much smaller than her parents. Her parents, Carol, quickly realized were the prayer warriors keeping them from running every block in their city. This small church that her parents belonged to was clean.

They didn't take bribes. The husband didn't have eyes for other women, nor did he have pinned-up anger or resentment toward his wife. She had nothing her witches could pull on to yank him down in the world or the spirit.

His wife was even more powerful than he was in the spirit, so she feared getting too close to her because of her influence. She knew if she did too much, she would be alerted, and her plan on too many levels would be postponed, if not canceled. If she played her cards right, she could take out the biggest church, not in size, but in power in the region, and reclaim her body all at once.

This was the jackpot, and she knew the window was short. She had less than 60 days to make her plan happen, and she was getting desperate. Her body was old, very old, and it had days to keep it together before a blood pack she made would come back to roost. She needed to swap lives with her daughter or granddaughter and let them go to hell in her place. She had too many plans to give up her reign now. They would understand, because there isn't one person who wouldn't do what she would to live another hundred years.

Now, she only had to focus on the plan to weave the web into a tapestry that would mean she got everything she ever wanted.

I Always
Get What I Want

It was a quick month that flew by, and Zoe's family had become more disconnected with each passing week. Their mother was concerned about the silence, but she also felt the silence meant everything was fine. Sometimes silence can be golden, right? Sean was busy with school, and he was being the best brother and protector he could be.

He was checking the doors at night. Staying off bad sites and living by the rules. He didn't invite even one friend over, and that made him proud of himself. He was tired, although he couldn't pinpoint why. Maybe he just wanted a break from the chaos of being a semi-parent and thought he'd get some fresh air.

Yeah, he liked driving the car, but what he really wanted to drive was the motorcycle. He looked at it every time he came home from an errand or took his sister around town. He wanted to hop on the bike just once, but where could he go and not be seen by the neighbors? He had to be stealthy and go when no one was up or would hear him peel out of the driveway.

He knew that meant a 3am bike run because what normal person would be up that late anyway? He feared opening the driveway, so on purpose, he let the door up at about 12am and planned to leave it up until he hit the streets. He looked out his window to make sure the block was quiet and most lights were out. He knew the old people who would be quick to call his parents were all asleep.

He fell asleep that night, and as he lay on his bed, there was a cool breeze that seemed to enter his dreams or cover him as he lay awake. His body was at rest, but he wasn't sure if he was sleeping or not. As he slept, he saw her face smiling and looking like an angel. Who was this woman that is now intruding on his dreams, he thought.

At first, she didn't do anything but watch him. She seemed to communicate with her eyes, and she started to raise a longing deep within his bones as she moved gingerly around the room that appeared to have no walls, no doors, and nowhere to run. There were soft whispers in his ears, but he didn't know what the voices were saying. Sean felt himself back up away from her and ensured she didn't get close to touch him ever again. In a quickness, she charges at him, almost like she was floating, and she comes before his face.

With a blink, he started to shout in his dreams, "I don't like you. Get away from me. I rebuke you, Satan. I rebuke you in the name of Yashua, Jesus, the Lord the Christ." His eyes stayed shut as he repeated, "The Bible says to resist the devil, and he must flee. Get away from me. I am not playing woman."

Then the woman, Jezebel, drifted away, and he woke up. The time was 3:20am. He almost overslept if it weren't for the crazy dream. His breathing was still hard as he tried to collect his emotions and pull his heart or spirit back into his body. He felt out of sorts but knew this bike ride would help him collect his thoughts.

Sean enters the garage and ensures the light stays off. Nothing like a bright light to blow the operation. He goes out of the garage by pushing the bike into the street and down the road. Wearing all black, with a black motorcycle and black tarp, he thinks no one will see him going down the road or think more of it than seeing a guy pushing a bike with no motor. He pushed the bike down the road about two blocks before he sat on it and turned the key.

The bike was quiet, and it hardly made a loud noise at all as he took off down the street. He missed the simple days of riding bikes, wearing glasses, and cruising down the road. The weather was perfect, and the breeze against his oversized shirt blew in the distance.

He felt at home for the first time, and it felt good. He was driving and was sure to be careful. He didn't lock eyes with anyone in case someone would recognize him or the bike. He pulled over after riding down the road to take his helmet off. He did think for a moment of how dumb this could be to see his face plastered everywhere.

The least he could do was put on the helmet and deny it was him riding down the road. They would have to have the license tag to show it was on the street, and maybe he wouldn't be toast. But who would be on the road to catch him anyway? He made sure to obey the traffic lights so he didn't get a ticket.

He pulled into a gas station to get some air. There was a girl who got into a nice car who winked at him. She likely was coming from a club and was tipsy. She didn't seem fully aware as she walked clumsily to the car. He didn't pay her much mind as he started the bike back up. He grabbed his helmet and clicked it into place, and planned to head home. As he pulls out of the driveway, he feels the breeze his body craves. His mind is at peace until he hears "Bam!"

He pushed the brakes, and the bike stopped on a dime. The girls who just left the parking lot turned their lights off and were stupid enough to drive down the road in the dark, with a black car! Who does that, Sean thought as they got out of the car? They came to him and said, "Hey, you hit my car!"

"Look, I didn't mean to hit your car. You didn't have your lights on, so I couldn't see you until I got too close. I barely hit you."

"But you hit me," says a girl who must have

been a few years older than the drunk girl entering on the passenger side.

"Look, I didn't mean to hit your car, but you cannot drive around with your lights out."

"Maybe, but you cannot rear-end people and think you don't have to pay for the damages."

"But this isn't my fault," Sean retorted.

"Really? Maybe we should call the police and find out."

"I don't think we have to call the police, but we do need to sort this out."

"Okay, I can call my mechanic tomorrow and get a quote. You give me the money and I will say we are all good."

"What about my bike?"

"You said it yourself, there isn't much damage. So you can pay for that out of your own pocket, or call this into insurance, and let them sort it out."

"I will give you a thousand dollars to fix this little dent, which I know is more than enough. I will cover the cost to fix my bike. Just give me your number."

"I am gonna need your license, phone number, and address. If you stiff me, I will know where to come and collect."

"I am not doing any of that. I will give you my phone number, and you can call me."

"Give me your social ID then. If you fail to pay, I will bug the hell out of you there. People are less likely to cut social handles than they are phone numbers. I want my money."

"I will give you that. But I need you to give me like a month to get the money."

"A month?"

"Yeah, money doesn't grow on trees. Give me a month."

"I will give you two weeks, then I will bug you nonstop until you pay."

They exchange numbers, and he drives the bike home. He needed to see the bike in the light to really know the damage he caused, but he couldn't check until Zoe went to school. He knew this entire process was going to be at least two or three thousand dollars. How does a college kid who doesn't work going to get that kind of money in a month or two?

He wasn't sure how he was going to do it or if he could, but he had to try. He needed a job, and he needed it yesterday if he stood a chance to pay this money back. He thought of how he could be so stupid to drive the bike at 3 am, knowing drunks would be out on the road. He blamed himself, but none of that helped him with what he had to do. He had to push it aside and focus on what he had to do and not what was out of his control.

How was he going to get a job and Zoe not notice it? That meant he would have to work nights to keep it under wraps. Maybe he could drive and deliver food at night and, ironically, do more of what got him in trouble in this first place.

This time at least, he would be in the car he had permission to drive he considered. So that would make it better, right? They never said he couldn't work after all. It would just be odd when they asked about the money he had made and where it went.

He didn't want the questions, so he decided not to mention that to his parents. He was living nowadays with more secrets than he liked. He didn't think any of his secrets harmed anyone, so he tried to keep them under wraps for as long as possible. He would only tell his parents what was going on if he must. For now, he will just figure it out.

He started his job search that day to find some kind of employment. He was looking at jobs, and many were not at the right time. So he tried delivering food because that made more sense to him for his timing. He arrived at work and met his manager. His manager was an older black man who would train him, but he explained that he works for himself as a contractor. He liked making his own schedule and being in control of what he could make and when.

He did have some advice for Sean to help him make the best decisions for life. "Drop the food off and be sure to take the picture. If you can include the address in the picture, do that so they can't say they didn't get it. I take a backup picture right after I get in the car because some of these people say they didn't get it when they knew they ate that food. Protect yourself."

"Got it." Sean heard him loud and clear. Protect yourself, no matter what, and don't trust people to be honorable. Good lesson, he felt it applied to all of his life. After the two talked a bit more, he asked, "Hey, can I ask you a question?"

"Yeah, man. What's up?"

"I met this lady right. She is beautiful, but something about her makes me uncomfortable when I met her. She kissed me on my hand, and that was weird. But I couldn't let go."

"Dang, you either got a lady that really likes you, or has a plan to haunt you." He says as he laughs. Sean's face told it all. She was haunting him.

He tried to give him comfort, "Look, if you think you are dealing with a witch. You gotta keep your distance. Don't eat their food, they mix that shit with blood, and have you loopy. Don't take nothing from them, that makes them feel you owe them. And whatever you do, don't sleep with them in your dreams or in reality. I know this shit sounds strange. But I've been there, and that shit took me years to get free from. That bitch was crazy."

"Yo, you for real, man? You really think this lady is a witch?"

"It could be a coincidence that she popped up in your dreams, but if not, you need to protect yourself. If you know God, you'd better dig deep depending on what they want from you. They ain't done. So keep your eyes open."

Sean heard every word he said, but he struggled with the reality of it all. Could this woman really be a witch? Is it possible that the devil himself was just using her face because he sensed or knew his feelings about her, and he is using that against him? He was in a mind twist, but right now, he had to go and deliver food in the dark.

He thought, *Why did I take a job that kept me in the dark?* That night was hard on his mind, but dropping the food made him forget about his witch problems for the moment. He said a quick prayer over his life and, for the first time, began to see the importance of prayer and having a covering, as his mom explained it. Did she always see stuff like this and just keep him protected from it?

The thoughts in his head kept him calm throughout the day, and he began to increase his alertness in his dreams and whereabouts. He started to pray at night and in the morning, starting that day forward. He didn't want to take any risk that the Father for a day wasn't with him. He woke up the next day tired, but relieved he had no dreams. He went to the kitchen to check on his sister. She wasn't down yet, but he knew she would be down any moment.

She came to the kitchen looking fresh as a daisy as she snuck up behind him and tapped him on the shoulder. He swung around intently, and she ducked to dodge any accidental blow. "Wow, Sean, you good?"

"Hey, my bad, Sis. You almost caught one."

"You need to relax."

"Yeah, probably."

She was wearing her pajamas from last night, so it was safe to assume she had slept the entire night. He was relieved knowing that the garage door didn't wake her from her sleep. He knew at that moment that he could sneak out nightly to work. She had the lipstick on, and Sean said, "Hey, can you wipe that off. You know if Mom were here, she wouldn't approve of that."

"Sean, it is not a big deal. She is not here."

"But God is here. You'd better wipe that off."

"Really, Sean?" He nods his head yes, and she goes to the sink to grab a napkin. "You are being ridiculous."

"That's fine. You are being a child. Thank you." Zoe sucks her cheek in objection, and she grabs an apple as she leaves through the door. The tarp on the bike was almost off somehow, but he was able to pull it up high enough so the damage wasn't seen. He had taken it to the shop yesterday to get a quote to repair the damage. It would cost him nearly $1,500 to fix the bike. He swallowed hard when he heard the price, but knew he had no choice but to pay it—and soon.

The drive to school would have been quiet, but the phone rang. It was their mom. Sean picked it up, "Hey, Mom? How's it going?"

"Good. Good, Son. It has been busy for more reasons than one." She doesn't tell them, but it has been a challenge for them across the board. The government was fighting some of their building permits. They had struck liquid gold on the property, and it had caused an unexpected stir.

It is great to realize money could be under the ground, but it also puts the project at risk. Now, they want to delay the building schedule, and that is concerning to her. To make matters worse, she is dealing with spiritual attacks by some of the people, too."

"Hey, how is Zoe? I don't hear her."

"She is right here."

"Zoe, what's going on? Are you having a good morning, baby?"

"Yeah, Mom. I am good." She is still in her feelings, and her mom can pick it up on the phone.

"Put me on video. I don't like how you sounding." Zoe pushes the button to go on video. Although she should be grateful now that she took the lipstick off, she was not. She was still in her feelings that she couldn't be who she wanted to be. She wanted to wear lipstick that had nothing to do with her trying to be grown, but to make a decision for herself.

She looks into the screen, and her attitude is still leaking funky vibes, "Hi, Mom."

"Hey, how are you? Why you looking like that?"

"Nothing," replies Zoe with discontent.

"She's mad she gotta listen to me. She thinks she is just as old as me," Sean chimes in.

"You know your brother is there to cover you, to keep you safe. You'd better listen to him, or I will be back on a plane to come and deal with you myself. Your father and I are dealing with a lot here, and it is putting a lot of pressure on your father, so I apologize that we have been busy. It is my intention to call more to stay connected. I don't like how we haven't really talked lately."

"Mom, it's cool. I know you are busy doing God's work."

"You are part of God's work for me, too," she says.

"I know, Mom." Feeling softer toward her mother, she replies, "I am sorry. But I am good, just figuring out my emotions, I guess. I am sure it will pass," Zoe says.

"If it doesn't, or if it does, let me know. Don't keep me in the dark, Zoe. If you keep me in the dark, I will go to God, and don't think I am not praying for you both, even though I am not there."

"We know, Mom. We got this. Don't worry and focus on helping, Dad."

They all three share love and happy thoughts before Zoe exits the car. They pull up to the school, and like clockwork, Charity is exiting her mother's vehicle. Jezebel catches his eye and waves. He waves respectfully but quickly drives off to get away from the awkward air. He drove home with Gospel music playing to help erase the presence of any spirits left behind. He was made light again and ready to tackle his day of college and higher learning.

Jezebel went home, and she looked over her list of actions. She made a plan for what she wanted, and her vision enlarged. She knew that the same information she had, her mother had, too. She wanted to beat her to the punch, but she felt like she was behind. Not being able to use her looks to tempt Sean was proven to be annoying and disruptive to her progress.

Her mom had her claws into Sean, and now she had to do something or bow out gracefully and watch her plan work. She wasn't sure what her mom was up to, but she didn't trust that her actions were part of a master plan that included her being on top for some reason. Growing up with her mother, she learned how selfish her mom could be with Charity's father.

It would have broken her if she had put her whole heart into trusting her mother. What it did was remind her of who her real enemy was. You keep your enemies close, and the tricky ones, closer.

She didn't tell her mother everything she knew, and her mom didn't tell her everything she had done. But for the parts of the truth they both had, it was enough for them to go forward with their plans. It was her mother who got Jezebel to realize that there is no such thing as family or love. Love is a happenstance, a circumstance that alludes them both.

Flashback

A young Jezebel was content to spend time with Curtis, and she thought to bake him something. She didn't cook much, but lately, everything she wanted to eat or smell seemed to taste like black licorice in her mouth. It never occurred to her that she could be pregnant, and it wasn't until this day that she thought to take a test. She went to the store, grabbed a test, and after peeing on the stick, within 3 minutes the results revealed she was, in fact, pregnant.

At first, all she could think to do was to tell the guy she had planned to run away with. She wanted to prove that they could be happy, and now get married and really start a family for real. For the first time ever, she saw a life away from her mother, magic, and the life she lived. She wanted to give it all up for this baby and husband she longed to have. She would give it all up for love.

She was excited as she baked the cake, which looked okay but not prize-worthy. She went by his house but didn't immediately see his car parked. She saw his mother come home as she waited across the street. Something told her to hang tight and not to call him. She wanted to surprise him. Maybe she could meet his mother since they were going to take this relationship seriously. If he wasn't going to marry her, he might at least want to introduce her to his mother so they could know the mother of his child.

She beamed as she waited to share the good news with him. It seemed like an hour had gone by, and she was tempted to leave. The cake icing was beginning to droop a little as the sun set on it. It was then that a car pulled into the driveway. It was a familiar face. It was the girl who, several months ago, she remembered dropped him off, whom he claimed was a friend.

He must have been out all night or something because his feet were barely beneath him. She had to hobble him to the door again. As she got him to stand up temporarily, using the house as a crutch, he fell slightly forward and tried to kiss her. She dodged his kisses and said, "Come on, Curtis. Stop, you're drunk and you don't mean any of this."

He replies, smiling drunkenly, "You know you will always have a place in my heart. How can I forget a face or an ass like yours?" He tried to kiss her again, and again she dodged him. It was at this point that Jezebel got out of her car holding the cake. She looked at both of them with eyes that were flaming red. Before she could say a word to either of them, Curtis knew this was going to end with cake flying.

He jumped in front of his friend, and the cake splattered him in the face. On cue, "Who the hell are you? You told me you are a friend, but is that true, Curtis?"

"Yes, it is true, Curtis. You need to get your girlfriend," the stripper said cautiously.

"Baby, it is not what you think. She is a dancer, and she is my friend. We are not in a relationship," replied Curtis.

"He's just my regular. Nothing more, I don't want to see him dead, so I drive him home sometimes," she said to deescalate the situation. That didn't work.

"That's it? What the hell do you mean that's it?" says a furious Jezebel.

"That's it. I am leaving. You can get it from here." She starts backing away, but keeps her eyes on

Jezebel, who is uncertain of what she will do next. The girl senses her hesitation to be calm, so she shuffles into her car, locks the doors, and darts out of the driveway. She throws his bag out of the car and into the driveway as she departs.

Jezebel looks at him on the ground, covered in cake, drunk, licking around his mouth. "Babe, this cake is pretty good. You should have saved me a piece."

"You idiot! Why the hell are you having strippers take you home?"

"What was I supposed to do, Jaze. Call you? Tell you come get me from the club?" She smirks but doesn't say anything. "No, I can't call you, so I don't. She doesn't want me, but she can help make my dark nights bearable. I know it is selfish of me, but it keeps me honest."

"You don't have nothing else to tell me, Curtis?"

"No, I mean, we had sex, but it was a long time ago. She doesn't want me now. She won't even let me kiss her. It was all just business to her."

"Well, that business is finished, from now on."

"Whatever you say."

"I have something to tell you, but I think we should go inside."

"I don't really want my mom to see me like this. Can we get out of here?"

"You want me to put your dirty ass in my car?"

"To be fair, you made me this way," says Curtis as he licks his fingers.

"Fine. Get your ass up and let's go." She helps him off the ground, and they hobble to her car. She struggles to open the door and keep the cake from hitting her skin or clothes. She has an issue with touching icky things, and this situation was messy. They got a hotel up the street, and it was nice to be somewhere other than the house his mother owned. She set her bag down, and he headed straight for the shower.

He hollers out to the open area, "You gonna make me shower alone? Come in here with me." She smacked her teeth because she was upset, but the invitation seemed so genuine. She didn't want to miss out on the opportunity to reclaim the energy and make things well again. She was mad, but she didn't want to stay that way.

She came into the shower with him, and they reconnected in a way they had both longed for. As they lie on the bed wrapped in their towels, Curtis is almost sound asleep. Jezebel looks at his face and is excited about more nights ahead like this. She was nervous to tell him about the baby and considered not telling him after the ordeal with the stripper.

Looking at him as he slept, however, she felt her life could remain like this. She could be in his arms and he in her lap for the rest of their lives. They could be happy and work through problems by communicating and loving each other through mistakes and problems.

Soon, they would have the money to match the plan and move forward with their lives. Why should she have to go back home and deal with the selfish bitch, whom she called a mother? Why did she need to feel pinned up when she could be here with him, free as a bird?

It was in that moment that she decided she wasn't going home. She wanted more for her baby and for her life. She wanted to build something that didn't have her mother's rubber stamp of approval on it. Who does she think she is to know what was best for her, and that was how she felt. All her life thus far, she lived by her mother's rules, but now it was time for her to look out for herself and get something that made her happy. Curtis made her happy, and she was excited to build this life with him.

She fell asleep with him, and they both lay together as the sun shifted down. It was about five o'clock when they got up and got hungry. The growl inside Jezebel's stomach was incredibly loud, and she couldn't conceal it. He asked after giggling, "You hungry?"

Sheepishly, she replied, "Yeah. I am starving. I should have saved some of that cake." She started to laugh some with him.

"It's all good. You want to go and pick something up or order it for here?"

"Can we just order it for here? I don't feel like going out right now," Jezebel said. The truth was, she didn't feel like going anywhere for a while. She had to think about what she would say to her mom.

Plan A was done, but parts B and C remain to be seen. He picked up the phone and ordered for both of them. She got cozy in the bed, and it felt good to be wrapped in a towel, propped up on the bed, watching him handle things.

Will he be like this as a husband, too? She asked him about running away, but would he be good with doing that today? Like right now, she thought. He hung up his phone and said, "Food is ordered. It should be here in about 30 minutes. I could think of something we can do until then." He comes up to give her a kiss, but she gently pulls him aside.

"I would love that too, but I need to tell you something."

"Yeah, of course," Curtis replies as he buries his lips in her neck.

"What do you think about us being together?"

"I would say that is what we are doing right

now."

"I mean, like being together all the time. Living together, maybe even getting married?"

"Woe, marriage? I mean, I care about you — you know I do. I am cool with us seeing where this will go and living together, even, but marriage is a big step. I don't know if we are there yet."

"Okay, but you do think we should be together and see where this can go, right?"

"Yeah, of course," replies Curtis.

Responding, Jezebel says, "Good. You want to hear what I think?" He gives her a kiss and a hug, then looks her in the face to listen.

"I think we should move out, take some time for ourselves, and have a baby. And go from there."

"Wait, you want to move in together? But where would we live? We both don't have a place right now."

"We have a place right now. We are both here, so what will be the difference?"

"It is different when we live together all the time. Right now, you only experience me in small doses. Who's to say you will still like me 24-7?"

"Don't be nervous. I know enough about you to know that I love you."

"Love me?" he says with a compassionate heart. He never intended for things to get this far. He knew then that this was the plan all along for Carol. She wanted her daughter to love him, but why?

"I know love is a big thing. I don't want you to feel rushed or confused by all of this."

"I am not confused, Curtis. I loved you the moment I saw you enter my shop. I knew it then. I have never loved anyone as much as I have loved you. But what if we got our own place for a few months, a year lease maybe? And we tried to become parents who love each other and eventually get married?"

"Why parents? Right now, we are both young and don't know nothing about the responsibility of raising a baby. Don't you think we should get married first?"

"That might be the right way, but that isn't our path. I've been trying to tell you–" There is a knock on the door that stops the conversation. Curtis gets up and grabs the door. It's the food. How did the time go so quickly Jezebel thought as she eagerly waited for her stomach to settle down. She opened the foil, and instantly her mouth was dry, her palms sweaty, and she felt sick.

She hurried up, got off the bed, and ran to the bathroom to the toilet that would catch the vomit lodged in her throat. Curtis, concerned for her, stood by the door and asked, "You alright? Are you allergic to garlic or something?"

A little annoyed, she replied, "No, Curtis. I am pregnant."

At that moment, the room started spinning for him. He slid down to the floor and sat there as the smells from their untapped food lingered in the air. He couldn't unhear the words, and he was pissed. This scheme not only meant he could end up with a wife he didn't pick, but he could be a father to a child with no say so?

Why or how could this happen? Yes, they weren't always safe, but he guessed she was on the pill to avoid problems like this one, considering her mother. How could he have been so dumb, lazy, not to ensure this couldn't happen?

It was moments later that they both sat seemingly in the same position. He wasn't sure of what to say. This wasn't part of the script; this was a whole new direction, a fork in the road, and he had to think of how to handle it. He asked the only question he could think of, "What do you want to do, Jaze?"

"I want you to be happy. I want you to want to be with me, and for us to be a family. What else do you think I want, Curtis?"

"I'm sorry." He got up off the floor and re-membered his manners. He gave her a hug and tried to comfort her because he could only imagine how she was feeling.

"It's alright. This is scary for me, too. I don't want to go home. I want to be with you and see where this can go. But you need to be here with me, Curtis."

"I hear you. Of course, I get it now. Sorry, I was selfish and on my bullshit. I will pull it together."

"Please, we are going to need you," Jezebel says through tears.

He said nothing as he held her in his arms. He held his woman, for the time being, and his unborn baby in his hands, and he felt nothing. Not happiness, not joy, not fear anymore. He was empty and hollow. He needed to get out of that hotel room, and anything could be the excuse.

"You want something else to eat? Ice cream? Water? Juice?"

"I could use some water and maybe fresh fruit?"

"Yes, of course. Anything you need. Let me get dressed and grab it. I will be right back."

A Change of Plans

He left out the door and, as he got downstairs and out of the lobby, he hurried to her car. For some reason, he felt her eyes could be watching him, so he didn't pick up the phone until he left the parking lot. These women were stressing him out. This is not a love triangle; this is a trifecta of chaos. He still had to call his friend and explain that this is temporary, and he will be back.

He needed to call Carol and explain he needed out right now. He had hoped that this baby wasn't his and that Carol knew something about it. It was hard for him to accept that he might be stuck with a woman he had zero feelings for, and to have a baby like this was not part of his plan. This is not what she promised him, and that was not what he wanted.

Carol had been calling her daughter all day, but she refused to answer. She was not so much concerned as much as she grew anxious. Where was her daughter and what was she up to? She was quick to answer his call, and the phone rang only once before she came on the line, "What the hell, Curtis?"

"Hey, sorry, it has been a long day."

"No shit."

"Look, I don't know what is happening right now, but this is not what we talked about."

"What is going on? Are you going to tell me or make me read your mind, Curtis?"

"No, your daughter is in love with me."

"I knew that would happen."

"I'm glad you knew, I had no idea, and I was railroaded today. How am I supposed to respond to this? I am a lot of things, but I ain't gonna do her dirty like this. This doesn't feel right. It's one thing to be a fuck boy, pardon my French, but this is a whole other matter. I didn't sign up for this."

"Will you just calm down? You don't have to marry her."

"But I do."

"Why do you think you have to marry her?"

"Because, because–"

"What, spit it out. Damn kids."

"She's pregnant, Ms. Carol."

The silence on the other end must have

meant Carol didn't anticipate this happening any more than Curtis. She couldn't stop the swarm of thoughts entering her head. She thought and tried to slow things down and replied with fire in her voice.

"What the hell, Curtis? How could you let something like this happen! This was supposed to be a hook-up with no strings attached, and here you are digging a ditch and preparing for marriage!"

"You think I am happy about this? The girl of my dreams, I just had to excommunicate because of a fake relationship I am not even into. This was supposed to be some fun for helping my uncle, and now I feel like you had a forever plan for me."

"Watch your mouth, I am still the one with all the power, and you better never forget it. What am I supposed to do with a pregnant body, Curtis? Do you even know what I am working on? I cannot have her weak and in this state to perform this spell!"

"Look, I don't know what you are doing, but this is ruining my plans, too! She thinks I am going to run away with her!"

"What the hell do you mean run away with her?"

"She is planning to live with me every day and not go home. She already said she wasn't leaving me. The only way I got out of the hotel was to get her something from the store. I am an errand boy right now for your daughter. What the hell is going on with my life?"

"So that little ungrateful bitch would leave me for you?"

"She is trying to be happy, Carol. I don't think she is thinking all the way straight. She is pregnant and scared. It might be her nerves talking."

"Or it might prove what I thought, she is just as selfish as I am and only cares about her damn self. I will show that little bitch what it means to cross me. Here is what I need you to do. I need you to do everything she asks you to do. Stay as long as you can, and try to pretend you are happy. If I can speed up the spell, I will try to fix the shit you just threw into my plans. If I can't resolve this, you are in this with me."

"Wait a minute. You told me I had to do this one thing, and I was done. You never mentioned us being one big happy family. I don't want that shit."

"If you were able to keep your dick in your pants, maybe we wouldn't be here. If you don't know how to use it properly, don't pull it out! And another thing, witches lie. Don't you watch movies? Gullible and stupid."

"You really gonna talk to me like that?"

"All you men are exactly alike. I think it is my daughter's turn to figure out what it is really like to fall in love with a man. You get her to feel comfortable, and when she is most vulnerable, I want you to leave her high and dry. Leave her with no one to call but me. She will beg me to help her, and I will be the only help she will have. If I have to share my body with some baby, then it belongs to me too. You don't have to worry about the child, I will take care of that, but I own your ass until you do what I am asking."

He doesn't say a word, but for the first time, he is concerned about how deep he has gotten into whatever this is with this lady. He never thought this would turn into anything like this. He didn't expect a baby or marriage. He didn't expect to hurt anybody, but just to have a little fun and play childish games. This was way beyond his heart level. He was torn between what he should and who he should fear the most.

Annoyed that he hadn't already agreed, Carol repeats herself through gritted teeth, "Do you hear me, Curtis?"

"Yes, yes, I hear you." Carol hangs up and says a slew of curse words that only she and the devil knows. She had plans to switch bodies after her daughter was broken and weak enough to be conquered, but now, she wouldn't be weak; this fake love affair has given her hope. Hope deferred will make a heart grow sick, so if she cannot have this relationship, she will get weaker and weaker, and Carol planned to kill her right after birth or before it. She didn't have plans for the daughter and couldn't care less about what happened to her as long as she got the body she had "preyed" for.

Curtis still has a mind that feels more like scrambled eggs than anything. He is trying to stay focused on the mission ahead of him, but he is freaking out. How could she be so cold as not to care about her grandchild or her daughter?

Could a human ever be so cold? He got to thinking about if he had made a deal with the devil and how he felt about it. No baby deserved to come into this world like this. He didn't deserve this, but neither did Jezebel.

He didn't love her, but she was sweet, and he believed she loved him. Would it be easy to love her, to be so nice, and build her hopes up for them to be together, then to leave her high and dry? Was he capable of doing that? Or would he rather treat her badly and force her to leave him? Wouldn't that be better for Jezebel for her to see him as the bad guy and not like something is wrong with her?

He wasn't sure of what kind of game Carol was playing now, but this isn't just a game to him; it is his life. He had to deal with the choices he was making, and he had to somewhat agree with them. He would not ever think about abortion, but could this be a time where aborting a baby might be better than bringing her into a world filled with such evil? Would she be guaranteed a place in paradise if she were to leave now instead of in the future?

He wasn't sure of what to think, so he allowed his mind to wander as his body was on autopilot, grabbing things he had heard pregnant women like. He got what she said and other items in case she would ask for them later. He brought bags of food to the hotel, and Jezebel was shocked at the sight. She replied with a laugh, "Well, this explained why it felt like you abandoned me and headed for the hills. You went and bought up the entire store. I am only pregnant with one baby, Curtis."

"Are you sure? Have you done all that already?"

"No, I haven't even told my mom yet. You are the first person I am telling, and I think it should stay that way for a while."

"Yeah, of course. That makes sense. So what if we just stay here for like a week and get our heads together, then we plan on where we go from here?"

"That sounds nice," she says with a smile and a twinkle in her eyes. How could he be so cruel to take this young woman's dreams and crush them in his hands? How can he be so heartless or selfish that he would rob a baby of her future to get what he wants temporarily for his uncle? Was he any better than Carol by what he was willing to do for magic and power?

He held Jezebel that night like his stripper friend often held him. She had a way of calming his inner demons, and tonight he needed her badly. But for now, he will have to learn how to hold himself, because he was alone on this road with no paddle. His instructions were simple, but the dedication will take more work than he has ever committed to anything.

Curtis knows he is best in small doses. He doesn't have the best temper, and he is afraid of what he can become under pressure. With a lack of sleep, he is a madman. He was sure to only show Jezebel his best sides, but what would she think if she saw the parts of him no one sees, not even his mom? He was dealing with his own demons, and now he had to share them with someone else. This is the closest someone would be to him, and it is not even with a woman he loves.

Several months passed by, and the baby bump started to show more and more. Jezebel was a conscious eater, and she never ate for the hell of it, even when she felt she could. She wanted to keep her figure and skin as tight as possible. She knew the value of a pretty face and fit body. She knew how men could become disinterested in a woman long before she grew old.

No, it is not fair, but it is life. She knew this relationship was still one-sided, but she believed that in time, he would grow to love her. Only if she could get under the layer of protection he held like an extra layer of skin she could get into his heart.

This was a part of life she didn't want to use magic for, although she could. Something made her feel pathetic to resort to magic to get someone to love her. She wanted it to be real, and by choice. It was a choice that she turned her back on her mom and chose to be happy with Curtis. She doesn't regret the arguments they have, the nights she feels alone and misunderstood. If she is honest, this living together thing isn't all that she had imagined it to be.

They got a two-bedroom house in a nice part of town. Turns out Curtis can be really resourceful when he needs to be. The house that was gifted to her previously, he upgraded it to a nicer area, and the deal she got was sweet. She was no fool, so she made sure the deed was in her name because "We are not married. I earned this house," was always her position and thought.

She knew better than to put all of her eggs in one basket. Curtis could be a jerk sometimes, but she knew all men and women, for that matter, had that streak. The stress of the baby, too, she felt, could be weighing on him.

To her surprise, he was very active during the pregnancy. He wanted to go to all of the appointments. He was there for her, but after each appointment, he would get drunk out of his mind and get irritated and want to fight the walls. He would start rambling about things she couldn't understand and slap the wall until he got tired.

He once slapped her when she tried to stop him, and for a moment, he got sober. He didn't stop the behavior, and things only got worse. Instead of seeing her as a help to him, Jezebel started to feel like a target. She didn't know where this anger was coming from.

He didn't talk to her; he would just go on these wild binges and say how he was being robbed of everything he had ever wanted. A family, to be loved, to have it all. She would try to be there for him and tell him with love and affection she would tell him.

"I am here, Curtis. You are not alone. We are in this together. You don't have to be afraid. We are a family."

But her words brought little to no comfort. He would only start crying, and sometimes uncontrollably. She had never seen a man so all over the place with his emotions. If she didn't love him, she would have thought of leaving him.

The stress of his mood swings would send her into borderline panic attacks. She never said anything, but the doctors had some questions about her irregular breathing. She said she was a bit anxious, and they chalked it up to first-pregnancy jitters and didn't pry.

It was stressful being in the same house with a man she felt was bipolar at best. One moment, he is happy and content with life. The next time, he is crying, angry, mad, or sad. She didn't know how to comfort him, so she started to take her distance, which only made things worse. He started going out and taking late-night rides. A ride to where she wasn't sure, but at the time, she didn't care.

She was five months pregnant and will soon find out the sex of the baby. She would read up on all kinds of things on the internet and wanted to buy up the world for the baby, but needed to know what she was having. She would ask whether his mother might need to know she is having a grandchild, but he would insist on waiting until after they knew the baby's sex to let her know. He really hadn't thought about how to tell his mom, and it is all still a big secret to her.

He did try to tell her once about his situation, and her response was a bit alarming. She said, "What have you gotten yourself into now, Curtis? Why are you asking me about an abortion? You know we don't believe that we are followers of God. God doesn't like ugly, and killing an innocent child is evil. It's wrong. If you were big enough to lie down and have that baby, it looks like you're going to be a father, whether you like it or not."

He knew telling her anything more would invoke her Christian hat, and right now, he needed a regular person to tell him what he wanted to hear. He wanted a way out. During that week, they stayed at the hotel. He went to his uncle and asked him the same question, "Unc, what should I do?"

"I wouldn't kill this baby because this baby could be the key to what you always wanted. You want power, you want wealth, and you need to create your own legacy. Having a baby with a woman like Jezebel will level you up in ways you don't understand."

"But I don't love her."

"Fuck love. You don't need love to get power, money, and the life you've always wanted. You think that stripper loves you? No, she loves money and power. Keep your heart there if you like, but the baby and her mom don't blow that."

His uncle smirked and said further, "You are getting a baby out of this and a baby with one of the most powerful witches in the tri-state area. What more do you want? This is like a necessary marriage a family has to make to advance their bloodline, Son. If this goes through, you need to be prepared to take one for the team."

"That's how you really feel?"

"If we were regular people, I would tell you to man up. Carol never told you to get her daughter pregnant; you did that. Sure, you didn't mean to, but we have to own up to our mess-ups the same way we deal with the shit that was personal or intentional. Maybe this is a blessing in disguise?"

"Did you really just say blessing? We are not the kind of people that get blessings, Unc. This could mean very bad news. Am I the only one seeing this?"

"Maybe you are the only one seeing it. You need to let this play out, and remember why we got here in the first place. Your mom is not coming off none of that money. There ain't a spell known to man we can use against her with the hedge her God put around her. So, we have to figure this thing out ourselves or live hand to fist, hoping she dies, which is real fucked up. I don't love your mom like your father did, but I would never speak death on her."

He looks intently at him and says, "Do you really want something to be sent to your mother? You know how Carol can be; she is unpredictable, and this is a woman who gets what she wants. I would stay out of her way and do what she says. Yes, you have to deal with the woman you live with, but you have to deal with the mother-in-law from hell. Stay on her good side, and this too shall pass."

He nods, knowing this is no longer about him or his wishes; it is about his mother and her protection. He can't tell his mom about this baby. He can't risk exposing her to the mess he started. And although there is deadly poison being flung all around him, he has to find a way to piece his life together under these circumstances in a way that doesn't hurt anyone. He knows it will break Jezebel's heart for him to fall in love with her and abandon her.

He doesn't have the heart to make her pay for the crazy antics of her mother, so he decides to do what he hates to do. Grow up and start thinking for himself. This whole time, he has allowed his parents, a woman, or something else to drive his decisions. Now, he had to think about someone else, not just himself, but the baby. Just maybe, if he could make her fall in love with the baby, when he was out of the picture, she would love the baby and put the love she had for him into the child?

What if he could fake his death, or she decides to leave him because he was such an asshole, and she found out I was unstable? He thought of a plan to become the most hated, unlovable, and inconsistent man he could be in hopes she would fall out of love with him and even grow to hate him. It would be better on his conscience for her to leave him than for him to abandon a woman who loved him and his baby.

He thought briefly on whether this could be a blessing in disguise from God. Maybe this was God's way of helping him to do right and bring a woman in the dark to the light. But how could he do that? How could he get things together in his heart or his head if he was still seeing this as a high-stakes game? He thought at first that Carol was playing him, and that everything Jezebel was doing was to lure him in, but now he is convinced she really does love him.

It makes him sick to reflect on how he was nice to her and baited her with brief, fleeting gestures. He wanted to be a better husband, a better man, and father, but how? He tried to get his head together these past few months, but his inner demons and thoughts had been getting the best of him. He needed to do something; he had to do something to stop the voices. He wanted that someone to be Jezebel, but she didn't do it for him.

He stopped wanting to sleep with her, and he felt bad about it. He didn't want to hurt her, but every decision he made felt like a thousand knives into her stomach and heart. She felt like the baby was changing things, and she was, but not because of the reasons she thought. The bigger the baby got and the more he learned about her, the more he knew Jezebel deserved better.

He went out one night and, for the first time in a long time, he returned to familiar ground. He went to the strip club where his favorite dancer — and perhaps the woman who had his heart —performed. He didn't know why this lady had a hold on him. Was it the sex, attention, her voice, or the fake promises she could give at the right moments that gave him comfort and blurry vision? Francisca had a way of making men melt in the palm of her hands, and Jezebel knew it too when she saw her.

She had a feeling it wouldn't be the last time he saw her, and when he dared to see her again, she had already made plans for how she would deal with him. She followed him on this dark night. She followed him because she needed to know if he was serious about this woman.

Was it sex? Or was it just her? Why could he not love her or find a way to love her with all that she had given him? She left everything she knew to make a life with him, and he put her under a rock and pretended to love her only when he had to.

She started wanting more and asking questions. She wanted to get married, but was he ready? If he wasn't, she needed to know why. Was it a person, or something with her? She could accept if she weren't his type, but if it was another woman, she couldn't accept that. She sat in the car that night, knowing he would leave the club with her. It was slightly after 3am, and he walked out of the club with the stripper she had seen twice too many times with her man.

This time, Francisca was not holding him up, but he was walking just fine. He was talking to her and even trying to hold her hand, which she playfully stopped many times. He leaned her up against the car, and his hand gripped her thigh as he talked sweet nothings in her ear that made her tickle with laughter. Her laugh was like nails on a chalkboard in Jezebel's ears.

He kissed her, and she didn't stop him. How could she allow him to kiss her, Jezebel thought. How unprofessional and sickening they both were to her. She could imagine how many men she had probably kissed and done unthinkable things with. What did Curtis see in her that he couldn't see in Jezebel, she thought as her temperature rose within her. She was gripping the steering wheel so tightly that her skin was turning pale and flushed as she grabbed and released it.

He nibbled her neck, and that was the straw that sent Jezebel's car into drive. She knew what would happen next, and she refused to be his fool anymore. He clearly didn't want her, and she was okay with that. But she wouldn't let him get away with it. She would see him when he got home and make sure to deal with him.

When he got home later that early morning, he tried to be quiet, but he was not. He tripped over a small side table, and she pretended not to hear it. He was relieved that he didn't hear her feet and fell asleep on the couch with his mouth open.

He was snoring, getting some good sleep, and she knew nothing felt better after a nice screw than sloppy sleep. As he lay there on the couch, she poured a mixed brew she had made especially for him down his throat. She knew this was a mistake, a trespass he would pay with his life for violating her trust. It was hours later, she tapped Curtis on the shoulder to tell him it was time for her to go to the doctor. She liked that he went with her; even seeing the girls flirt with him didn't bother her, because she was happy about her life choice.

But today, she wanted him to see what would forever be out of his reach. They went to the appointment, and the appointment went fine. They poured the cold, clear gel onto her stomach, and the doppler was placed. As the tech scanned, the baby squirmed around in her stomach.

She saw her baby girl for the first time. She was pretty even in her womb. She could make out her little hands, feet, toes, chest, arms, and legs. The technician measured everything, and Curtis was there crying, "with his cheating ass," Jezebel thought.

He was trying to be nice today, but he was a day late, and Jezebel had plans to reveal. She told him, as they drove home, that she had a surprise for him. He was surprised and couldn't imagine what a woman who gave him so much could possibly have for him still. When he walked in the door, he felt a strange shift in his appetite. He felt hungry like he hadn't eaten all day.

He asked Jezebel, "Hey, babe. You hungry? I think I got the munchies or something from you." He started to laugh at his terrible joke, but Jezebel didn't join him. He called out his bad joke and apologized for not being sensitive, thinking that was what Jezebel wanted to hear. It wasn't.

He sat on the couch, thinking that was what he needed to do. Plus, he felt dizzy and lightheaded, so he needed to find a stable place to keep the room from spinning. As he sat there holding his forehead, she said. "I know you probably feel like shit right now. As you should." he didn't say anything; he just listened.

He thought, did she know about Carol? Was he busted? Could she have followed him last night? He thought he was careful. She was asleep, wasn't she, he thought.

"I know that you don't love me. I thought I knew why. I thought it was because I had gotten fat and unattractive. I blamed myself for why you hit me, sometimes thinking I was in the wrong place at the wrong time. I accepted it, thinking this was what love feels like. People make mistakes, and I can deal with that. But what about disrespect?"

She leans down to look him in the face, and she shouts the question, "Have you ever felt disrespected, Curtis?"

He clears his throat, "Look, I don't know what you think–"

Before he could finish his sentence, she slapped stars into his vision. He was a bit slow to respond initially and then said, "What the hell, Jezebel? What the fuck you slap me for?"

"Maybe you should tell me why you fucked the stripper last night?"

"Come on. You know, men do dumb shit like that to blow off steam. It wasn't anything personal."

"Really, so that is why you were nibbling on her ear and whispering you love her?"

"What? How did you hear that?"

"I didn't. You just confirmed it. I knew it was something between the two of you, but I couldn't put it together! I didn't want to believe it. I thought it was me, but it was that bitch who had your heart this whole time. You played me."

"Look, it is not what you think. We are all losers in this Jezebel. I am a victim!"

"A victim. What the hell do you take me for, Curtis? Have I done something to you to deserve this shit you pulled on me this morning?"

"No, but this is not about you, Jezebel. It never was."

"You need to explain yourself, Curtis, because I am not understanding this."

"It's your mom. She told me to do this. All of this. I never meant to hurt you or anybody. I was in love with the stripper long before I met you, and I apologize for lying to you. I didn't know how to tell you, and your mom swore that if I told you, she would do something to me."

"So I was a game to you. All of this was a lie, Curtis!" Jezebel and her pregnant belly seemed to be bouncing around the room. Curtis couldn't stay focused on her whereabouts. His head was ringing, and his body was not right.

As Jezebel kept on yelling, sometimes at him and then into the air as if the scream was toward her mother, he feared the once-loving woman standing before him. He was in no shape to defend himself if she wanted to fight. He questioned, Was I poisoned? When? By who?

"You are a coward and a weak father. I was right to decide to give a damn about myself and say fuck you, and for sure, my mother now. Here, my dumbass is trying to make a family with you, and you and my mother have plans for me— what are they? What is she planning, Curtis?"

"I don't know?"

"So what are you getting out of this? Sex? Can't be. We haven't had sex in weeks, so what is this really all about?"

"She said something about switching bodies."

"She wants to switch bodies with who? What does that have to do with me? She wants me for the spell?"

"I think you are the spell, Jezebel. Look, I don't know if you know this, but your mom is really old. Your mom and my uncle are long-time friends. My uncle is a voodoo priest with Creole roots. His friend agreed to father a baby with her if she would give him powers. He told my uncle, and lately we have been having an issue with my mom, so we thought your mom could help."

He tries to go on, but his head is in excruciating pain. "I am sorry, but can you get me some water, food, or something? I feel lightheaded, and I think I am about to throw up."

"Shut up, just finish what you wanted to say. What did you get out of this? What did she tell you to do?"

"She told me to have an interest in you. She watched my every move. There are cameras in your shop, and she tails me everywhere. I am looking over my shoulders, paranoid and shit. I never meant to make you fall in love with me, and I surely didn't expect a baby. I wanted you to hate me and leave me instead of me loving you and leaving you.

I tried to give you every reason to hate me and leave me, so I didn't have to do what she wanted. I couldn't leave you high and dry, Jezebel. I have love for you even though I am not in love with you. You are carrying my baby, and that matters to me, although I didn't know what to do in this process. I will marry you if you want."

"You think this is a game, Curtis? This is my life. Do you think I need your pity, or something?" Curtis knows better than to respond. He remained silent as he squirmed from the pain.

She is quiet for a moment as she realizes that the whole time, everyone was playing games with her heart. She was the one with her heart all in this. She was thinking about everyone but herself. And now she is the only one left raising the baby. She asked, "So what does my mother expect you to do after you leave me?"

"She thought this would be what it would take for you to come crawling back to her. She said you needed to know your place, and she would figure out what to do with the baby. But she had no clear plans, she told me, if the baby would live or die. I was not, I was not okay with that. So I want to help you be better than me, Jezebel. I want you both to be good together. I wanted you to put the love you had for me into her, and for her to get all that you had in store to give to me."

"I don't give a damn about you anymore, so I have nothing to give to this baby. You will never for-get this night or the night you lived yesterday. You don't know this yet, but this morning while you were sleeping, I gave you a dose of your own medicine. I want you to know how it feels to eat food, and can't keep nothing down. What it is like to grow big, and to think yourself ugly. To watch your body go out of sorts, thinking it is for love and good intentions, when those who you show love to, turn their backs on you."

She goes on to say, "I want you to see how it feels to be me. To watch another man with the woman you love. To see her happy with someone else, because you will no longer be able to perform in any way to make any woman happy or to bear another child. This baby will be the only one you have, and after her, you will have no more. She will be part of your legacy, but she will have nothing to do with you. You will be forced day and night to eat, or feed this hunger that will never be quenched. You will feel every pain I have ever felt or will feel, given birth. And you will know what it is like to lose everything like I did last night and even today."

She takes a deep inhale and gets him a napkin with a glass of water. "It's time for you to leave, you are starting to sweat on my furniture. Good luck with making your life work and doing whatever you need to, to live with your trifling self. You are a piece of scum, and now you will know what it is like to mess over a witch." He drinks the water, but as it goes down his throat, it feels like hot water boiling his throat.

"What the hell did you do to me?"

"You haven't seen nothing yet. Good luck with finding something to quench this fire." She starts laughing, and he gets up to run. "Oh, and if you breathe a word of this to her, you have no idea what pain is. You pretend as if you loved and left me as you both planned, and I will deal with my mother. I never want to see you or anyone from your family ever again. You are dead to all of us. Charity will be my precious treasure, and I will decide what is best for her. Not you or my mother."

To the Moon and Back

Rachel is sitting at home in her living room speaking to her mother. The day is slipping into early evening as they discuss the plans that Rachel's Mom has brewing in her mind. She insists, "Now is the time to turn up the heat. Charity is 45 days away from the biggest change in our district, and we cannot leave this to chance. We have to turn up the heat and get her to fall in line and become a pillar of what we are building."

"But why would she do that if she knows her mother and grandmother are both seated above us. Who knows anything about her father?"

"Girls run this show. I am not worried about him. But the biggest mistake they made was keeping her in the dark for so long."

"Why do you think they did that? I get they wanting to protect her light, but to what expense? She has to want magic for the spell to work anyhow."

"Right. I am not sure what was going on, but

I do know that if we can introduce her to the arts and get her to side with us, it might be enough to not harm her light and win her to our side. I know her mother hasn't told her a thing, and neither has her grandmother. I think Carol learned from all the shit she did to Jezebel that wasn't the way to go."

"She has a sad story then. Maybe I shouldn't be so much of a bitch to her."

"This is magic. Nothing is fair in witchcraft; we take what we want and do not ask politely."

"Fair. So what next?"

"She didn't eat the cupcakes."

"No, that damn Zoe couldn't keep her mouth shut, or we could have read her cards, too. She would be eating out of our hands now, drunk on the spell."

"That girl is either not as dumb as we thought or she has something on her side, too. Who are her parents?"

"I don't know. I didn't think to look her up."

"Girl, what the hell is the internet for if you don't look up people, Rachel?"

"Sorry, Mom. My bad. She sits with a bible group at school, or at least she used to. Now, she sits with Charity and whoever she sluts out her wisdom to. She isn't that loyal."

Her mom looks her name up on the computer. She turns her computer around and says, "Is this the girl?" It was a pretty picture of Zoe with her parents. "Yes, that's her." She looks over the picture and says, "That's the guy who dropped her and Charity off at the party."

"Looks like her brother, based on this picture. But I recognize her parents. Aren't they…" she looks up her suspicion and replies, "Yup, bingo. This girl is the daughter of that pastor of Holy Temple Church, shit. You've got to be kidding me."

"But word has it, her parents are out of town. I think they have a mission trip or something, Mom. She's been at Charity's a lot lately, so I am thinking she will be there more often than not."

"Stay away from her mom. When she is on it, focused, she is ready. We have to see what we can find and see if Jezebel planted something already to monitor her."

"You think she is after Zoe?"

"You think she doesn't know every move her daughter makes? Her life is in the balance. I know one thing to be true: Charity's dad's side of the family has to be posing a problem for Carol's plan because she wouldn't have gotten to be this old if she had her way. I know of too many spells she must have tried that failed. She's got some kind of covering over her. I wonder from who?"

"Her mom never talks about her father.

Charity doesn't even know his name."

"That's smart on her behalf. I know for a fact she gave birth alone, and he never came to the hospital. We were praying that night, and her mom left to keep her company."

"Her story does sound more and more pathetic the more I hear."

"Just don't feel sorry for her. She is not your friend, but your enemy." She looks at a picture of Charity and Zoe on her social media, and marks an x with her finger over their faces.

Back at Charity's

At Charity's house, dinner was cooked by her mother to her surprise. She hardly ever cooks, and when she does, it is either for therapy or to prove she is a good mother who bakes. Charity is always nervous to try her food, so often she pretends to eat but throws it out when she isn't looking. She doesn't know if she is aware of it or not, and doesn't care.

She has been a practicing vegetarian, and her mom would know that if she were ever home. Zoe had never stayed as late at her house as she did today. Her brother had errands to run that he was super secretive about. He had to pick up a day shift to help pull in some more money. The repairs for the vehicles jumped an additional $1,000 for parts they had to scurry to find on the internet and bid on.

At first, he was pissed, but he knew getting mad wouldn't change anything. He had to pay off the repairs, but he also had to give them $1,000 or risk his phone being blown up and the mistake he had tried to cover being exposed. Like clockwork, this girl called his phone and pestered the hell out of him. He gave the first $1,000 to her, but she didn't stop, so he had to block her.

He was relieved that he only gave her a fake social account he never checked, so if she called that, he wouldn't feel any kind of way. She was a lazy stalker and only called him from two other numbers before she stopped trying to extort more cash from him. He arrived late at the house, and when he had to knock on the door, he was nervous. He called Zoe's phone, but it was still on silent from school. He hated when she had a phone but didn't use it as intended.

Cell phones give you the right not to have to go into people's houses or be around people who give you the creeps. Although he couldn't prove Jeze was a witch, he didn't want to find out the truth either. He remembered the advice he was given and had no intentions of violating his instructions. The door was opened, and a beautiful mother who didn't look a day over 26 opened the door. She was really captivating, but he knew that meant nothing good.

"Hey, Sean, was it? Come in. We were just about to have dinner. Did you care to stay with us?"

"Aww, no. That is too kind of you. I really think we got it."

"Zoe, tells me your parents are away on a mission trip to Kenya. That's pretty amazing, but I know it is a lot of responsibility for you, is it not?"

In these moments, he wished that Zoe had no friends. Why is she telling the world they are home alone? Is there a sign on her back that says our parents are out, come and bother us? He snapped out of his thoughts and saw the pot of pasta on the table. With a quickness, he walked over to his sister and grabbed her by the hand.

"It is time for us to go. I have food on the stove, and Mom is really picky about your diet. We have to go." He grabbed her backpack and threw it over his shoulder as he almost bolted to the door. Jezebel, trying to slow him down, replies, "Are you sure you don't want to take a plate with you? I would hate for you to miss out on good food after I slaved over a stove for you."

"No, thank you. We cool. Ya'll have a good night."

"Sorry, I gotta go. But I will see you at school tomorrow, and thanks, Ms. Jeze," replies Zoe as she is rushed out the door.

Jezebel stands at the door and waves with a grin, "Of course. It was my pleasure. Anytime."

Sean hurries them along to the car. He tells

her firmly, "Get in the car. Let's go." She gets in the car a little out of sorts and upset. "What is going on?"

"Be quiet and don't say anything until we pull out of this driveway." He smiles as he pulls out toward Jezebel and waves. He gets to the main street and drives for about five minutes before he address-es her questions.

"I hope there is really food on the table when we get home because I am starving! What happened to you today?" says Zoe angrily.

"I got busy with school," replies Sean.

"Until almost 6pm, Sean? We know you get out of school in the morning, and none of your classes go past noon. What's going on?"

"That woman is not fit to be trusted. You don't be at people's houses eating their food, and you don't know what they've got going on. Come on."

"Really, we're going to talk about food now? I was hungry and you left me stranded at school."

"I knew you could get home, and you have a key," says Sean.

"Only, I told you this morning I left it on the counter. I had no way to get in when I got home, so I had to wait on you."

"Look, that was my bad. But you can't go to

her house no more."

"Why?"

"Because I said so. I get the creeps, and I don't like it."

"Her house isn't haunted."

"You don't know that. What do you know about her mother, or father, Zoe?"

"I know she doesn't know her father, and her mother works a lot. She is mostly home alone, Sean. Her mom was only there tonight."

"Convenient."

"What are you trying to say?"

"I think she could be a witch."

"Come on, Sean. You've got to stop playing these games. It really has your head going into a fantasy island."

"Really, I think you need to get your head out of the make-up and fashion store, maybe you would see that this family has "crazy" written all over it."

"Why? Because she never met her father?"

"No, because her mother has this drawing effect that pulls you like a magnet. Her eyes are like ice sculptures with heat in the center, ready to suck the life out of your soul. That shit is not normal. Sorry, I shouldn't be cussing. I am working on it. But I am serious, Zoe. You have to watch yourself."

"I will be careful. But can we please stop and pick up something to eat, please? I am starving." They pull into a local drive-thru and order. The guy in the store says, "Hey, whose order are you picking up? You have to come inside."

"No, I am not here to pick up. I just ordered."

"Oh, my bad, I thought–" Sean snatches his bag past the cashier as they are handed to him by another associate. He replies quickly, "No worries, you thought wrong," and drives off.

"Why did that guy think you worked there?" his sister said, puzzled.

"I don't know. I guess everyone has a twin in this city."

They drive the rest of the way home in silence as the hot fries and burger smells fill the car. Zoe thought that she might be hungry, and that is why she smelled the scent even before getting her order. Or was she just that hungry, and it was all in her head? She couldn't decipher which and happily ate her dinner. They pulled into the garage and got out of the car. The sheet was knocked off the bike when the door slammed, and Zoe got a glimpse of some damage on their dad's bike.

"Ohhh, what did you do? How did you damage Dad's bike? He's gonna kill you."

"Don't say that. It was an accident, and I am working to get it fixed so that he will never know."

"Wait, you didn't tell them yet?"

"No, and if you want to live, you won't either."

"I can keep a secret, if you can keep mine. But if he asks and I feel threatened, I am not holding water. You'd better match everything because he loves that bike. I mean, like a second you."

"I know it was just one time, and it was stupid, I see now. But it is out of my system."

"Good. Because that looks bad."

"It is costing me a few thousand dollars to fix."

"Dang, I hate to hear that, Bro."

"Me too. The people tried to suck me dry, and then these extra fees with imports were killing me. I think I have at least another month to work before I am free. But I may have to leave you at school sometimes to get home on your own, if you can deal with it."

"Yeah, I can just take the bus or something. I will figure it out."

"Try to get a ride from a friend or someone who stays close."

"You got it."

Jezebel is sitting at the table, looking at her dish. How many lives does this kid have? she thought to herself. Why won't he just get in line and go with her program? She thought about Sean's character, then thought of herself. She was a calculated thinker, and she couldn't fault him for being cautious. She was actually impressed, considering he is green.

She liked the kid, but not enough to change the plans she was making. She had to get him to compromise and felt he would be like any other man in time. No man could resist her sexual charm and addictive allure. She knew what it meant to be caught up in her grasp, but no one knew the power she had better than Curtis. He was the first piece of dark magic she had ever performed. Most of the stuff she had done prior was just charms and cute spells to bring small fortunes, wealth, and puppy love. But this was the spell that brought her into the big leagues.

This spell was the one that pushed her from being a blind witch to a practicing witch out for blood and her own gain. This step did push her down a dark path, but no one could have imagined how this turn of events would delay the plans Carol had. In a way, this baby who no one thought about, started to become the center of how everyone would get what they wanted.

That night, Curtis didn't feel right in the head, so he thought about going home. He knew no one could love him like this, especially Francisca. He only came to her when he had money or drugs. She was a coke head, and she couldn't resist a line. He had done powder before, but never had a problem with treating it as casually as drinking. He had a problem, but it never wore on his skin like it did in this moment.

He had a fix, and he didn't know how to quench it. Did Jezebel's hex make him a coke fiend? What did she do to him, really? He went home and sweated, shook, and felt it all night. He couldn't face his mother, so he stayed in his room and suffered in silence for as long as he could.

The night air was brisk, and he felt it hit his body. He was cold and hot, sick but functioning. He was hungry but had no appetite. His body was confused, and he didn't know what to do.

He couldn't go to his mother, but maybe he could make it to his uncle? But he was in no position to drive. He tried to walk, but that lasted for a few moments before he started shaking as he walked the street. He looked like a drug addict, and he hated it. He opened his phone and called his uncle. "Unc, I am hurting real bad. Can you come get me?"

"Where are you?"

"Walking…" there is a thud as Curtis falls down to the concrete. He is vomiting, and he doesn't know if he is dying. He blacks out. Several hours later, he wakes and sees his uncle singing over his body. Unsure of what was happening, he says, "Unc, what's going on?" His uncle is in a trans and doesn't respond. He feels better, so he keeps quiet in case whatever this is could be erased.

It felt like his uncle performed some kind of ritual for twenty minutes or more. When he was done, he asked his nephew, "How do you feel?"

"I am better. Thanks. Can you tell me what is going on?"

"Yeah, you got a curse on you."

"What do you mean I got a curse on me?"

"She put something bad on you. It is a mix between voodoo and spellbound. I don't know if I I can get this off. I've been trying for over a hour with no progress. You might have to grow through this for a bit."

"What do you mean grow through it?"

"Your body is going to change over the next few months as her body changes. Until she delivers, you won't have any control over your body or how it responds. To mimic what she feels, you will go through an extent of pain. You are essentially teth-ered to her pain."

"What the hell, Unc! This shit is not fair. You got me caught up in this, and you know this ain't the life I should live. Set me free!"

"You are a grown man and I ain't never made you do shit for me. You chose this knowing the risks and rewards. I never said this was going to be easy, but we can make this work for us."

"How are we going to do that? It looks like we lost across the board?"

"That's where you are wrong. Because you are tethered to her pain, we know their plans and can think ahead of both of them. Together, and with this baby, we can piece this thing together and come out on top."

"Are you serious?"

"As a heart attack."

Curtis looks at him but doesn't say a word. He tries to sit up, and in that moment, the room starts racing again. "Unc, I don't feel too good."

"I think I know why?"

"What? There is more?"

"You're not going to like this, but I had to give you something strong to control the pain."

"How strong? I don't do hard drugs, and you know that."

"I had to give you a shot of heron to get you here, but I got you on a drip now to reverse it."

"That stuff will have me blow up like a doughboy!"

"I hate to say this, but I think that's what she was hoping for. If your system mirrors hers, you have to gain weight as she gains weight. You are going to look pregnant by the time she delivers in four months."

"Are you shitting me?"

"No, you are going to blow up, and there is nothing I can do to stop it. I tried to reverse it."

"Try this shit again. I cannot live like this, this shit is embarrassing."

"What do you think I was doing? The hokey pokey? They ain't changing it. Whatever she gave up must have been big, because I can't move it."

"This is bullshit!"

As Curtis lay in the bed trying to make sense of his life, he replayed the conversation with Jezebel. She had intentions to ruin him and ensure he never saw the light of day. Even if he were able to kick the habit, he would look like an addict. He would be embarrassed to step foot in front of his mother like this. How could he ever have the heart to tell her what he had done? He messed up, and now he regretted ever getting mixed up in all of this.

He stood the least to gain, and he feels like a target hit by all three sides in a three-way duel. He hated being the loser, but he was learning that day that magic comes with a price. He would lose his good looks, his house, a woman who loved him, and never meet the baby he loved. She was innocent in all of this, and he worried about her future. He knew that being close could mean disaster, so he had to be distant.

He thought hard about what he could do, and the only thing he could think to do was to call his mom. She answered the phone. "Son, did you leave the house? What time is it? Where are you?"

"I am safe, Mom. Just out. Um…I need to ask you for a favor."

"Are you in some kind of trouble?"

"Nothing like that, I just think I messed up, real bad, Mom."

"Baby, you know there is nothing we can do that God can't fix," she replied with a sweet and tender tone.

"I think I would give God a run for His money on that one."

"You should try Jesus, Son."

"Maybe, or maybe I just deserve what is coming to me."

"We all deserve hell for the sins we commit. Mercy and grace pays it all and takes our place."

"One day, I want to learn more about that. But I am a bit tired right now."

"Is that a medical machine I hear in the background? Have you been hurt, shot, or something?"

"No, nothing like that. I just got something I am dealing with. I wanted to ask you to pray for something or somebody for me."

"Okay, of course, Son. What's their name?"

"Charity."

"Anything specific?"

"Just for her to be protected and for no harm to come to her. I owe her my life, and I want to be sure I did all I could to protect hers."

"Seems like a special girl. Father, I am here today because I know you are a good God. You know how to keep people from harm and danger. If we are in the valley of hell or the edge of the earth, you can be with us. You are not afraid of the arrows by day, nor the fiery darts by night. May you watch over this precious one, Charity, who my son is willing to bring to me in prayer. Father, I know you will do anything but fail me now. I entrust this beautiful soul into your hands, for now, and forever more.

Keep her surrounded by your angels. Cover her with 10,000 angels to her right and 10,000 angels to her left. Keep her focused on the things above and not beneath. Father, I don't know who this mighty woman is, but I know you have plans for her. Plans to bless her and to prosper her. May she obtain all the favor you have for her.

May every life she helps to bring to the Kingdom of God be a victory for the angels and all of heaven to celebrate. Father, cover her no matter her age or circumstance. In the mighty name of your son, Yashua, Jesus the Christ, and it is so!"

She is released from the power of the prayer and says, "Wow, Son. I am not sure who this woman is. Is she a girl or a woman? I was wanting to say girl for some reason?"

"You did good, Mom. Hey, I gotta get some rest. But I love you."

"I love you to the Moon and Back."

Satisfied, Curtis lay back and allowed his body to transform in ways he didn't think possible in a short span. He saw his feet swell, his cheeks grew chubby, and his belly went round. He looked like he had been drinking for years and had a beer belly to prove it. He had withdrawal symptoms for months, or morning sickness. He couldn't keep food down, and he needed drugs to wake him up and to put him to sleep. He would try something, and it would work for a short while before the effects wore off. He was miserable but knew he deserved to feel every bit of the pain.

He went from wanting justice to feeling

justified in his punishment. Maybe this was the punishment of magic and selfishness. He couldn't bring himself to go outside, so he looked out the window and watched life go by on his cell phone. It wasn't long after that that he saw the woman of his dreams start posting pictures of a single man he had seen before. She was happy, even happier than he had ever seen her. She had forgotten about him, or would soon.

He saw the life he had planned to live implode, and he knew no apology would reverse the scorn he put into her heart. He feared coming to her begging would only make things worse. He couldn't go to her mother for help because Jezebel had all the cards. She outsmarted him, and he had hope that she would outsmart her mother, too. What did she do to make money, and how would she get back into good graces with her, he thought of occasionally.

He didn't think too long because the cravings kept him busy, longing, hoping, waiting for rest that never did come. If he didn't have his uncle, he would have been wandering the streets, going from high to high and doing any drug imaginable to keep him numb. He hadn't eaten for days, and he would have been thin if it weren't for the curse. He couldn't control what was happening with his body; to be skinny or fat wasn't his choice.

He feared what would be the outcome of his life after the baby. Would he return to normal, or remain fat, skinny, or nothing? Would he try the wrong drug or do the wrong thing and end this misery that seemed to have no expiration period? He never imagined hell to feel like this, or to even be real. If he thought it was real, maybe he would have made a different choice. Maybe he needed to get saved, then he could clean his life up.

He had two more months to go, and they were bitter to his soul. He would wake up in night sweats, have heavy breathing when walking the floors, and his oblong stomach made it hard for him to buy clothes. He looked like a grandpa and hated it. He didn't like what he saw in the mirror and imagined how Jezebel felt. He empathized with her before, but now he understood her. Maybe he could be the only one who would ever get it, truly.

Maybe this curse was her way of ensuring she was never alone. For the first time ever, he started to realize he could actually learn to love her, the woman who had now cursed him. The woman who had the guts to show him, himself. His problem was that she wanted nothing to do with him.

What he would find out years later, as he tried to win her back and make his way into her life, was that she blocked him in the spirit and the natural from ever getting close. With each attempt he made to rekindle what they could have, she would send him into a drug house to get high as a kite to forget about his plans. He was a slave to addiction, and only she really knew why.

He became alone, and the loneliness was only accompanied by regret. He became bitter of soul as time went on. He had learned enough magic to make it into his daughter's dreams. He wanted her to know something about him, although he could only last for a few moments before his soul was snatched back to his weak and feeble body. He was useless to her, but he got the chance to warn her. He got the chance to see the prayers of the righteous availing much.

Whatever he was told, he made it a point to tell his daughter. The love he wanted to give to Jezebel, he knew now, he had to give to their daughter. The same thing he told Jezebel, he told himself. This is what made him stop several times from hiding in parking lots. This is what gave him the strength to believe he could be set free. He needed a touch from something, someone, mercy, but he couldn't see his mother, and his soul wasn't at rest for anyone else to slow him down.

He craved the high in body, soul, and spirit. He needed to be the monster to talk to his daughter, but he wanted to be the saint to live free from addiction, the curse that followed him everywhere. No amount of money was worth the penalty he had to pay.

It was in his travels that he heard of the danger that would befall his daughter leading up to and after her thirteenth birthday. He had to warn her about who she was and where she came from. She needed to dig deep and get rooted in truth because the storms of hell were coming, and in fact, were already there.

He wanted better for her life than he could

obtain for his own life. She was the hope of him, but also the hope of everyone around her. She was a young lamb in danger of death for reasons she did not know. She didn't deserve this, no matter if her mother was a witch, her dad was a misfit and failed voodoo priest. He would give his life to spare hers.

As Charity lies in her bed, looking up at the moon from her window. She had always been attracted to the moon. She was never sure of why it seemed to call to her and bring her comfort growing up. She would close her eyes, and in her soul she would hear, "I love you to the Moon and back."

Her mom never said it, but why does she hear it in her soul? She wasn't sure if she had heard it in a dream, and then repeated it while she was awake. But the sound brought her comfort, even hope, that the night would be a good night.

She allowed her eyelids to close for her to enter a dream world that held her in perfect limbo between reality and spirit. She never got scared when she saw the overweight guy in her dreams. She never saw him on the streets. He seemed to know her, but she never knew him. He was kind, though, so she never told her mom about him. He wasn't creepy, or maybe she would think he was a demon or ghost.

This man had been whispering encouragement and reminders in her ears for years. She welcomed the voice and felt connected to it. It would pop up randomly and without being summoned. He usually carried broken messages of warning, and on this night, it would be no different. The message was blurry because dream memory sucks.

"Charity, I need you to know I love you. You are in danger…Be careful…forgive…love." The voice left, and she would awake sometimes looking around her room, thinking to see him. She never did. She never said she loved him back, but he never minded. She was just looking at him and wondered who he was. Maybe he was an ancestor or a random person she saw in a dream while sleeping. She had heard how you can see things in your dreams when you sleep, listening to music or watching videos.

Maybe the man was some kind of hologram or something, or a connection from God to earth? She wasn't sure, and she allowed her mind to wander as she drifted into a deeper sleep filled with peace. One thing about the man's voice that made her pay attention was that he was always right about what he said. Once, he told her to remember that when underwater, don't panic. Her foot got caught in a piece of coral, and she went underwater. As she was underwater, she felt the waves rush over her head, and a lifeguard who saw her came rushing to her side.

She learned to trust the voice after a few more moments like that. The voice wasn't a threat, but like a guardian angel in her mind. She doesn't know what a prophet is, although Zoe tried to explain it many times. She is not connected to God, and she is also not a witch, because she is not connected to the devil. She is in this gray space. A space where life exists, but it will demand that you choose a side. Her "D" day is coming up.

Big Plans, Presents, Oh My

Turning thirteen is a big deal. It is the age where you become accountable, and everyone has all eyes on you to see how you will turn out. Will you be like you were as a child, or will you morph into this being no one recognizes for a spell, and then mellow out over time? Charity is the talk of the underworld. She doesn't know it yet, but her sweet thirteenth birthday will be anything but.

It's morning, and she is in the kitchen, grabbing an apple. Her mother enters and takes a seat at the counter that holds nothing edible. The counters are swept clean, and if Charity waited for her mom to cook breakfast to eat each morning, she would starve. "Hey, Beautiful."

She looks up from the fridge door and bites into her apple. "Oh, hey, Mom. You up? I thought you worked late last night?"

"I did, but I wanted to talk to you, and nights are harder."

"Yeah, that makes sense. But a phone call is always good too. We are in a modern society."

"Yeah, but this is about something important, so I wanted to speak to you in person if that is fine with you," replies Jezebel in a joking but firm tone.

"Of course it is, Mom. What's up?"

"I wanted to talk to you about your birthday. Was there a theme or something special you wanted?"

"No, not really. Just something nice, I guess. I figured you had planned this months back since you talked about it so much. You would think I was turning sixteen."

"This is an important year for you and a moment for me. Some of everything will be going on. Your body can change. I know you haven't gotten your ministration yet, but it will be coming soon. So just be prepared for it."

"I'll be ready for it, Mom. You gave me every kind of pad or tampon in the store. I keep them in my backpack, plus period underwear."

"Good, girl. So, no ideas for me to stay within? I can go all out?"

"I trust you, Mom, to come up with something fit for a queen. Just remember, I am not, and you will be in a good space. Can we head to school, now?" She gives her mom a light peck on the cheek and heads out the door.

Charity can be so charming that her mom really hates herself sometimes. She wonders if the life she wanted could have ever worked out. Will she have the heart to follow through with whatever was necessary to win at this cold game? At moments like this, she wasn't too sure.

She thought about her plans. What could she get away with, and what must she have? She knew she wanted gold, white, and soft pink to be the color scheme. The party must be fit for a queen, and the stage set. She prayed that the heavy covering over her daughter would be removed so that her plans and Charity's wishes wouldn't be hindered.

Since Charity was a child, there were limits on what she or her mom could do to her. Her grandmother tried spells on her, and none of them worked when she was young. She couldn't figure it out because she wasn't blocked before. What kind of magic was this, she thought. How come this little girl, who had no teeth, was able to out-power her spiritually, physically make her laugh, and, for a moment, steal her focus on her future plans?

This baby, Charity, was always a miracle, though neither understood why. Their hearts were to use her for their will; they never considered that she had a purpose for their lives. She was an open book, who didn't know her complete past. It didn't occur to either one of them to tell her a word about her father or his side of the family. She grew up thinking she was alone, and they secretly feared that they, too, might have plans for her on this magical day.

How could they prevent a war from breaking out across families? Why would they try something now, after so many years? Surely they must assume she was aborted or died. Carol was careful enough to tell them everything she thought they needed to hear.

But some magic is so pure, so powerful, that no dark magic can hide its light. Love is still the greatest weapon to overcome darkness. Although Charity was unaware of all the dark magic around her, it didn't stop her from having enough power to find her way in the darkness.

The light of a flicker can stand up to a dark room. She was a light flickering in the darkness. She went to school, and it was a normal day. Her friends were her friends, but today, everyone seemed to laugh and joke a bit louder than before.

If she weren't popular, she would have thought they all were a little crazy to stare so hard at her. She thought at times, was there a bug on her face, or something odd about everyone else she had missed. She sat in her seat feeling warm.

It was like she felt sweaty as her legs clung to her seat. Was it her nerves? She struggled through the class, put on her backpack, and hurried to the bathroom to erase the ick she felt. Entering the bathroom, she went into the first stall and heard the girls come in shortly after her. She saw why everyone was snickering, but she didn't get why everyone made a big deal of it. She wore light pants, and on a day like today, she regretted it.

"Did you see it? This is how I know young kids ain't shit. Why did nobody tell her?" says a concerned student, Carla.

"She should figure this stuff out like the rest of us," replies a familiar voice from Charity's last class.

"That's not cool."

"Hey, she is your friend, why don't you warn her?"

"Me? I will tell her, but how do I tell her?" replies Freda.

"You help her, cover her. You don't let the whole school laugh at her."

"Charity has embarrassed a lot of people with how she talks to them. I can't tell you how many times, so today is just a piece of karma. I will let her know at lunch time, if she hasn't figured it out yet. I really don't know how you can't feel it and know?"

There were a few familiar voices. She didn't recognize them all, but she knew that at least one of them was a close friend. She was embarrassed and wondered why no one, not even a friend, would pull her aside to tell her. How could children be so cruel when she hasn't done anything malicious like this or wrong to anyone? She felt misunderstood, wronged, and betrayed, and that feeling burned in her chest.

They were right, she didn't have any other clothes she could wear. She had the underwear, but what would it do now? How could she stop the bleeding heart she had from embarrassment? A few moments later, she sat in the bathroom considering her options, then she heard a tap at the door. "Charity?" It was Zoe.

"Yeah?"

"Hey, you good?"

"Let me guess, you heard about–"

"I got my PE uniform. It is not fashionable, but you can wear it."

"I will take it. Will this mean you get an F today for not dressing out?"

"I will figure something out. If I get an F for one day, it won't bring my grade down by much anyhow. I will be fine." She hands the clothes under the door. Charity says a silent thank you and moments later reemerges outside the bathroom, more confident and still radiant.

She added the shorts to her top, and she was still in fashion. She could make a PE outfit look like a put-together idea. The girl was gifted. Zoe thought that must be the reason everyone was jealous.

How could her so-called friends see her in a bind, or hear about it, and do nothing? She assumed they must not have heard, and she was glad to help. Charity didn't mention it to them yet, but she would be keeping a close eye on them. She guessed the guy was right again. Can't trust everyone, but if you can't trust your friends, who can you trust? She was on edge that day and remained bothered.

Her mom asked her about her day, but she didn't feel like reliving it. She would tell her about her period later; she didn't feel like speaking about it in the car. She honestly wanted a moment to process the whole ordeal at home. Figuring things out couldn't be that difficult anyway. Her mom gave her pretty thorough instructions with demonstrations using hot sauce, ketchup, and pads.

She got home and desired to take a nap to ease her troubled mind. As she entered dreamland, a familiar voice called out to her. "Charity." She could hear the voice but not see the face. She walked around, hoping to find the voice, for years, it had been a sort of guiding light. Today might be the perfect day to ask questions and not just get information. She heard the voice again, "Charity." She thought she found where the voice was coming from, and so she walked into a room that was not dark but had a strange light.

She saw a large stone and she sat on top of it. For a moment, she thought the voice had given up on finding her, but then she saw the man. He was a round man —not incredibly fat, but not slim and trim either. He was aging but still looked handsome. He said, "Hey, Charity."

"Hey," she replied, not showing her emotions entirely, but lacking enthusiasm.

"You alright?"

"It was just a hard day at school."

"Yeah, you want to talk about it?"

"Yes, I do."

"Okay, you go first."

"I just don't know who to trust right now. I want to talk to my mom about it, but I feel like she isn't the right person just yet. I had one of my friends today talk trash about me. I just didn't realize she could feel the way she does about me."

"You have to pay attention to everything around you. Welcome to womanhood. Right now, you are entering a new timeline for your life. Growing into a beautiful adult is a great thing, but it comes with its own set of challenges. Not everyone you see and hear, you can believe. You get to choose what you pay attention to from now on."

"How did you know, and how is that different from before?"

"You might not know this yet, and I don't

know how long I will have to help you through this. I want you to know, you are special, and no matter where you think you come from, you were made with love. I know you might ask questions on why you had to be alone so much, and I apologize for the messed-up people around you. But I know that God has a plan for you."

"What are you talking about?

"I wanted to tell you something, and have been trying to tell you for years. I am part of your family. You don't know me, but I am fighting for you to get to know me. I don't want to scare you, but my side of the family loves you too."

"Your side? Are you my grandfather or something? My mom never told me much about him."

"No, I am not your grandfather. I am your father."

"My father?"

"Yes, I can't explain everything right now, but I need you to listen to me. Your life is in danger. There are people in your family who hate me to the core, which is why I cannot get to you or my parents. This is the year that will change, if you allow it. I will find a way to get to you, and if I fail trying, I want you to know that I love you."

"Look, I am not sure if you know who I am? My father, I was told was dead."

"Sometimes I feel like I am. But no, I am alive. I am in my own bondage right now, but I will do what I need to get things right with you. I just need you to trust that I won't fail you. When you need me, I will find a way to find you. Just call me."

"How am I supposed to do that?"

"With magic, you don't need phones. The same blood in my veins is in yours. Close your eyes and pray, dream, and I will be with you there."

"So are you just going to stay in my dreams?"

"Your mom and grandmother keep a tight control over your life, but after your birthday, that will all change. Everyone will want to have you influenced by them. I don't want you to feel forced to do anything you don't want to do. You get to choose."

"Choose what?"

"Choose the life you want to live. You don't have to become what you don't want to. Don't sacrifice your life for any of our happiness. No one deserves to ask you for that or demand it of you. Do you hear me?"

"Yeah, I hear you."

"I gotta go, it's calling me. Remember what I said, Charity."

Then the voice, the presence, the image of the man was gone. She sat there in the dream, thinking, could this be my father? She never even saw a picture of her father to compare the features, so who really is this man?

Was he an angel? He didn't seem like how she had pictured an angel to look. Strong, handsome, and warrior-like with wings. He definitely didn't give her God vibes.

Maybe this was a depiction of her watching too much tv she thought about as she lifted her eyes to take in the room's air. Waking up wasn't something she wanted to do, but she needed to if she hoped to finish her homework. She entered the kitchen and there was her mother sitting at the table. "Charity, up from your nap?" she said as she entered the room.

"Yeah. I was tired."

"Yeah, of course. I've been working on the menu. How do you feel about rabbit stew?"

"Are you serious?"

"Yeah, I was thinking of an old-world theme. I mean royal gowns, crowns, food, and design."

"I think–do you think we are going to eat your menu, Mom? We are teenagers in the 21st Century."

"You will love it. Rabbit tastes like chicken anyhow."

"Are you sure about that?"

"Yeah, I had it a few times."

"Okay, but we need regular items too."

"Of course."

"Oh, and uh, I started my period today."

"So that's why you had the gym shorts earlier?"

"Yeah. It was eventful but not too crazy. I have it under control, I just thought you should know."

"Thanks for telling me. How do you feel? Do you want to go out and celebrate your coming into womanhood?"

"I do, but today, I really need to get my homework done."

"Okay, so this weekend we will do something."

"Sounds good."

"I am going to head out in a bit. You want me to get something for you?"

"No, I will just make a salad from the fridge."

"You are going to turn into a rabbit eating all

that lettuce."

"Haha, Mom."

"You know I can keep the rabbit's foot for you. I can dye the fur a wild color like pink, blue, yellow, or orange. When I was growing up, we all had one on our key chain."

"You kept a rabbit's foot on your key chain?"

"Yeah."

"Ugh, that's nasty," Charity said as she faked gagging.

"You are thinking too hard. It was just a good luck charm, is all."

"Well, you can hold the rabbit's feet and keep all the luck it can bring."

Jezebel laughs and replies, "Maybe you would prefer something else, like a silver bullet or head of garlic?"

"Mom, this is not a vampire or werewolf event. We are just some teenagers trying to have fun."

"In this era, there were plenty of monsters, vampires, and werewolves. It is kind of the backdrop to the period. What would this time be like without a monster, or black people who ain't the help? We are going to change the game!"

"I don't know, but I will try to envision it. I want my party to be elegant like a high-end tea party, I guess. You can make a menu that would work with that. I think we can do finger foods, bite-sized stuff we like, and keep things small and moving. Good?"

"I guess. You could do more, but if this is what you want, who am I to change that?"

"Thanks, Mom."

Carol's Home

She is walking frantically through her kitchen, searching the cabinets, but not finding what she is looking for. Her kitchen is dark, and seemingly very little outside light can be seen. Her cabinets are black, and her countertops are black granite with speckles of silver that make them shine. Some of her cabinets have peekaboo spaces that allow you to see her dishes displayed on the inside.

In her prized cabinet, she holds her special dishes. Six ribbed stem glasses that held the blood of her last victims. It is some kind of power to take a life, but to drink the soul of a person is the ultimate power that Carol knows too well. Five times she drank their life and took their powers, but this time has to be different.

Reaching six is the age of man, and where an unfriendly demon as of late wants her to rest, eternally. There are many gunning for her head and power, but she is gonna fight with every fiber of her being and rise to the top like she always does, and strike a reassuring fear in her subjects' ambitions. There is nothing new in witchcraft; everyone wants more power, and to get it, you have to go through whoever is in the way. At the moment, that is her.

Her hands shake as she looks in unmarked jars on her counter. You would think it would be hard for her to find anything in a space so dark. She finds some kind of root and goes frantically to the pot boiling wild herbs. She is waiting for the mixture to finish, but her hands shake more violently as she tries to grab the pot's handle. She filled the pot a bit too much, so she lost a good portion, as the pot's weight weighed heavily on her feeble hands. She is able to save seventy-five percent of the brew in the pot as she sees the other twenty-five percent slip out and onto the floor.

"Shit." She sees the brew she needs desperately to turn back the hands of time falling on the floor, and her heart wants to sink or light up with rage. She knows she can't stop moving or attempt to save what is missing. She is a stingy woman; if she could have anything to the last drop, she would, and has. She needs to move the mixture because if she doesn't stop this shaking, everything will be on the floor or down the drain.

On her counter, she has seven vials preset for pouring the mixture. The vials are the same size and a murky dark gray. They don't look clean, but perhaps the heavy use is causing the residue in the vials to linger and stain. It looked like squid ink was used, given how dark the liquid swirling around in the pot is.

Looking at the pot, she might have enough for five vials if she is lucky. The mixture is piping hot, and the pot is growing heavier in her hands. She tries to balance the pot with both hands, hoping to nail the angle of pouring the strange black shots.

She blows over the top of the pot, but the heavy steam has a force that pushes back against her lips. She tightens her lips because she knows that twisted friend is playing tricks on her. "What the hell are you doing?" She says seemingly to the air. But the voice replies, "Do you think I was going to make this easy on you, Carol?"

"Why would I? You were never a good sport."

"You owe me."

"Yeah, get in line. I owe a lot of people, but I have this funny thing about paying. I don't."

"You will pay this time, Carol."

"Shut the fuck up." She realizes the steam won't die down, and there is only one way to pour this out. Fast, and as steady as she can get it. It seems like the pot is now releasing liquid, popping up like she is popping popcorn.

She takes the pot over to the vials that beg for filling. As she pours the liquid into a vile, she feels her hand shoved by a force that makes her lose a portion. She turns up her lower lip and tries to focus more, but misses more than she saves.

She realizes slow and steady won't win the race. She pours quickly, but as she pours, she loses some and barely has enough to fill five vials halfway. Carol, frustrated, says, "Now, you know that this is nowhere near enough for what I need. How the hell am I supposed to do what I need to do if you kill me early?"

"That sounds like a personal problem, Carol."

"Haven't I been good to you?"

"Do I need to remind you of what you did to me?"

"No. You don't."

"You watched me push away everyone who was ever close to me and then made me believe you loved me. I would have given anything to be with you. I loved you."

"That's where you went wrong. There can be no love in magic, Pookie."

"I learned that late. But fool me once, shame on you, you will never fool me twice. The power of love has no authority over a woman as wicked as you! Hell is your home, and I am on assignment to ensure you get there."

"Well, you are going to have to wait a whole lot longer."

"You really think you can kill your daughter and granddaughter, Carol?"

"Those bitches won't see it coming. I never liked the little girl. She always thought she was better than everyone. My daughter was gonna turn on me as soon as she got the chance, after all I had done for her. Serves her right to die for me, and I live to protect our legacy. This body will die, but I won't be in it when it does. You will continue to be lonely."

"You will come and visit me, Carol. You will be here with me in hell for all eternity, where we both belong."

"Speak for yourself. I never agreed to be there."

"But you did."

"I *Lied*. There is still hope for me yet."

"You are a selfish bitch."

"Yeah, maybe. Or I just learned to play the game and I play to win."

Carol's hands are shaking almost uncontrollably. She is running out of time, and they both know it. She picks up the vile with both hands locked in, but no matter how hard she tries, the liquid pops out and onto her flesh. As the sting of the liquid hits her hands, she can't stop, moving the vile to her mouth. She needs this to survive, to buy her time. As the liquid goes into her mouth, it cools the fire inside her belly. The snake, long since buried, awaits the flesh of another, and if it goes hungry, she is next.

She drinks a vile, but it is not enough. She is shaking too badly to get anything done with her left hand, so she had to drink another vial. Now, she has three remaining at various heights.

"What the hell am I supposed to do? I was told I had forty-five days!"

"Guess what, Carol, we are all liars."

"I thought you were better than this."

A voice replies that has no face, body, or tangible aspect. "We had a deal, Carol. I am not changing my dates, so you'd better figure this out. If not, we will claim your body."

"But I am close."

"Close isn't good enough if you want to live. Want your hands back? Give us what we want. What I want is you, but what they want is them. You decide."

"How am I supposed to get anything done

when you got me shaking worse than someone with Parkinson's?"

"That's your problem. A deal is a deal."

The voice goes mute, and whatever heavy spirit hovered over the room was gone. Carol thinks about what she can do to speed up the process. With three vials left, she had best a month to figure out how she can restore her energy. The truth is, she has been dying, and her days are closer to an end than ever before. She has less than 30 days before the spirits she bartered with want to claim her soul. They don't care who the soul is, but someone is going to hell with them, and Carol was gonna make sure it wasn't her.

She calls Rachel's Mom, and she answers after a few rings. She isn't surprised to hear Carol's voice.

"Hey, I need a favor."

"I knew this day would come. What exactly do you need from me that you can't get from Jezebel?"

"Look, I am not going to beat around the bush. I need you to do a few favors for me, and I will do a favor for you."

"How do you know what I want?"

"What do you want? Money?"

"No, money is fleeting; I want status."

"You know how this is going to end."

"Indulge me a moment. You and I both know that my mom was queen before you, and the throne you or your daughter sits on should have been mine."

"Only, it is not. Rightfully, it is in my hands where it will remain."

"I am not coming for your seat, but I do intend on becoming your second. Make me a grand witch."

"You and I both know that seat is claimed by authorities that go beyond me."

"I think you have a way with magic that could help me. Or maybe you can teach me something that I don't know?"

"Teach you what?"

"How to switch bodies like you."

"Who told you that?"

"You are not the only one who knows magic, Carol, and a bit of voodoo. But I am not after what you have; I have my own plans. I just need your help for this piece, and we will be even."

"Magic always comes with a cost."

"And I am willing to pay it. I want what is mind, plain and simple, and nothing personal."

"You know, I thought you would be bitter towards me after everything with your mom. I know you two were close."

"She was a selfish son of a bitch. She didn't give a damn about me and the things she promised me, she is dead, and can't keep. I want what I should have had to hell with her."

"Well, if you feel this way. You should know, the spell you want is going to require sacrifice, and I am not talking about cats, dogs, or birds."

"I understand the risk, and I am ready."

"Then let's get to work. There are six snares we need to lay between my daughter and Charity if we want this to work."

"Why six?"

"Because I am the teacher and you are the doer. I will tell you when to ask questions. But I will answer this question once, don't make me repeat it. We have to crush the light in both of them at the same time, so we both can get what we want. In order to learn this spell, you have to take possession of a body at the start. There is no practice run. Can you do this?"

"Yes."

"We need to release six powerful demons as old as time. I do mean that literally. Robbery, Injustice, Unfaithfulness, Betrayal, Jealousy, and Anger. My daughter is not difficult at all to disrupt; the process has already begun. With my granddaughter reaching her prime, the last thread of hope will be lost, and the spirit of robbery will be released that will spew out the kind of rage I need for dark magic."

"Okay."

"Now, your job is to work on Charity."

"What do you mean, work on Charity?"

"I mean, you need to do the hard work of building her up and tearing her down in three weeks. I would suggest doing this before her 13th birthday or near it. My time to help you is closing, and I cannot make guarantees beyond her 13th birthday."

"Three weeks is not enough time. Shouldn't we have months to prepare for something like this?"

"Time is not on your side. If you can't do it in three weeks, I need to make another phone call. Don't waste my energy."

"No, I can do it. It's just, I'm gonna need your help to tell me how. I mean, what do I do?"

"I am telling you now. How you accomplish these six things is up to you. Get creative. I have my own problems. I need you to keep Charity distracted and pushing closer to our road."

She swallows laboriously, and says "I cannot help you directly, but I can answer any questions you have. I warn you, she has a strong hedge of protection around her. I am old, so maybe that's why I am feeling it more than you. Or some other twisted spell, but don't take long to do what you must," as the snake in her belly coils growing anxious.

"I will figure it out and contact you if I need you." The ladies hang up the phone, and Rachel's Mom's mind starts to run. She is wondering how she will cause hell to break loose in Charity's life and not alert her mother, or why she should trust Carol. Her mind is working, but she must address one fire at a time. The first: Which of the six demons will she unleash first?

Nothing stirs up trouble for teenagers like a good party. She knows that getting drama circulating, which usually results in the six demons being released, would start the ball rolling, and she would follow up on any lead she has to move forward. Now, her focus needs to be on making the wildest party ever.

Back at Zoe's House

The girls, Zoe and Charity, are sitting in the living room with a bowl of popcorn, watching tv.

Zoe is in the thick of watching tv, but Charity's eyes are all around the room staring at her pictures. She thinks of a million questions, but only one comes out of her mouth. "Hey, why do you have so many people on your walls?"

"I have a large extended family. People we meet at church, on crusades, and even just random people we pray with. My parents have been active in ministry for years. I love that they do it, but sometimes, I just want them to be normal, and it is like they don't know how to do that."

"I love that you have a family. Staying at home can be quiet. I used to always think what a house would feel like to have siblings."

"Annoying. You would want them gone as soon as possible because when you have them, you understand the need for quiet."

"My mom would never have any more children anyway. I think she just grew content with having just me."

"Or she was smart and realized having a whole lot of kids is not the way to stay slim and trim or get what you want. When I get older, I want to be like your mom. I want to wear nice clothes and follow my passion. Nothing wrong with being an artist if that's what you like to do. I could never get away with that. My mom and dad always tell me to find a practical interest that could survive the age of the robots."

"Here I am thinking I have an active imagination," replies Charity.

"Don't laugh. It's true and not in a creepy way."

"Sure, you keep thinking that. Technology and AI aren't going anywhere. I think we have to get used to things changing because that is happening one way or another, and there is nothing we can do about it."

"Or is it? We have to go along with it to catch hold. If more people fought against artificial intelligence for food, information, writing, or drawing, in health, communication, media, etcetera maybe we won't have a fake world in our near future."

"What AI does for many people is save time and money. For the world, that is more important than humans."

"Do you really believe that?"

"I mean, no, but I do see it. People die every day, go broke or rich, and the cycle of having and losing repeats. Life is just life with money being a motivator and not the end-all, for sure. We are already in a technical world. When was the last time you got up to change the channel?"

"What do you mean?"

"TVs back in the day had knobs and antennas. We don't have any of those things now, and look

228

at how much time we save, options, buttons, and other services we have because of technology. AI is just a progression and shouldn't be intimidating."

"I think it is a sad day for AI to take over every category in our lives, where we can no longer tell the difference between what is real and what is fake. It might sound good to shortcut in the moment, but it will backfire over time. It always does."

"You should run for office." The girls start laughing. Charity continues, "So, what are you doing this weekend?"

"Staying home. My brother has to work. What about you?"

"I might be hanging out with Rachel and Freda. Don't know if John is going or not."

"You might want to do that yourself. I don't gel all that well with your friends," Zoe said as she shook her head from side to side.

"I told you, we are all friends."

"Okay, you can believe that. But I know what I know. I will be here watching tv or looking at my phone."

"Hey, in your room, you have a lot of pictures of fashion. Do you want to be a designer? I meant to ask you that."

"Yeah, I want to design clothes that can be

on the runway or just worn around. Nothing too crazy, but I think a designer always has those bizarre pieces they love that break conventions."

"Yeah. Maybe you can make it big in fashion."

"Remember, I need to be practical to beat out a machine."

"The world is changing, not much you can do about that. But like you said, creativity is something that isn't duplicated, even though it is emulated. Maybe you can pursue both?"

"I could live vicariously through your mom's wardrobe any day, but I doubt when my parents get back, I could even get this close to the dresses I want to make."

"What do you think about designing our dresses for my birthday party next month? You do know how to sew and make clothes, right?"

"Yeah, I can make them, I just need to know your style." The girls start scrolling through images and discussing options for design. Zoe is in heaven talking about cuts, stitch lines, material, and the overall look of the their possible dresses. The girls both agree on what they want, and Charity sends her some money to get started.

"This is just some old birthday cash I've kept. My mom buys me everything, so I don't need much."

"Thanks for supporting a young business owner. I won't let you down."

"I am sure you won't. Well, I gotta go. Not sure what my mom has planned, but she's been asking a million and one questions for this party. I might go out later tonight. Maybe you should come with me?"

"Who's all going?"

"You know who. But it should be chill and fun."

"I'll think about it and ask my brother."

"Okay, just let me know."

A Party for Two

Charity leaves out the door and Zoe sits looking over her design. She didn't know how much she missed fashion. She knows this is like a forbidden passion that might turn into nothing serious, but the thought of becoming a designer still brings her joy, even if it fades after high school. Why can't she live her dreams now?

She looks in the fridge to see what she wants to prepare and decides on chicken alfredo. One thing her mom always taught her and her brother was that, when in doubt, cook pasta. She knew her brother would be getting home soon from school, and she thought to ask about hanging out with Charity. She made enough to include him so he would be in a good mood, she'd hoped. He was a bit cranky with working nights and going to school.

But it's Friday, the start of the weekend. Her brother came through the door on cue and smelled the food in the kitchen. He washed his hands in the sink and opened the lid. "You cooked?"

"Yeah, of course. I can cook."

"Why didn't you cook before? I have been slaving away trying to think of stuff you would eat this whole time."

"I think you are doing a good job, so I wanted to do something for you."

"Hmm, that sounds fishy, and I can smell BS."

"Aww, don't be so skeptical about everything. I can just be a good person."

"Or you are a baby sister who wants something."

"No, just being nice."

"Okay, thanks. I gotta work later tonight, so I will eat before heading out. I am just going to go up and change. What are you planning on doing?"

"Nothing much, I was asked to hang out with my friends, but I wasn't sure if I wanted to do that."

"I really don't like you hanging out with that girl, Charity. Her mom gives me the creeps. I think you should have Mom or Dad meet her to feel them out."

"Don't be so weird. Not everyone is a witch or something. You just get nervous around pretty women."

"I have seen and dated lots of pretty women who don't give me the hibbee-jibbees. That woman is weird. I can't really describe it, but it ain't natural–and before you think it, it is not sexual. I do know the difference."

"Yeah, okay."

"Alright, let me go change."

Zoe saw her brother disappear from the kitchen. She heard what she needed to hear, an open invitation to do what she thought not to do, but never said she wouldn't do. His reluctance wasn't a no, but not a yes. There was a gray space in the conversation, just enough for her to go with Charity if she liked. He wouldn't know anyhow if he was driving, she thought.

The pasta was good, not as good as her mother's, but better than a frozen dinner. She sat at the table, and although she wanted to start working on the dress and could think of a million good things to do with her time, hanging out with Charity and being a kid seemed to win out. She texted her bestie to see what the plans were, and wrote them down just in case she needed to call her brother if the worst happened.

He left on cue, and she felt she would get home before him, so she didn't think he would ever read the note. She heads to her room to pick out her outfit and figures jeans and a cute shirt would suffice. But she needed something for her neck to make the look pop. As she searched the drawer for socks, she remembered the necklace she had forgotten about from Charity's mom. She pulls it out and places it around her neck, and now, the outfit looks amazing. There is a new wind blowing in her hair, and she likes it.

She put on the lipstick she got and added a little oil to make it shine. She looked like new money and a pretty picture if she did admit it to herself. She met up with Charity outside, and the girls laughed as they headed to get Rachel and Freda. John said he would drive to meet them there.

Rachel seemed a bit surprised to see Zoe in the car, laughing and having a good time with Charity. Her smile was more of a grin, and she reluctantly got into the car and said, "Hey…"

"Hey, I invited Zoe."

"Yeah, I see. Hi Zoe." She tried to be friendly, although her tone had a sense of sarcasm that walked dangerously close to insulting.

"Hey, thanks for letting me hang. I am working on something for Charity and thought this could be good."

"Yeah, I told her we were looking for our dresses, and Zoe offered to make me an original dress."

"Oh, so you are going to trust her to make you a dress that will not look cheap? Doesn't it just make more sense to buy a dress you know is what you want? I mean no shade to you, but something out of the stores is probably going to be better for the kind of party your mom is throwing."

"I get it. And I know I might not be an established business owner–yet, but I have an incredible eye for fashion, and I know how to use a sewing machine. I have been using one since I was like five or six. Nothing will look immature or cheap about her dress."

"I would feel bad to upstage her at her own event," says Rachel with a sarcastic laugh.

"Trust me, that won't happen," replies Zoe in a playful but firm tone.

Breaking up the tension, "Where does Freda live again?" asks Charity's mother. Rachel directs the way as Jezebel watches Zoe in the rear-view mirror. There is something about the girl she likes. She reminds her of herself when she was thirteen or fourteen, full of dreams and ambition.

She liked hearing the girls banter in the backseat, knowing that the trivial things they argued over now wouldn't matter as they aged. They won't matter in the next few months. No one cares about these moments that seem to be a simple part of life. If she could have had a party thrown for her, with friends, and had someone like Zoe to defend her, maybe she wouldn't be what she chose to be, she thought.

The thought escaped her quickly because

powerlessness doesn't look more appealing than power. She never wanted to give up the power, but if there was a way to have the power and the life she could have lived, she wanted both. She never saw herself as a simple woman, because simple women get hurt. She would much rather be the one who wins, no matter what. She drove in silence, taking in the moment and fishing for details to help her solidify her plan to move to number one.

Everything you need to take down parents can be said through the mouth of a saucy teenage girl in time. But how much time did she really have? She knew the clock was running, and she could only pray she got things in order before her mom did. She has a plan, but she knows her thoughts would collide with her mother's. Now was the time she had to dig deep, deeper than she ever had, and she thought about who else she could seek for help.

If she were really desperate, she could ask people in the coven to help her, but she knew they were all hunting for blood. They seemed content with being under her, but every witch is, until they are not. She couldn't take a risk and expose her weakness. She didn't see her weakness, and she prayed that her mom was equally in the dark.

The drive seemed to go in slow motion as she shifted her focus to Charity. She truly was a wonderful child. Maybe if she had a pinch of a good mother, she could have been more loving towards her. It almost pains something in her to think what she would look like, feel like, after what needs to be done is done. She hated to think how much evil can rob you of your gentleness, softness, that she misses in her own face.

Although she is in her thirties and looks great, she can't help but notice how many of her soft curves have become hard lines, strong lines that shape her chiseled smile, look, or grin. The soft laughter she once experienced in her life felt close in that moment. She thought of Charity's father and what kind of life she could have had if only he hadn't been a scam. If he had not been a selfish asshole, she thought, they could have built something for this girl, and continued to mend the heart that was broken and craven love, that now has grown as stony as her eyes.

She worked hard to feel what love was and whatever it was meant to be. She now hates it and sees it as a vile thing sent to break her focus. She vowed to never let love have its way because that is what led her to unshakable pain. Pain that was not physical, nor completely understandable. If she had been honest with herself, she would have known she needed to release the pain and not hoard it for fueling her revenge against him and her mother. She stopped the vision of family and bright, sunny days filled with laughter and replaced it with a mumbled remark: "Stupid asshole."

Freda walks up to the car, and her eyes are locked on Rachel. She speaks to her before she opens the door, and the two make eye contact. "Hi Rachel?"

Rachel who was deep in thought breaks her glare at Zoe and looks to Freda, "Hey, girl. How you been?"

"Good. It's been a good day so far. Zoe, move over, I can't fit." As Zoe scoots over to give her space, Freda smiles. The car is not as talkative as it was before. They are all a bit transfixed on their inner thoughts, and the music playing in the vehicle happily fills the air. They arrive at a plaza with shops, where walkers are on a mission to find gifts, as waves of people cross paths.

The girls are huddled together as they exit the vehicle. Jezebel looks out at them through the passenger front window. "I will be right here if you need me. I have one store I need to visit, but when you are ready, just call me, Charity."

"Alright, mom." Jezebel, satisfied with her reply, drives off.

"So, where to first?" asked Rachel, sounding slightly bored already.

"Let's start with the dress. We can at least get our styles and then focus on the accessories and makeup." The girls hear her out and all agree to follow her lead. Charity happily starts walking to her favorite spots. Naturally, Freda walks alongside Rachel, and Zoe walks up to keep in step with Charity. The pairs were naturally selected, but Rachel wasn't satisfied. Freda was in her own world talking, but Rachel didn't hear a word she said, although she could hear her voice.

240

"So, Rachel. Are you going to have a date to Charity's party?" Freda didn't see Rachel respond, and she looked a bit distant, so she grabbed her hand gently, which caught Rachel's attention. She looked at her and said, "Sorry, a lots on my mind. What did you say?"

"I said, were you thinking to have a date for the party?"

"No, I don't think an event like this really needs one. It's not like this is prom."

"For us, it is kind of like one. I mean, it is fancy dresses, nice shoes, and matching purses. We are not in the 1600s where this would be commonplace." Freda talks in a playful and proper tone, emulating European accents of the time period.

She has a perfect blend of curiosity and nonchalance. If you weren't an eye expert, you would miss the passion that burns behind her question. She wanted to have an entrance, but what must she do to be seen by Rachel? Is it really hard for her to walk through a door she leaves open, or does she have no interest in accepting Freda's advances?

She nods her head, seemingly accepting the answer. But she can't help but think about who Rachel will choose to dance with during songs. Who will she spend her time with if not her? If they came together, she thought they could dance and be together without distraction. She could grab her drinks, laugh, and maybe–just maybe they could kiss, even if it was once.

"So, I mean, you don't think you would want to dance with someone? I mean, at parties, it will be music, lots of talking, and stuff," Freda inquires.

"Yeah, of course. I am sure I will dance and talk to guys. But I am not trying to tie myself down to one of them for the night. Some guys talk way too much."

"Yeah, I know what you mean," replies Freda with a light-hearted laugh and smile. They walk on in silence. "That's what you have girlfriends for, right?" They both laugh, Rachel blowing off the comment as comical, and Freda hiding her wounds.

Entering the store seemed to be the perfect transition for the conversation. The girls get caught up looking at the manics against the walls. They were pondering what color they wanted for their dress. Zoe thought about a white and silver dress. She didn't bring any money, and to ask would have meant telling her brother, or worse, her mother, what she was up to. She liked looking at the dresses for concepts and seeing colors she liked.

She watched Charity a bit more than she paid attention to what she wanted for herself. She thought, *this is my first client*. I want to nail this. Charity was attracted to stones, crystals, white, and straps. She had a dainty, almost regal style that seemed beyond her years. She picked dresses that seemed to match the styles of hundreds of years ago more than those of the present day. She was classy, and Zoe wanted to be like her.

She would never admit it, but she wanted a little more each day of what Charity had. The freedom to choose what she wants for herself. To have days where she can be alone in her room to sew. She wanted to be like the dainty but confident girl who hunts through dresses in seconds to say what she liked and didn't like. She didn't overthink what others would say, and didn't appear to care.

Zoe can not think of a day when she didn't have a running list of who would judge her decision and render them good or bad before she could speak up about it. It was normal, but does that make it right? Is it right to question so much and get few answers that really make sense to you? She kept watching and asked questions when she had them. She wanted to watch for Charity's smile.

Freda was also looking for smiles. They weren't to affirm affection but to show a glimpse of what she could experience if Rachel could ever see her. She wanted the smiles she saw on her face, looking at dresses and turning others away, to be what she could do for her. If anyone could peek into her thoughts, they would quickly notice how her entire world was wrapped up in her.

"Freda, what do you think about this? Do you think this could be the dress?" Her eyes squint as she compares two dresses while looking in the mirror. Her head turns to the side inquisitively as she tries to imagine what it would look like. Finally, Freda replies with a suggestion.

"Why don't you try them on? Sometimes it is about how you feel in the dress, not what it looks like on a hanger, right?"

"Freda, you are so smart." She comes close to her and gives an air kiss as she walks past her and to the dressing room. Freda melts as if the kiss landed anywhere on her face.

"Bring your dresses back here, too," says Rachel as she finds an empty dressing stall. Freda, without hesitation, grabs two dresses she barely looked at. She really wasn't into dresses. It was always her mom's idea for her to wear them when she did. She is dead now, so she doesn't have to wear them at all, and on most days she would be in pants and a shirt.

But to be around Rachel and Charity, being uncomfortable to fit in or be around the love of your life, seemed like a small pill to swallow. As the girls change into their first dresses, Charity suggests to Zoe, "Hey, let's try some things on too."

"Okay," replies Zoe as she picks up the three dresses she likes. She is out committing the ultimate sin. Shopping while broke! She doesn't mention it and prays no one asks about it. Freda and Rachel come out of the dressing rooms first and gaze in the mirror.

"See, we look good together, Rachel," says Freda as she admires the dresses.

"Noo…I am not really liking this. Let's

change into another one." The girls re-enter the dressing room. Charity and Zoe both come out of the rooms and stand in front of the mirror. They both laugh because they look fantastic. The dresses seem to fit both of them so well. They laugh and dance a little in front of the mirror as they play around.

Rachel, hearing the noise, rushes out of the room to see what is making them so happy. She sees their dresses, and envy wraps around her, its tentacles gripping her mind, heart, and hands, growing stronger with each passing moment. She thinks, "Why does everything she does look so damn perfect. No one is perfect. So why the hell does she get so close to it? This shit is not fair."

Rachel comes up behind the girls and breaks up the merry time by jokingly bumping Zoe out of the frame. She replies, "Now, you both know I look better. I pray those are not your final picks?"

Charity has a light-hearted laugh, "No, I told you Zoe is making my dress. This is something I will add to my closet for a different occasion. But your dress looks nice, buuut. I know it won't look better than what I will have. Right, Zoe?"

"Yup," replies a confident Zoe. The praise or verbal battle that Rachel was fighting seemed to quickly lose steam as the girls seemed uninterested in battling with her. They both felt great in what they were wearing, and they reconnected near the dressing room doors with a smile and a hidden truth that they didn't give two cents what Rachel said, and she could feel it as she watched their reaction in the mirror.

If her eyes were lasers, they would zap them both. She tossed her hair as she left the mirror, and Freda exited with no one to take in her dress. She quickly looks into the mirror, but only sees the lonely face she had hoped to turn into a smile at the party. Will times change or be more of the same, she thought. She was last and hated being last.

Her mom was last in the witches' nucleus. She knew very little about what she should do and felt the only reason they kept her around was that her mom had been sacrificed on a bad spell they tested to see what would happen if crap hit the fan — and it did. She was the first line of defense, and she wasn't a match for the magic she was playing with.

Freda missed her and wanted to find a way to remember her. She had hoped that being a better witch could be a way. Her grandmother never agreed with playing with books, crystals, and spirits. She felt it was all demonic, no matter how they tried to convince her it wasn't all bad. She would throw her hands up and say, "You mess around with Diablo and you're gonna catch hell. Don't bring that into my house. I will be the first to say I am not perfect. But that is dangerous."

Freda heard every word but never knew what it meant, nor how or why it came to be. Even after her mother died, she never connected magic with danger. She just thought it was an accident because witches lie, and most of them do it well. She believed what she was told, and her friends, whom she needed desperately to learn weren't coming out with the real facts either.

The girls grab their dresses and start walking toward the counter. Zoe sat her dress back on the rack and tried to stay away and look at accessories to help buy her time. Charity, without saying a word, picked up the dress and carried them both to the counter. She wasn't sure of the circumstance, but if she was making her dress, she might not have time to make two, no matter how good she was. These dresses were the backups.

One thing about teenage girls, she knew, they could smell blood in the water. She was last in line and stood two guests back to make sure Freda and Rachel would be lost in their own thoughts, and didn't see her purchase both dresses. Freda was going a mile a minute again, and Rachel started to walk off, hoping to get a break. Sometimes she felt like Freda was a stray cat she hated that she rescued. She never would leave or shut up.

Charity checked out and walked up to Zoe to save her from her distractions. The two of them walked out of the store smiling for what was to come next as Charity joked. They walked and almost forgot that John was even coming. He spotted them and jogged over to them. "Did I miss anything?"

"Yeah, we got our dresses," replied Rachel.

"That's nothing important. I don't wear

those."

"You take a lot of them off, though," replied Freda loud enough to be heard by Zoe.

"Why don't we take a break from shopping and do something a bit more fun?" replies John.

"Like what?" inquires Rachel in a playful but bitter tone.

"I don't know. Maybe check out my family's shop?"

The girls, uncertain of what shop he had in mind, hesitantly agreed. He notices their hesitation and replies, "Don't worry, it's not sex toys or something. Chill. Plus, you have to be 18 to go into places like that."

They all breathe out with a sigh of relief, but inhale with curiosity. They walk over to a shop that looks dark and low-lit, filled with scented candles. It looked like a candle and body bar shop more than anything.

But there was something odd about the air, the emptiness, and even the music that played low but steady in the place. It wasn't familiar songs, but almost noises or instruments that reeked of creepy. Zoe's necklace started to warm her chest. She nearly forgot she had it. She grabbed it to help her calm her nerves. Normally, she would have felt ultra uncomfortable and bolted immediately, but she was somewhat relaxed.

Zoe leans closer to Charity and asks, "You ever been here before?"

"No, I don't know what this is. I am guessing a soap bar that sells scented candles and incense?" She looks around, but she too feels an odd energy in the place. The two girls stay close as they look and smell. There is a lady who emerges from the back, and she comes to John first and greets him with a kiss.

"How are you, young man?"

"I am well, Auntie. Just hanging with my friends." She looks to the girls, and carefully she scans each of them. She lingers on Charity, "Child, how are you?"

A little taken aback, Charity replies, "Me? Oh, I am good."

"You are a radiant child. There is a beautiful aura around you. Do you know that?"

"I mean, I know I am special, who is not?"

"No, you really are special. A key that links to a lineage ages and ages old on both sides of your family. There is a lot of power flowing through your veins. Do you want to know who visits you in your dreams?"

"What are you talking about?"

"You know, the man?"

"Wait, how do you know about that?"

"Come with me, child." The two of them walk away from the others. Zoe looks on to make sure something doesn't happen weird, and if it is weird, what would she do, she thought. Her first mind would have told her to pray, but in this moment, that wasn't what she chose to do. She just decides to watch."

"Darling, you have a powerful family."

"Ok."

"A girl like you is not born every day, and everyone is going to want to influence you. You need to learn to trust your gut, even if your mother, father, or grandmother approaches you."

"What are you talking about? I barely talk to my grandmother. My father, I never met, and my mom is a jewelry maker."

"Child, everything is not what it seems. You need to know that not everything you see is all that there is. There is a lot you won't see until you see with this eye."

She touches her forehead and says, "Your natural eyes will let you down. Don't put your faith in them either. Trust me, child, the man in your dreams told you right. You must choose a side, and your mother and father represent a side. Your grandmother, too, but you, you get to choose who will live or die."

"Die? Why is anyone dying?"

"That's the way magic works. The price of magic is always death. Even good spells lead to death of something. A rabbit, a cat, a dog. You can know them, or it can be a stray. But the stronger the magic, the closer the deaths become, the more powerful the magic. A light crushed is more powerful than a live flower."

"I don't understand."

"You–" her voice is paused. Zoe stands closer to them, and the necklace around her neck is burning as it sits on her chest. Although it heats up, she is not empowered to remove it. It sits around her neck and holds her isolated, present, but powerless to move. She looks at what she thinks she hears, but she is uncertain of what to make of it. The woman's voice is muted, and one of her arms is swung back around, wound up like a clock and going in reverse.

She grunts in pain, looking towards the ground, she says words that none of us can decipher if it is English or an ancient language, the sounds she whispers are loud enough to be heard, but not known to write or speak and repeat. Her eyes signal that someone is there, but who? Who is she talking to when there is no one else in the store but them?

John comes over and tries to move his aunt, but she is transfixed in her position. John says, "What happened? What's going on, Auntie?"

She looks at him and replies, "This bitch is

trying to control me."

"Who?"

"You know damn well who. Everyone needs to leave."

The girls started backing up to leave the store. Charity starts walking over to Zoe, but Zoe grabs her, and they're both stuck. As Charity firmly tries to move her, she moves to look her in her eyes, standing in front of her, she says, "Zoe, Zoe, can you see me?"

Zoe shifts her focus away from the lady and to Charity. "Uh, yeah. Yeah. I am here." The lady is able to recover her arm and grabs it. She is released from the invisible captivity, and John's aunt says after Charity, "Mark my words. You are not alone, and you will never be. You get to–"

Zoe turns toward her, and again the woman is muted. She tries to grab her throat to get her mouth to open, but nothing is coming out. She can no longer speak, and John rushes to catch her because it looks as if she will lose her balance. The girls quickly start moving, and Charity pushes Zoe, saying her name, "Zoe, let's go. We gotta go."

Zoe's legs shift from the force of Charity pushing her toward the exit. The girls now outside the shop ask each other, "What the hell was that?" replied Freda. "I don't know, but I need something to drink. If I were older, I would want a shot, but we are kids, so let's get coffee." Charity and Zoe agreed.

They were on autopilot, moving with the flow. John pops back up and says, "Hey, sorry about that. She is old, and you know how they can be."

Charity tells him, "Yeah, but what was she talking about?"

"Old people have no filter, I guess. Don't mind her. It was a mistake to bring you there. I thought my mom was going to be there. We keep my aunt in the back for a reason, is all I can say."

Zoe and the girls nod, feeling a bit more relieved. Zoe grabs the necklace around her neck, feeling more encouraged. She felt an ease come over her that melted her concerns or cares about what she had just seen. She welcomes the cup of cappuccino that tickles her nose and leaves foam on her lips. The creamy coffee they drank in healthy silence resharpened their focus for shopping.

Charity couldn't help but repeat the lady's words. She mentioned her father. How could she know about her father, when her father was dead, she thought. How could he be in my dreams as a dead man, she asked. She wondered, did my mom lie to me about my father, and why would she?

The coffee got her calm, but her mind was far from considering the thought. If the man in her dreams is her father, why didn't he just find her if he were *alive*? What kind of game was she in?

She was growing frustrated thinking of the questions, and feeling silly because it all seemed animated and unreal to her. She didn't want to dwell on the idea anymore; she would just have to ask more of her questions when she saw him again. But, would she see him again, or was the last visit her last?

Her mom met them at the coffee shop. When she popped up, she said, "Hey, found you guys."

"How did you know we were here?" asked Charity.

"I tracked your phone."

"Sounds right. Why don't parents just call?"

"Because we don't have to when we can monitor you. You guys ready?"

"Yeah, I think we are good for today. We can come out again later I guess," replied Charity.

"Yeah, I need to head home. My brother will be home soon," replied Zoe.

"Dang, I just got here. I feel late," replies Johnny.

"Sometimes you miss the mark," replies Rachel.

The girls follow Jezebel back to their vehicle and pile in. Johnny heads back to the shop to check on his aunt. He arrives and finds her looking at a mirror. She is speaking to it as if she is having a conversation. He hesitates to speak, hoping she would hear his presence and welcome the conversation if she wanted it. She keeps whispering, then she turns her head quickly to look at him and speaks in a deeper voice.

"Johnny, Johnny," she says.

After waiting several moments, "Ahh, yes?"

"That's not the rhyme. It's yes, Papa."

"Uh, yes, Papa?"

"Eating Sugar?"

"No, papa?"

"Telling lies?"

He hesitates, "No, Papa?"

"Wrong answer. Telling lies, yes, Papa, because that is a good son. Do you want an assignment, Johnny?"

"Elevation?"

"Yes, of course, elevation, but think with me. I need you to tell some lies."

"What will I get?"

"Life, power, respect–"

"Money?"

"Whatever you like, you can have."

"Okay. What should I do?"

"You just do what I say. When I come to visit you, you will listen and not question my commands."

"Who are you?"

"Long ago, a friend of Carol's."

"The Queen witch?"

"Not for long."

"And my mother?"

"I cannot make choices for her. She has to be strong enough. But I can ensure a seat for you at the table. You won't fail."

Johnny doesn't speak a word, but in his eyes, he is thinking. The spirit speaks up again and asks, "Johnny, Johnny? Will that be a problem?"

He nods from left to right to signal that it is not a problem. "No, not a problem." In that moment, he thought about how he had to secure his own destiny. There are no partnerships in magic. Temporary arrangements are, at best, what witches can hope to have. Balance and partnership are only stabilized by power. He needed power; then he could give his mom something, so he could honor the human side, but the spiritual side, she had to earn that on her own.

His aunt's eyes returned to a softer shade of brown. Her body is less tense, and she speaks in her normal female voice. "Johnny, you need to be careful. That spirit is not familiar to me, and he came to me. All magic has a cost, and you didn't ask the main question before accepting and signing your name in blood. Nothing in magic is accomplished without shedding blood.

"I don't care whose it will be as long as it's not mine, or my mom's. You think it would impact you?"

"No one can be sure. I would like to hope it does not," she replies.

There is silence that fills the room. The heavy cloud didn't seem to shift away, although the room felt calm. Johnny left after seeing that his aunt was functioning like her normal self. She saw a figure in the spirit leave with Johnny and knew who he was; she recognized the scent as it blew into her nostrils. "Oh no, no," she says as she quickly moves from before the door and goes to the phone.

She picks up the receiver, thinking to call his mom. She answers, but is a bit preoccupied. She knows the urgency of what she must say, "Aurora, I need you to listen to me. I think "Diablo" just left with your son."

"What are you talking about?"

"Diablo, grand wizard, who died 65 years ago."

"How are you sure?"

"I will never forget his scent. He is here. He just–" Her hands raise up to hold her throat. She begins holding her throat, but it seems like a hand with long nails has seized her and has her suspended in thought. She is silenced, and her sister asks questions on the other end, hoping to get clarity. Tears run from her eyes, and then she hears.

"You know who I am. Good. So you know that what I am about to do, you cannot stop it. Don't meddle in this, or I promise you won't survive. I don't want you. You are too weak, but I will kill you if you step one foot in my way. Shut up now, and never speak my name again."

She hangs up the phone as she sleeps on the floor.

A New Friend

Charity was silent in the car on the way home. Jezebel noticed but thought it was no big deal. She thought to say nothing, but was pushed to say, "Charity, are you alright? You look like you've seen a ghost."

"Ugh, no. Just a little weirded out by John's aunt. She seemed off."

"People are weird, hun. Old crones can always make people feel on edge."

"Crone?"

"No, I meant crow."

"Right. Mom, if my dad were alive, would you tell me?"

"What's got you thinking he is alive?"

"I mean, I know it's crazy and stupid, but I needed to ask."

"Of course, I guess every child has questions about their father. Your father was a man who loved me but struggled to balance family. He didn't want to make the sacrifice to ensure our safety. And in the end, it cost him. He went out and never returned."

"What makes you think he is dead?"

"Wouldn't he have come to check on you? To be with me if he were alive? We were to get married, move, and buy a house. I got the house —the one we live in —but he was just missing, without a trace. He had debts. I hate to think of what people would do when they get desperate to get back what they loaned to your father."

"So, he might not be dead?"

"There is a very slim chance, so slim, I would say he is dead."

Charity doesn't say anything, but she listens. She nods in agreement, but if there is a hope she could see him again, she wanted to. As she sat there, she asked herself and anyone who would listen, "Please let me see my father at least one more time. I need your help to figure myself out."

With Cassandra

Cassandra was looking at her daughter's limp body in the bed. Something so sad happens when a person doesn't age on the inside, mentally, or in any other way, but their body grays, their skin wrinkles, and their body draws up. She is frail and nothing like how she was years ago. Her mom looks to God to deliver her child. She knows that all things are possible, and doesn't know why some have to suffer and others do not.

She is no judge of God's decisions, but she trusts His hand. She is not certain what her daughter could have done, but she knows what she didn't do. She never wanted to hear about God growing up. She was anti-God, and her father's side heavily influenced her power to choose nothing over the truth. She didn't like that her in-laws were so crabby.

Her husband, before he died, was a devout believer. He was the one destined to change his family, certainly. That is how it happens sometimes, though. It seems like the light in the family is stumped out by those filled with gross darkness. Cassandra didn't understand it even when it happened, and he got sick. She just knew to serve him and stay connected to God.

She tried to keep her family close to God, but they were pulled in secret to consider magic and dark arts, no matter how much she tried. It is breaking her heart now to see her two children in such a disarray with their lives. Some would think this is God's punishment because they wouldn't serve Him. She never believed it was. She knows her God is a good God, capable of saving her and her whole house. Her God gave her promises, and she intended on praying them until they came to pass.

On this day, like for the past several years, when she felt a huge urge, she prays. She prays for the grandchildren she hopes to have, the redemption, restoration, and healing of her children. She wants them to change, but knows the change also has to be in their own hearts and lives. The prayers of the righteous avail much, but it doesn't solve everything.

She stares at the sky and she claps her hands together softly. She knows she has the attention of God, but she also wants to revere Him. "Father, you are a good God, capable of great gifts. You say children are a blessing from the Lord, and Father," her voice trails off as she tries to push back her tears. "Father, I know you know my children, Curtis and Courtney. Father, they have not been faithful to serve you a day of their lives. And if I am honest, they have been doing everything but that. But Father, I need you to come by here. Kumbayah, My Lord!"

She continues with a renewed strength and certain victory, and says, "See about your daughter, Lord God. Hear my voice and humble your ear to hear your humble servant who is calling on your *Name*. I need you now. My son needs you, my daughter, and my grandchildren whenever they come, need you. If you don't save them now, Father, will I ever be a grandmother? If you don't mend my children, I will be barren. I will have no legacy and fade into the fabric of society."

She isn't done, but speaks, "Father, show me your favor. Touch my legacy, touch my children, and children's children. Give me an inheritance that I can share with the world. Bring them out of the hell they are in. For my daughter, this long and overdue torment. For Curtis, this spirit of addiction, Father, give him rest. Allow him to come to his right mind, even for a moment, to hear you and to do right by this family.

Make him honor his father, me, and those of us who sacrificed and poured into him. Father, this son is a jewel and crown to this family, and we won't give up on him because he is struggling now. We are believing that there is nothing too hard for you and you can *break* this off his life. Prepare his heart to receive the gift of salvation and keep him from choosing *death* instead of life."

She is intentional about her words as she repeats these words with power that is strong enough to crack the foundation beneath her enemy's feet, "Help my patience, Lord. Increase my *faith* and strength if either shall fail me. Father, you will *never* leave nor fail me. Be here with me now. Send your angels out to bring forth good news concerning me and my family. Lift up our hands to *fight* so that we are not consumed by the enemy. In Yashua's name, my Redeemer, My Savior, I say hallelujah, and it is so!"

The little lady sits there for a while, and the tears that started are still coming down her cheeks. The tears are warm, hot, and she can feel the Presence of God tingling all over her from the top of every hair follicle down to the soles of her feet. This prayer she knows touched Heaven.

Her tears are no longer of pain, but of victory. This is her war cry and the start or the part of a battle she will win. She is determined to see the full recovery of her family, and this prayer is the precipice of setting the house back in order with God.

This woman is old, but her body is young, and so is her spirit. She has not given up, and the Father has given her youth because of her faithfulness. He has not left nor abandoned her but preserved her to keep her daughter, and guard over her wondering son, attempting to heal in his own way from his guilt. She sees the pain in their eyes, but she cannot make them give it to God. She can only pray and trust Yah Almighty to do the rest.

Curtis Bedroom

Curtis tosses in his bed as a warm blanket seems to clothe his body. He feels the light touch and questions what it is. He doesn't remember the day, the time, or even where he sleeps now. Yesterday was a haze and a cloudy day filled with pills he could find and alcohol he bought after begging. He learned how simple it is for people to give him dollars on the street than for him to attempt to get a job he would soon lose.

No one wanted to hire a washed-up man to do anything. He tried to get his life together, but one step forward resulted in five steps back. He would try to give his life to something else but find himself getting lost in the details. He would lose his feet from underneath him and go scratching, aching for a high. He thought this was who he was. A man who craved to be high. A man who needed to be moving to keep alive.

There was a burning in his stomach, and nothing he did distracted him from it or cooled it down. He felt like his mother's prayers were being wasted on him. He was unaware of all that she did, but knew it was more than he deserved. He tried to go to church a few times, but more shame than freedom filled his heart. He would go in bound, and life would somehow get worse for him when he left.

He stopped coming to church after listening to the voices that seemed to convince him that running was better than staying and feeling the fire of guilt. Torment would raise a pitchfork and poke his heart, testing the temperature and maturity. But he was broken. He lost the love of his life, a baby he would never see, and nightly he dreamed of the woman he abused and misused on repeat.

But what could a man like him ever do to regain control over a life littered with pain, regret, and hell? Everything he could do, think of, hurt. Drinking hurts. Not drinking hurts. Looking to the future hurts. Looking to his past hurts. He could not live, and he could not die, because they both hurt.

He was lost and beyond confused. He was bound, wrapped tight. Some days, he felt like a hostage bound, drenched in gasoline, and everyone had a match ready to toss into his direction.

With so much hell, how can he fight to live? His dreams are the only place he can still be awake, inside, he was a resemblance of what he had hoped to become. He wanted to connect with his daughter and rebuild the family he never got a shot to have. He wanted the impossible, sure. He couldn't manufacture the dreams anymore. His uncle went on a sabbatical to preserve and build his power.

"He told him the powers are stirring and the time is growing nearer, and nearer." Curtis struggled to remember it and live consciously considering it. If he was honest, his life had no strategy and lacked focus and purpose. It was on grace and mercy that any of these actions could lead to something good. This was the prayers of his mother working to make all things work to his good, even being lost and broken.

This night, he thought it was good to be in a blank dream filled with nothing, but this night was a dream he had not recalled before. He was sober. Sobriety is a fleeting dream for him, so in this dream, it felt like a wish come true. He was dressed in white, clean. He looked out, but he didn't see anything for what seemed like miles. He saw a body of water that looked refreshing enough to drink from.

The water was clear, so clear that, as he scooped it up with his hands, it looked like a mirror, a glass door. He considered whether to drink it. He couldn't decide but enjoyed feeling free and playing with water like a kid. Happily, he sat by the water, looked down to see his reflection, and then looked to see if anything under the water could be seen.

He saw through the clear water to the beauty beneath the earth. He longed to touch it. He leaned his face closer to see the colors and what looked like jewels just beyond the surface. As his face gets closer, he thinks, "I can almost touch it." He reaches for a stone, and he slips into the water.

The water, he thought was going to be cold, was warm. The water surrounded him, cradling his face, putting power beneath his arms, and although he thought he would sink to the bottom, he floated with unseen power beneath him, pushing him up. He didn't realize it until now, but he was breathing.

Breathing underwater. He wasn't struggling, and he wasn't in fear. He was at rest. "Oh no God, am I dying?" he thought as he remained suspended in the body of water with no depths beneath his feet he could see.

Then he heard a voice, "Curtis, do you know who I am?"

Curtis searches the water for the location of the person whose voice he hears. The voice is like rushing water —firm, powerful, but welcoming, like a grandfather's voice that tenderly misses his grandchildren. The voice speaks again.

"Curtis, are you searching for me?"

"I don't know, who are you?"

"Isn't it obvious? I am the Creator, Yahweh. I am breath. I am soul. I am light. I am good. I am all-powerful. I am steadfast. I am God."

"Oh, oh. Hey, I am–"

"I am that I am. I am HE."

"I know, I know you brought me here to kill me, didn't you?"

"Why would I kill you?"

"Because, because I know what I have done."

"And, you think I don't know? You think I don't know the plans I have for you, Curtis?"

"Honestly, I don't know what you would want from me. I am a nobody, washed up, lost, and no good for anyone. I am a addict with no purpose but to live out the hell I caused a woman and my child."

"And if I want you? Can I have you?"

"Me?"

"Is there another?"

"There are plenty better than me."

"Yet I choose you."

"But God, I really think you should choose my mom. She knows you and–"

"Do you want to be mine? To be set free?"

"I need to," he says, filled with the emotions of regret. Tears, warm his face and scroll down in neon white, glowing.

"I didn't come here to shame you but to set you free. Word, come to him. Comforter, wrap your arms around him." There are other voices.

"Do you understand what you see, Curtis?"

"No, what am I looking at? Where am I?" A spirit-filled being comes to him, bright gold, glowing, where you cannot make out his pigment. He is neither black, brown, white, nor other. He is just a being filled with power, light, and peace. He has a reflection that mirrors his every move, and it can be seen even underwater. His eyes are like fire, but the blaze is gently filled with orange, white, and black.

He reaches out his hand and touches Curtis's body. He feels the touch, and instantly he is rushed to see the top of the body of water. He is out from beneath the water and back on dry land. He is not wet as he checks his clothes. He thinks this is a dream in a dream. But as he looks up, he sees the glowing being with fire-enriched eyes. "Am I awake?" he whispers to himself, but looks to the figure for reassurance.

"Yes, you are here. This is the spirit realm,

Curtis. Here you are free, you can bind, or release. You can be set free here."

"Free from what?"

"Everything. I came to set the captives free."

"I see."

"No you don't see. What you saw was the surface. You see how clear the water is?"

"Yes."

"The Word is clear. You can feel it and see there is no evil in it. It is not cloudy, confusing, nor does it hide the jewels beneath the surface. When you live it, you will find your breath and receive the power to move and breathe under water. Do you get it now?"

"No, I am not fully following."

"I speak in parables because if I tell you, use the Word it will deliver you. Take my Spirit, and it will be your comforter; you would think I was crazy. You will say it has no power. That is to call the clear water you can see cloudy and deny everything you just witnessed beneath the surface.

That would be you saying everything you just did, you couldn't do. And the truth, without me, you cannot. You cannot breathe underwater without me. You cannot break addiction and the chains you have, without the living water I offer you; without my Spirit, or the living Word."

"You want me to drink this?"

"I am the only way. I am the truth, the power, the light. Drink this water, and see the great depths I will carry you. As you walk by faith, I will be with you. When you think you fail–or if you do, I will carry you. Either way. I will never leave nor forsake you, Curtis. But now, you must choose. Will you choose life or death?"

"I don't know. I don't know."

"You must use this precious time carefully, or wait until I knock again and you can come to your senses again for a moment."

"This isn't the first time?"

"No. I have come many times. I stood at the door, at a street corner, when you were at a club. While you were in church. All the other times you ran from me. You ran from the very living water you hold today. What do you choose, Curtis. Your body is wanting to wake up."

"I choose–I choose." He stumbles with his words; he doesn't want to feel the heaviness, the pain anymore. He speaks up, "I choose life. Oh God, please, please, save me."

He drinks as if he had never seen water. The water goes down his throat and washes over his face. His face glows, and his power is being harnessed from within. His body remains at rest; the addictive hold on his body was made to relax by the authority of the living water circulating through his body.

He would usually wake to drink. Search ash trays, tables, counters, for something to snort or put on the tip of his tongue. He woke up thirsty many days for things that didn't water, didn't nourish, and had no power except the influence it had over him that he yielded to.

He was in a new space and he wasn't quick to leave. He wanted to rest in this peace. To soak up the sun, the power, and the energy he had long lost. He wasn't tired like he normally is. He had real hunger and was not crazed. He didn't know the depths of his healing, but he knew something transformed him in that dream.

His eyes slowly awoke and he set up. He looked around the house and saw the mess he made. He could see his mom's influence over the house and he thought to get sad about how he had been treating her over the years. Then he heard, "Don't cry, Curtis. The old things have passed away. The new has come." He recognized the voice from the dream. It wasn't scary even out here. He thought of doing something different, cleaning up his mess.

He went and started cleaning the counters, washing the dishes, and taking out the trash. He cleaned the floors and did the laundry. He didn't realize it but three hours had passed. He knew where his mom must have been seeing that she wasn't home. She let him move back in when he got beat up and left in an alley for dead the last time. She thought he would have died without her influence.

The house was clean, but there was no car to follow after his mom. So he went to a cafe near a middle school. He ordered and surprisingly enough, he had enough money in his pocket to have what he craved to eat. He wasn't sure how it got there, but he was grateful that it was.

Across the street, school had let out. Children came out of the building like an ant mound releasing baby and midsize ants. They crawled and went to where they needed to be. Some went on buses, others got in cars, and a few looked like they were walking. There was a pair that caught his eye.

Leaving School

Charity was leaving school when she heard a ding on her phone. She looked down and saw a short text from her mom. "Hey Charity, I am running late. Get a ride home or walk. Be there soon."

Charity knew what that meant. Walk. She didn't trust her middle school friends, knowing where she lived, or their teenage siblings, with her life. Plus, she preferred to walk whenever she could. She liked nature, and the trees seemed to allow the sun to poke out just perfectly to kiss her face as she walked.

She walked in silence thinking no one would join her then she heard John. "Hey, wait up." He came jogging over to her and said, "You know you could just ride home with me?"

"Yeah, no thanks though. I like walking."

"You sure?"

"Yeah."

"--Well let me walk with you then. I can come back to my car."

"Suit yourself," she continues walking, not looking behind to see if he is walking to keep up or not.

"I never got the chance to talk about the other day with my aunt."

"It's cool."

"No, I mean, I wanted to ask you, what did she say to you? I didn't hear it."

"Nothing, really. She just talked about my family."

"Yeah?"

"Yeah."

"Uhhh, so there is something I want to ask you." He starts to look fidgety for a boy. He is not shy so this version of John was perplexing to Charity, but also annoying.

"What do you want to say John?"

"What do you think of magic?"

"It is for movies."

"No, I mean real and practical magic."

"I never thought about magic, John."

"You should. You are a pretty big deal."

She stops and looks at John observing his eyes, "What are you talking about? Are you high?"

"No, I am trying to tell you that you are a–a"

"Oh my goddess John–" she starts walking hoping to lose him.

In a different and commanding voice John speaks this time. His voice is slippery, commanding, and no longer timid. It is a different tone, deeper, richer, older, more mature, and full of confidence. "Charity, I don't think you are understanding what I mean and I am to blame. Forgive me."

She snaps around to look at him, "John, what the hell? That shit is not funny."

"No, I am not John, although I am."

"I'm confused."

"I know you must be child. But please, try to keep up. I am here because in less than 30 days your life is going to change for one reason or another. I come to bring you an option you must not refuse.

I can give you the world, Charity. I can make you the ruler over cities, countries–even if you want it. I can make you rich, prosperous, more beautiful, and have the body of your dreams. I can do it all. I have done it all."

"John, you sound like the devil. You cannot promise all those things, and what the hell is wrong with your voice. You are starting to creep me out."

"I am not John. John is a dumb teenager more content with sleeping with every girl in school, and he could never have the knowledge to build something that I am proposing. I am promising you a life of easy living. One where you can be and do whatever you wish. You can command something and it will happen."

"What kind of magic is this?"

"Dark magic."

"You said that quickly."

"Don't you know who you are, Charity? You should believe in dark magic. You were born in it. Do you not know who you are, Charity?"

"Of course, my name is Charity Masfield."

"No, it's not. You are the granddaughter of a grand witch of four generations. A daughter to a grand witch, and a granddaughter of a voodoo priest with three generations of commitment. All of them serve the kingdom."

"What the fuck?"

"Oh, language princess."

"Look, you got me twisted with someone else. There is no way in hell I believe you."

"How could I prove it to you?"

"You can't."

He laughs and says, "I am sure I can."

"Look, I am done with this conversation, John. You need to go find your ride." Charity turns to walk away and has no intentions of turning around.

"I don't think we are," John moves to grab Charity and stop her from leaving. "I am not trying to hurt you, just try to calm down."

As the two are wrestling and tugging in the streets a man comes over seeing the commotion and says, "Hey, back off. You cannot force her to do anything she doesn't want to do. Do you have a problem?"

John looks at the man, his eyes narrowing in on his. The bold voice that was there moments ago, is not as bold, and is not as loud. "Sorry, I ugh. I was just trying to talk to her. I wasn't trying to hurt her. We are friends."

"Do you know this guy?" the man asks Charity plainly.

"Yes, we are friends–but I am ready for him to leave."

"Then get gone. She don't want to talk to you right now." John raises his hands up as he moves on down the road. He walks back to his car. The man turns to her uncertain if she is alright, she still seems a little shook up. "Hey, sorry about that. Some guys can be dicks–sorry, boneheads. You sure you good?"

"I'm a little fucked up. Sorry, just a lot to take in you know?"

"Yeah, I don't have to walk you home, but I can walk with you until you are good."

"Thanks, I would like that."

"So what's your name? My name is Curtis."

"My name's Charity."

"That's a beautiful name. How do you like it?"

"It feels ancient to me. It makes me think of a

box with treasures inside."

"That's interesting. Last night I had a dream where I saw a ton of treasures beneath the surface of water."

"Like what do you mean?"

"I was able to go underwater and see stones, rubies, gold, and it went as far down as I dare look."

"Dang. I pray that it means good fortune for you."

"Me, too! It was a powerful dream that I think changed my life and I am living day by day to see how much."

"That's good."

"What about you?"

"I am gearing up for my 13th birthday party. I think it is going to be a lavish party."

"Yeah?"

"Oh, yeah. My mom is going all out for it. We are doing a time period event of the 1600s. It should be fun."

"That does sound fun. Growing up, we had all kinds of mask parties with my dad's family. My mom wasn't into Mardi Gras or themed parties, but on my dad side they were. She thought they were a bit devilish."

"This party won't be any of that."

"So your mom and your dad are hosting the party?"

"No, my mom is single."

"That's cool."

"Are you single?"

"Yeah, I'm single. But I am not looking for anything."

"Good. My mom isn't either. But maybe you should come and meet her. I have money to give you for helping me."

"No, I would have done that for my daughter if she were in the same situation."

"Well, that guy will be at the party, too. So if things get out of hand, maybe you can help with that."

"I see. So you want me like a bodyguard type?"

"If you want the job. I can pay you."

"That's how you teenagers got it nowadays?"

"Yeah, I get an allowance, and I don't buy

much. So I can pay you."

"Well, alright. Sure, I can be there."

This is the first job Curtis has thought of having where it was offered to him and he didn't have to defend his gaps in employment. Today was turning out to be a powerful day. He didn't have a craving or a pain in his gut like normal. It was strange. Did that water really make him a new creation he wondered. He got the details from the girl for the party and he gave her his number.

Charity carried on home content John wasn't coming back and relieved she had a bodyguard in case whatever that was came back. She made a plan to avoid John at all costs from then on because something was off about him. She couldn't help but wonder what he meant by her mother and grandmother being witches. She never saw weird brooms, candles, or things that make you say dark magic. Surely, he was mistaken and the only one dealing with something was John.

She buried the thought for the time being because to continue to think would kill her lighthearted mood. She wanted to focus on getting good remarks on her upcoming school assignments. She had a ton to do if she wanted to be in the clear to focus on her party details. She felt confident with her dress direction, but she wanted to see the material and be more involved. Her dress needed to be perfect; if it would outshine Rachel's dress, and it had to.

Making the
Perfect Dress

The weekend took long to come, Charity felt. She needed a break and a great escape from her thoughts. School helped a lot, but it wasn't what she wanted to deal with. She wanted to deal with this magic conversation and put it to bed. Who really wants their mother to be a witch anyway? All the ones she could think of were old, unattractive, unless they were sucking a youthful person bone dry.

She's seen enough of the fairytale movies, and her mom doesn't seem like any of them. Her grandmother, on the other hand, was never a nice lady, so she could see that being more possible. But what would their aim be, she thought. What would they want if they already had everything? She thought about how they live, what they have, and how simple their lives are.

She struggles to see the reason to channel the dark world for things. Just get a job and it will work out, she thought. She did consider she might be too simple in her thinking, but what should they expect from a nearly 13-year-old? Pure logic and understanding? She is piecing her consciousness together as she pieces the dress of her dreams to match Zoe's esteemed sales pitch.

Today, the girls were supposed to be picked up by Jezebel, but she was stuck at work sorting out a necklace that lacked the oomph the customer was expecting. She is good at what she does, but some cases just need more. They use their phone to call a driver, and within moments, he arrives. The girls quietly file into the backseat and await the driver to take them to their first destination.

To pull this dress off, they were going to need variety, perfection, high-quality materials, and more than they needed to account for mistakes. The girls were both excited for the assignment. While exiting the car, Charity asks, "So I have something I want to ask you if that's okay?"

"Yeah, of course. You can ask me anything," replies Zoe.

"What do you think of my mom?" The girls are looking at fabric, row by row, searching for what they can find to match the vision of the dress they both have in mind.

"I think your mom is cool. She has her own business. She is very smart. Beautiful," replies Zoe.

"Yeah, I mean–do you see anything else?"

"What do you mean?"

"I mean, you know God, right?"

"Yeah, I think so."

"So do you know the devil, too?"

"Ughh, what do you mean?"

"I mean like, do you know the devil when you see him?"

"I guess. He is not really out there and in your face. It is more like with your thoughts and what you do, I think."

"So, more like a good angel and pitchfork devil trying to help you make decisions?"

"Yeah--to me."

"Do you think he talks?"

"Girl, I don't do scary movies because of that. I ain't got no time for hearing no deep scary voices. That stuff plays out in your dreams."

"Yeah. I think I heard the voice of the devil."

"Really?"

"Yeah."

"What does he sound like?" Zoe asks as she stops looking to hear this. She didn't take Charity for a spiritual person at all. She seemed more black and white and like an agnostic, if anything.

"I can't describe it but to say, confident, deep voice, but it is like the voice is slippery. It's enticing but also filled with like dark power."

"How long you talk to him for? And what did he talk to you about?"

"He was trying to tell me about my family."

"The devil knows about your family?"

"Yeah, at least that's what he said."

"You know the devil is a liar and you cannot believe what he says."

"So you think everything he told me was a lie?"

"Probably. The devil doesn't tell the truth–maybe, unless the truth is a big deception in itself. Maybe. But girl, that sounded so deep, I don't know if that is possible either."

"What did he say anyway?"

"Oh, that my mom, grandma, and dad's family are all witches or voodoo people."

"Really? You believe that?"

"I didn't know what to think."

"I think that sounds crazy. I am sure that was all in your head."

"I pray so." Charity seems bothered and Zoe picks up on it.

"Really, Charity? Your mom? I don't know the others. But your mom is very cool. I wish my mom were like her. She is about your freedom, and she raised you to mind the rules and be a fairly decent kid."

"Fairly decent?" The girls kid around.

"Yeah, when we first met, I thought you were a bit selfish."

"And now?"

"You just have standards for what you want, and you make no apologies for knowing what that is. You cuss sometimes, which could be improved," Zoe kids, "But again, I think you are a good person, and I can learn from you, which says a lot. I feel like everything I think to do, want to do, is scrutinized, and I tend to overthink what I want to do. It's gotta be nice to just breathe and be yourself, and say what you want and mean what you say, you know?"

"Yeah. So do you think John is acting a little weird?"

"No, why?"

"I don't know. We talked the other day, and

he weirded me out a little."

"Yeah, maybe he is sneaking and drinking what his aunt has. She was odd the last time we saw her, too. Not sure what's going on in their family, but they should sort it out."

"Yeah."

"Be careful for what he might try at your party."

"Girl, I was thinking on if I should still have him come or not."

"If he is your friend, he should come. It would be weird for him not to."

"Yeah. I thought that too. So we are stuck with weirdos a little longer. But I did get a body-guard."

"A bodyguard?"

"Yeah, he was a guy I met helping me out the other day."

"Really, from school?"

"No, he is an older man. Got a bit of a dad's bode, but good looking."

"Okay, did you ask your mom?"

"She will be fine, I am sure of it. I got the

money to pay him anyhow."

"Okay, what do you think about this? You've been quiet."

"I am just thinking–"

"Do less thinking and more shopping, please," says Zoe. The girls laugh, and they start looking and commenting on the fabric to gauge what Charity likes. They enjoy each other's company and are excited for the outcome of this dress. As they shop, the driver stays outside, parked, awaiting their next ride request. He is on the phone, talking and getting instructions. He watches the girls like a hawk to be sure they don't drift too far away from his sight.

The girls are oblivious and missing his burning eyes filled with mischief. The girls spent what seemed like an hour in the store searching through fabrics and accessories to accentuate the dress. Just when they thought they were done, Charity says, "What about your dress?"

"Um, I will figure it out."

"I figured you would say that. So I got the dress you liked."

"Charity! Why would you do that?"

"Because I want you to be as stunning as me. I will give it to you so you can embellish it. Just think of what you want to add. Here's a picture of it because I knew that would help!" Zoe smiles, thinking of the friend she has, and she starts looking for ways to make changes to increase the appeal of an already stunning dress.

After another thirty minutes, the girls head to the counter and check out. With bags in their hands, they start walking toward the coffee shop on the corner. They order cappuccinos, and the milk flirts with their lips and noses. They are excited to feel like little adults as they enjoy their cups. Charity asks, "So how are your parents? You haven't talked about them hardly at all."

"Yeah, they are still out of town, likely for a month to go. They keep running into issues with the government to build and do what they plan to do. I know my mom is getting anxious to get back. She hasn't been away from me this long ever."

"That's good. You miss them, too, right?"

"Yeah, of course I love them, but I am not in a hurry for them to come back. I wouldn't be able to do all of this if my brother or parents were home. They would watch my every step. Now, I get freedom and I am liking it."

"Are you being a good girl, Zoe," she says jokingly.

"Of course, for the most part. I am home by curfew and only told a few white lies."

"Is that good?"

"For me, very good. I mean, don't get me wrong, I am not a liar. But I realized my parents can relax a bit, and I won't turn into the devil. Being a goody two-shoes is hard work. I would say it is impossible, so it feels good to do what you can do and just learn. I am not gonna do anything stupid."

"That's good."

"So what time are we heading back? I need to get started."

"Yeah, let me call the ride." Charity reaches for her phone and calls the ride. The ding is almost instant, and her ride is showing as 1 minute away. "Good news, the ride will be here in a minute. Let's walk out because you know they will leave us."

"Yeah," Zoe says as she gathers the bags with Charity to exit the shop. They exit and stand on the curb waiting for their ride. They checked the window to see the driver's face and looked at the plate. Both are good, so they enter the car. They chat in the back about the dress and what Zoe will start with first. As they chat, the car doesn't seem to be going in the right direction, or at least taking a different way Charity is unfamiliar with. She has been in the area a million times, and so has Zoe.

"Hey, where are you going? You missed your turn," replies Zoe.

"I apologize. I am going another way. It's faster."

"Let's stick to the main roads, please. Or I will report this ride and call my mother," says Charity.

"Relax. You will get to where you are going."

He goes through a questionable neighborhood. There are bums and people struggling to walk straight down the street. They are zigzagging, and the girls assume they are either drunk or high on something. The area looks like hell. Those who are fighting inner demons to keep their mind roam the streets like the zombie apocalypse, and the sad part is that they didn't look like they were winning the war.

"Hey, where the hell are we? I want to go where I put on this app," replies Charity.

"Again, this is the way," replies the driver.

The girls don't trust the ride, and they agreed through their eyes that they will jump out at the next light on the corner and take their chances. They weren't sure of his plans, but they didn't seem like they were up to any good. As the girls' hands grip the bags, they each put their hands in position to grab the door closest to them.

The light seemed to come faster than their hearts were beating, and their feet were tapping silently against the carpet. They both felt the stop of the car, and they grabbed the handle to escape the vehicle. The doors are locked from the driver's seat, and he asks.

"What the hell are you doing?"

"We want out now!" says a bold Zoe.

"You cannot get out mid-trip. I am getting you to where you paid to go."

"You can keep it. I am leaving now," replied Charity. The girls start hitting at the windows.

"Look, relax, I will let you out. Just let me get you to a real business. I don't want you to jump out in the middle of the hood."

"The girls look at each other and nod. The warmth of the necklace around Zoe's neck goes hot. She didn't take it off for days, and her brother hadn't recognized it because she wears it under her shirt. If she were looking at it, she would see the colors within the stone swirl around in a colorful dance. As the car continues forward, there is an unexpected accident, a bump toward the front driver's side that stops the driver.

The girls didn't see what happened but imagined he might have hit something or someone. He got out to inspect what he had hit and what damage was done to his car. While he was yelling and cussing, the girls hopped into the front seats and locked themselves inside the car. The guy turns around when he hears the jerk of the locks and says, "Come on, this is my car. Open the door."

"No, we said we wanted to go home. That's where we are going," replies Zoe.

"You can't steal my car! Open the door," he says as he slams against the window.

"The girls are trying to figure out how to put the car in drive and take off, hopefully avoiding a collision. The guy went to the curb to get something, and feeling the pressure and danger, Zoe pulled the shift out of park and into drive. She puts her right foot on the gas as the left hovers over the brake. A loud *screech* noise could be heard throughout the block. The car got enough gas to take them from that spot to the corner in several seconds. They were gone.

"Did we just steal a car?" asks Charity.

"Did we really have a choice? Who knows where that guy was trying to take us? We had no choice."

"But how do we give the car back?"

"I don't know? I guess he can come and pick it up?"

"He knows where I live? You think he will come back to harm us?"

"He would be stupid to. Your mom ain't gonna go for that."

"Yeah, if she is home."

"What can you do?"

"I have to ask for help." She dials a number on her phone. "Hey, you got a moment to help me?" Charity nods as she listens intently to the male voice instructing her. "We can head toward my house."

"You sure?"

"Yes." Zoe uses the little driving skills she learned from her brother and dad to get them closer to Charity's house. The park is less than ideal, but she made it without killing anything, although she got close to swiping a few cars parked on the street. There is a guy who comes to the window and knocks. His knock startles Zoe, and she jumps.

Charity smiles at the handsome man, clearly middle-aged, with a dad bod. He smiles and says, "Hey, ladies. I am here. What do you need?"

"We need to get home. It was a challenge to get us here, and I don't know how much more luck we will have before getting into a real accident. You can bring Zoe home first."

Zoe exits the driver's seat and hops in the back as he goes around from the passenger side. The cap that's on his head blocks his face, and Zoe hasn't gotten a clear look at him, but she is glad she was saved from the driver's seat. She sits quietly in the back and turns to look out the window as she sees the trees and houses pass by. Getting home in one piece was something she learned to breathe through.

She didn't want to think of the plans the wicked man could have had for them. She did think about what they should do with the car. The guy decided to park it at the police station and wipe our prints as he exited the vehicle. The guy was inside filing a report while his car was found outside. He didn't seek to pursue the girls, but he was curious about how his car got there without an accident.

He got into his car and turned the corner. There was a car that pulled up behind him and watched him. Every turn he made for the past ten minutes, the car mirrored staying two cars back. The guy arrived home unaware that anyone had parked across the street from his small home's front door. He enters the door and starts taking off his shoes. Then he realized he had forgotten something in the car. He opened the door to go and retrieve it, and a blunt object hit him in the face.

He falls, stumbling back away from the door. "Woe, woe. What the fuck?"

"What the hell were you thinking?" replies an angry woman.

"I did what you said. I was trying to get them there, and they stole my car and left."

"What are you talking about?"

"Aren't you the lady from the phone?"

"What did she tell you?"

"She told me she would pay me $500 to fol-low these two girls and bring them to an address she sent me."

"What was her name?"

"I don't know." She slaps him again.

"Shit. She didn't give me a name."

"How did she pay you?"

"On a money app."

"Let me see her profile." Jezebel looks at the screen; she knows the face, but she wants to be certain. "What's her phone number?" Without hesitation, he shows her his phone. She knows the number."

"What did she want?"

"I don't know. But she told me to bring them to this address." He shows her the phone as his nose bleeds, and his forehead has a new bruise forming.

"If you follow these girls or do some stupid shit like this again, I will kill you. Do you hear me?"

He shakes his hands as he tries to protect his face from a possible blow. She kicks him and heads out the door. She drove by the location, and it was a run-down building. Full of hooligans and people who didn't want anything good for young girls. She guessed her plan was to gang rape the girls and initiate them into some cultic thing. She knew based on her m.o. She was likely working with her mom. This is too bold for a dumb witch like her with no power for over five decades.

She guessed her mom must be speeding up her plans. Could it be she is dying? That evil hag needs to die. She has never cared about anyone, and now her eyes are set clearly on harming Charity, and likely before her birthday. Jezebel needs her alive, healthy, and submissive. She doesn't want her destroyed and powerless. She needs to be pure until the time of decision.

But this ordeal doesn't have to be bad. This can demonstrate how innocent girls are prey for the powerful, for men. She could use this to create fear of men and further extend Charity's chastity. Her power is locked into her virginity and choice. Even as she decides, if she wants to solidify her power, which Jezebel wants to control, she needs to stay pure. Jezebel now had two of the pieces of the puzzle put together. She knows who this guy is; now she needs to figure out who this bodyguard is.

That necklace has proven very helpful. She knows Zoe will be alone for another month, so if they had to sacrifice someone, she would be an ideal and willing candidate with persuasion. Maybe she could join them and be stronger than the small church she goes to. Jezebel always saw potential in the girl; it's not her fault her parents are bible thumpers.

Back at Rachel's place

The calls coming through to the driver's phone were blocked, and Rachel was frustrated to find that she didn't have any calls to confirm that the girls had made it to the drop-off location. "What the hell happened to them?" She kept saying as she looked for a way to find the girls. She was left with her wondering thoughts. She didn't have a way to contact the driver and considered whether he kept the girls for himself.

She thought if he did, that wouldn't be bad either. Violating the girl for whatever reason doesn't matter to her. It was all a means to an end. Her initiation into a coven wasn't much different. Her mother surrendered her to the hands of ten people who all delivered her a spirit. She was bound for 30 days to battle the thoughts and voices that swirled in her head from the soul ties. She can sense all ten at different times, and she doesn't know where to point the blame.

She started smoking weed after the ordeal, and that seems to keep her memories and demons in check. She cares less, and the pain is more un-recognizable. She thought about hating her mom, but what was she supposed to do to get her power? Her mom didn't know about voodoo. Her magic was limited because Carol took everything for herself and fed us scraps. She gave us enough to make a living, but not enough to thrive or rise to replace her.

This was a chance of a lifetime to get knowl-edge and avenge her bloodline, or at least herself. She wanted the power she was promised and not just the pain. Pain with no power is just suffering. She wanted more. She wanted it all. She lit her blunt as she tapped her leg. She looked at Rachel and asked, "So what do you think?"

"I can call her. If she answers, she is fine. If she doesn't, I can seem concerned or curious about where she is. But I can find out."

Did she want to know? Was she ready to stop celebrating so early? Or had she lost and didn't see it?

She blew out a puff of her blunt and said, "Yeah, call your friend."

"Pawn?"

"The pawn."

The phone rings. Charity sees the phone ringing but debates answering it. Did she feel like dealing with Rachel? No, not really. She let it go to voicemail. Rachel replies to the beep, "Hey, Charity. It's me, Rachel. I wanted to check and see what you were doing today. Not sure if we might want to hang tomorrow? Let me know. Bye."

Her mom watches Rachel's face; the sinister smile brings a bit of dark light to her day. She felt accomplished and thought she had done something, and was unaware of the setup she had lined her life up for. Jezebel guessed she would be glowing from her error. She thought on how to turn the tables against her and banked on her ignorance being her downfall. A simple witch can only see one step ahead. Jezebel was no simple witch; she is the Queen now that she knows her mom is too weak to do anything to stop her.

The only person she is warring for right now for the crown that poses a threat is Charity. Is Charity ready to know what she doesn't know? Should she come clean now or wait until her daughter builds up the stomach so she is not rejected when she finds out, but seen as a mentor for training her in power? Although Jezebel knows much of the knowledge her mom knows, she still doesn't know how to tether spirits and then how to overtake bodies. She needed to know this if she had hope to live forever.

Is this her mom's dream or hers, she would think sometimes. Does she want to live forever or live really well once? If she decided to live and die once, Charity's life was safe, but if that changed, she wanted a body worthy of snatching from purity to knowledge. A body that doesn't know sex is far easier to control than an experienced one who falls in love. She wants Charity to be as she is now.

Everyone thinks they know what they will do when they get an opportunity. But how many, if they are honest, would say what they would do if what they would do is vile? If it is wrong or even evil? Jezebel thought she knew herself, but from day to day, her ambitions change, and so her mind, although strong, is not the most stable.

She loves the little girl, but does she love her enough to sacrifice her life, or what she wants to see her happy? Why must everyone seem to benefit from her efforts? Her being here is a decision she made to complete a pregnancy and provide for Charity with no support or genuine care from anyone.

Charity's father, likely, never wanted her. She was a mistake born from an evil game. Her mother was a wicked witch, only concerned about her own preservation. And her father is a mystery to this day; no one knows. She, too, never met her father, and likely never will. She had to deal with it, so she knew that Charity could too.

One thing Jezebel didn't want to do was to raise an entitled child. She knew it would take work to be the grand at anything. Charity had to know that she was part of the elite her entire life, so she never second-guessed her authority, superiority, or placement. It had to be earned, inherited, but also feel like it belonged to her. She wouldn't be able to deny her throne, if it were hers, if she always saw herself worthy of having it.

Charity is snooty, and Jezebel made sure that she was. She didn't want her to ever feel like a future she could have was ever outside her reach. She wanted Charity to have options, but not follow in her footsteps. She wanted to be better than her mother's errors, but also be seen as a guide who knew best. In a weird way, she wanted Charity to want her heavy influence in her life so it would feel different than her mother's grip around her neck growing up. She had a plan in her head and in her heart, but she just battled with which voice would control her actions.

Rachel's Mom still has questions

There is a ding on the phone for Rachel. She hears it and looks to answer. She lost focus on eating her food and burned her lip, forgetting to blow on it before eating. "Shit," she replies as she drops her fork and touches her lip.

Her mom looks up and says, "What, you forgot how to eat? You knew the shit was hot."

"It's not the food."

"What do you mean you just burnt yourself?"

"Mom, I just got a text from Charity."

"What? So she is where?"

"It seems like she is home, getting ready for school tomorrow. Said she would call me later."

"Shit, let me see what the hell is going on." She puts her fork down and grabs her phone. She sends $500 to the driver with the subject, "Talk?" She awaits a reply and looks at her phone. Soon after, there is a request for $500 more.

"What the fuck? This little bitch wants $500 more to talk?" She looks at Rachel, who has eyes that say, "What you gonna do?" "I don't want to pay this money. This little shit made nearly $1,500 off me, and I don't think he is gonna tell me what I want."

"Don't pay it then," replies Rachel.

"But if I don't pay it, how the hell am I supposed to know what is going on now?"

"Ask Carol, she got power. Sounds like you need a lifeline."

"This isn't a game, Rachel."

"Sorry, Mom," says Rachel, sensing the seriousness in her tone.

"I know things are supposed to be funny, and you kids can't take anything seriously. But this could be the key to us getting back everything. You do see that, right?"

"Yes, sorry. Pay the $500."

"Dang, right. Not because he deserves it, but because we do!" She pays the $500, and the driver's number pops up on the screen.

"Good of you to call me."

"Sorry, it's been a long day."

"Do tell. I paid you some money already to make sure you got the girl where I needed her to be."

"Yeah, well, I had a bit of car trouble.. And there were two girls and not one."

"Yeah, probably her friend. What kind of trouble?"

"I tried to get to the spot, but the girls started freaking out. They threatened to report me. And even tried to jump out of the car!"

"Okay, the girl is tactful."

"No, it was the other girl, Zoe, who had some serious balls. She stole my car!"

"Now, you have to help me understand how two barely teenage girls stole your car and why you weren't driving it!"

"So that's the thing–"

"Here we go."

"No, I was doing the job, and the girls seemed to calm down when I assured them everything was good. But then I hit something."

"You got into an accident?"

"Well, yeah, sort of. I don't know what the hell I hit, to be honest. I thought it was a person because it was a good thud, and it felt like we rolled over something. So, I had to get out to inspect the car and everything."

"Let me guess, and they took off with the car? Who the fuck are you, Sanford and Sons? Slow as fuck."

"Yeah, but I never found out what I hit. There was no dent or nothing in the street. The only person who could have gotten ran over was me, by my own damn car. I banged on the glass and tried to get them to open up. But they told me "no." When I went to get a brick to bash a window out, they took off."

"Where did they go?"

"Hell, I don't know. I wasn't there. They went home, I guess. I went to the station to report the car–"

"Did you tell them about this?"

"No, I kind of left this part of luring girls to some building out."

"Anything else happen?"

"Yes, it did. When I left the station, the cops came to tell me that while I am describing the theft, they found my car. I didn't tell them the girls' names because I wasn't sure of what that meant. I just said some kids took the car when I stepped out to look at a tire I thought felt flat."

"Get to the point."

"Then they came in and told me they found

my car. I was prepared for the worst, but my car was in perfect condition without a scratch. I didn't think the girls could drive, but I guess they could."

"So, where was the car found?"

"At the station."

"So, they steal the car and bring it to the police station? Why the hell would they do that?"

"The cops said it might have been a joyride someone took, and after the ride was over, it is not uncommon for them to bring the car back in near the same condition. He asked if I wanted to press charges or sort it out because they had 'shit to do.'" I said nah, got to the car, even the keys were in it."

"What did you do next? This is like watching a flip book. What do I need to know?"

"I drove home not thinking of anything. Got home, took off my shoes, but I had forgotten my smokes in the car. Just when I opened up the door to get them, I got hit in the face with a rock from my garden."

"Wait, what?"

"Yeah, I guess someone tailed me because they asked about the girls and what I was doing."

"What did you tell them?"

"Only what I could after they beat my ass. I

told them I got paid to drop them off at a different address."

"Did you tell them my name?"

"I don't know your name. I am glad I don't. Keep it that way and don't tell me shit."

"Okay, any way you think this could come back to me?"

"I don't know. I ain't no detective. They beat my ass and told me to stay away. I am doing that. If we good, I gotta go."

"Last question, who beat you up, a man or a woman?"

"If it matters. A woman."

"You let a woman beat your ass?"

"Anybody capable of breaking my nose and having me bleed from my forehead can have you sit down and rethink your life. You good?"

"Yeah," Rachel's mom breathed out, and the puff of smoke she inhaled after the conversation seemed to be the calm she needed. She wondered, who would follow him? Who would get this close, and could it be Jezebel? She thought, "Could Jezebel be bold enough to beat someone's ass, or how could she even know where to find them?"

She was lost in her thoughts, and Rachel

wanted all the details as she impatiently looked on at the silent conversation. Rebecca didn't want her daughter knowing everything, especially not anything that could make it easy for her to slip up when around Charity. Rachel wasn't the best at discretion. She can be an emotional girl who lashes out at the worst times. She kept the findings personal and just said, "I am working on it. Don't worry about it. Just be cool."

She said, "If it were a problem, she knew the drama would be at her doorstep." She assumed that if it were Jezebel who started the fight, she would have been at her door too. She wasn't, so maybe this was a nosy person, or even Carol's doing. Could she have two or three people working on this, and today, they were colliding? She didn't know the answer, but she considered that she might not be the only one working to get what she wants, and Carol could have other allies.

She mumbles under her breath as she eats, "Witches ain't loyal for shit." The girls continue eating in silence as she thinks. Her daughter heads up to her room for some R&R, and Rebecca sits smoking, getting higher and higher. While the crackling noise she hears intently in her ears could be the tip of her blunt, she doubted it. Something or someone was there, watching her. Who?

In a slithering voice, she hears, "Tired of this?"

The Unholy Trinity

"I know your voice is ancient. You gotta be old as fuck," replies a hazed Rebecca.

"You're not as wet behind the ears as some think, then," replies the voice that temps men and women souls.

"Who are you?"

"Someone who can help you."

"I have help," she replies as she taps her ashes.

"From a dying woman, who can't save you."

"She has powers?"

"I am the best one who gave her her powers."

"Shit."

"Carol is not what she seems."

"Are any of us?"

"All is fair in hell and magic," the voice replies.

"What do you want?"

"Shouldn't you tell me what you want?"

"You gonna be my genie?" inquires Rachel's mom.

"I am better than a genie. But like a genie, I want my freedom."

"Carol took that from you?"

"Temporarily. But I got plans on how to get things back. I just could use a faithful witch to nudge things in the right direction."

"Will Carol know about this?"

"When it is too late to change a damn thing."

"So, you can make me grand witch, money, status, and power?"

"At a cost, but yes. That stuff is easy."

"What do you want?"

"To make Carol and her entire family pay," he says with grit in his voice, and fierceness that lets Rebecca know this man is serious. He's not the devil, but he is related to him. She breathes in and tries to remain calm.

"I take it you two aren't close?" she asks.

"Carol took my life, and I am gonna take hers and everything that came from her."

"Sounds like love scorned? I know a bleeding heart when I see one."

"No, that's another man's story. You know nothing of the pain I feel, the anger, and bitterness."

"Try me."

Diablo and Carol

There was an old brown house that didn't seem welcoming at all on the outside. Anyone who wanted to enjoy love and life would stand clear of the home. Even the birds didn't fly above it or land on the awkward trees that were scattered around the grounds. This country town left little to do but to spend time with your family, and Carol grew up with such a life.

Carol was always a curious little girl wanting to understand the gifts of her mother and grand-mother. She was an old soul even at birth, although she didn't quite know why. She was born into a family of witches, and her mom and grandmother made sure to show her everything they knew and made her learn it.

She, too, didn't have a choice on who she would become; it was already decided she would become a witch. Her grandmother was a mean old lady who would pop her for touching her knick-knacks or sitting on her couch with dirty fingers. Digi is what everyone called her. She had a terrible history of burying husbands. As a brute, strong woman, she managed all of her life on her own and hardly called on any family, if there were such a thing. She was a loner, and her female best friend, an appealing young woman, seemed to be all she confided in.

After having her daughter, Effie, she stopped having husbands and spent her remaining years alone with her best friend. It was uncertain of what kind of affection she had for the woman, although there was gossip in town that suggested otherwise. The two women happily raised Effie, and it wasn't until there was a freak accident and Digi's female friend met an untimely demise by slipping and landing at the bottom of the stairs.

Death seemed to follow Digi, so many would stay clear of her house and all that belonged to her. Effie was a loner, likewise, and under constant surveillance of her mother. The two of them were close, and anything that could be taught or done, she gave Effie. She was seen as a prize because Digi knew all that she would have hoped to become would be carried on by her.

She wasn't big on dressing; she wore more

manly clothes if you asked her neighbors. She wore pants, which were outrageous for her time period. She was brazen and seemed to be led by her own opinions. You had to be desperate to come by her farm and ask her for anything. Sorry, saps who found that their spouses were cheating on them would come and visit her after swallowing their fears.

She started a business that was not about love but heartbreak. Perhaps this doomed Effie to see love as something to ward off and ignore. She didn't have a traditional upbringing filled with love and affection, though she had attention. Her heart was more tender than her mom's, and she could only blame that side on her father. As Effie grew older, she loved plants, grass, trees, and things that made the land more beautiful.

Digi was a neat freak on the inside of her home and knew every speck of space. It was hard for Effie to get something from her. Seeing the loneliness in the eyes of Effie, she knew she had to give her something to love because the strongest magic is birthed for something had and then lost. When you are robbed or disenchanted the energy can be redirected and that's what Digi needed. So she appealed to Effie's desire and spruced up the landscaping for the outside of the home.

Love for a man was not something Digi could build in her, so she gave her the love of things and money. Repeatedly, she enforced the power, the glory of having wealth and the means to live how you desire. She ingrained in Effie that life wasn't worth living if you couldn't control your own destiny. Nothing should be off limits for you to have your freedom.

The death benefits from her three husbands did afford her the freedom to dress and be different. Some thought the men were bewitched who had fallen in love with her, but none questioned it. Many were drawn by it. There were unsightly marriages in the town that many gossiped were her doing. She never smiled, and her home was just as cold as her mood.

Inside was dark, cold, but clean as a pin. Digi could have been a vampire with how much she chose to stay indoors and in the dark. She always said keeping the room cool allowed spirits to breathe. Effie didn't know anything about ghosts, what she called them, before she learned they were demons and pawns for her bidding. Her grandmother saw herself as a sea witch who had demons pulling her dreams, plans, and body to where she wanted to be. Since Carol could remember, her family had some degree of affluence.

At a time when she couldn't remember, there was a brief time when her family was threatened to lose it all. There was a merchant, new and unfamiliar with the land. He thought of uprooting the seemingly small family of two. Her estate was large and more could be done with it, he judged. She had power, but he had money.

The battle ensued with an accusation that her

land ownership was improperly filed and was being contested. She laughed at the note, but after going to court and speaking her peace, she was baffled by how they sided with the wealthy banker. She was now fighting to regain control of her estate by needing the money to legitimize her land.

This crisis couldn't have been better planned; it served the point that Effie needed to see and experience to believe in the necessity for power and magic. The ladies were forced to eat bread and live like peasants, something altogether unfamiliar to them. Digi came up with a scheme and devised a plan, using the siren's call to woo not just men to fall artificially in love with her, but to bring powerful men to the feet of the sea monster. The monster was good at swallowing men whole.

He fed off fear, false bravery, or brazen pride. Nothing seemed to feed it more than the pride of men. Bringing the banker to his knees through a curse was the entrance into a long, dark history of using magic to build status and not just wealth. The monster told her not only how to humble the banker, but how to reposition herself in society to rule as a queen.

Having money is a good reflection of how well you've learned to leverage the magical arts a witch possesses, Effie believed, and she shared that with her daughter, Carol. She also told Carol growing up, "Nothing is worse than a broke witch, except a broke bitch. If you are gonna be called a bitch, get the money and live how you want to. People will have something to say always–the quicker you get to saying, fuck em', the better."

Death was the only reason why the duo was broken up. Everything Effie ever did was based on the advancement of power. Love was never part of the equation. She married one man, and after he died spontaneously, she never remarried either. Digi made sure to give Effie the means to use dark magic to get what she wanted. What they both wanted was to be immortal, to live forever in the essence or presence of their bloodline.

The monster was teaching Digi all kinds of things, but she never learned how to possess another soul or to shift consciousness. It wasn't until Effie that the bloodline learned how to shift consciousness from themselves to another. One dark night, she channeled and positioned the demon to reconnect her to her long-lost mother. It was a deadly spell that nearly cost her life, but she survived.

When she arose, she had the consciousness of her mother. Spells she never could learn to repeat, she now had pristine vision to recreate. She could feel the power in her blood deeper than she had ever felt it. She was drunk on power, but knew the power would come to an end with age, as it did with her mother. She vowed to find a way to keep the family together, and Carol was the key to this unholy trinity.

Carol's grandmother would cuss like a sailor, and it always made her uneasy as a little girl. Her mother, Effie, was more gentle, but she too was not loving but distant. She treated her like a puppy she had compassion for, fed her, gave her a bed, but she never told her she loved her or gave her hugs that lasted more than a few seconds. Carol, like her mother and grandmother before her, was regarded in society as a woman of power, although she didn't have the beauty of other women.

Her match was also political and based on power. She was of a ripe young age when she first married a man she had no love for. He was an older man with a fetish for younger girls. Effie knew he had possessive intentions and a perverted mind, but that didn't mean much. She had a plan for dealing with him, as was a family custom. Carol only had to survive a few years, and she would be free, she thought.

She waited for the two to conceive a child. It took years, but the two never did. She saw the lack of compassion on Carol's face and was moved to do something about it out of vengeance rather than love. She saw from Carol's eyes the horror the man was capable of, and so she sent monitoring spirits to follow him and search for his weaknesses. After learning them, she put her plan in motion to ruin him publicly, so no one would care about him but welcome his untimely demise.

When he died six months later, no one blinked or hardly attended his funeral. He was a broken man with a broken name, and taking his wealth was like stealing candy from a baby. With husband number two, he was more kind. He had notoriety in town, and people did love him. He had a gentleness about him that attracted something within Carol she knew nothing about.

He was kind to her, patient, and seemed to do things without her asking. He wanted to tend to her himself. He would cook her dinners and light up their bedroom with candles on special occasions. She hardly smiled, but he found a way to make that happen more often.

His notes would make a bad day for her seem like a non-issue. He didn't care if she worked, and she started to work less. Her mother would call her, trying to get her attention, but she became more distracted by him. She didn't care what was happening around her; the two of them could get lost in each other's eyes, smiles, and laughs.

She often thought, "Is this what love is supposed to feel like?" Her mother, sensing the distance between her and her daughter, channeled her consciousness to experience life as she does, and she was appalled. She was jealous. How could she turn her back on family and purpose, to be laid up all day in bed staring at a man? She didn't see her as faithful or virtuous.

It was on this account that she vowed to separate this union and not allow anything to come of it. Carol, although young, knew her vision was surveilled, thought of a plan to protect him. David didn't deserve to die, and she knew it. She tried to be cruel to him, thinking he would pull back from her, but he only became more patient. He never raised his voice to her or his hand.

She would get angry and unyielding, and still, he would be there to give her a bath, to brush her hair, and to love her. She couldn't find a way to separate herself from him because he wouldn't let her. She planned to run away with him, to live how she wanted and deserved. Wasn't freedom the point of all this?

She began to think and was compelled to live for herself. Why should she give them what they want and suffer to live under their restrictions? This was her life, she started to say within her heart.

She soon discovered life wasn't as simple as it appeared. The day was dark and cold, and the sun cracked through the window. She awoke to look at her loving husband, who seemed to sleep like an immortal angel, glowing. He was always a marvel to look at, and she would do it often. Today, though, she reached out to touch his face.

Her hands touched death that day, and it cut deeper than it ever would. He was cold to her touch. His skin still moved, but she knew the early signs of death, and she hated herself for ever involving herself with a cursed family. If she only knew him better, she would have tried to save him before any-thing happened between the two of them. But it was too late. She cried that day like she never cried and would never cry again.

Losing her first love broke something she never knew could be, her spirit. She no longer saw people as people but as a means to an end. She switched her thoughts for the points of her mother. She threw herself into every form of magic; anything new she could hear about, she made it a point to discover. As Effie grew older, she reinforced, "Don't fail us. We gave you all we have; it is your turn to give us what all you have. No one is greater than the other."

These were the last words her mother spoke to her before she passed. She handed Carol an expensive gift and told her not to part with it. "At the time you obtain the knowledge we need for immortality, use the blood to bring us together." She understood the assignment. For weeks, she searched for such a power.

One night, she went to a dark alley on the streets of Mardi Gras. She had heard there was a guy there who knew magic better than anyone in her small town. She had to venture out and dig deep to find him, but she did. He was a well-groomed man who appeared to be in his early forties by appearance. Although time and communication would prove that he is much older.

The two greeted each other in a low-lit alley by him extending his hand from behind a cloak that draped over his shoulders. He wore a well-tailored suit, clean shoes, a cane for decoration, it appeared, and a top hat. His words were like strange fire, warm but eerie to the ears. He was electric, but was it attraction or power? As she touched his hand, she could feel the surge between the two of them.

He leaned down to kiss her hand and said,

"My beauty. What brings you down such a dark alley?"

"I'm looking for something."

"Something? Or someone?"

"Could be both," Carol replied.

"Would you indulge me with a drink?"

"I have some time," she replies with dreamy eyes.

Nothing is more fresh, sweet, than a woman who has been in love. Fresh from her relationship, she still had the glow of being in love. Or was it pregnancy residue? She didn't chart because she was irregular. She didn't imagine she was pregnant or would be, and didn't know it. But Diablo sensed it right away. She was with child, and he wanted it.

He put her arm around his and they walked down the alley into the lights. There was a light on in a dark home across the street where he walked toward. She didn't anticipate going to his home that night, but she couldn't turn back now.

With each step she took, she could hear a pounding in her belly, but what was it? She continued on, and she entered his home, and the room instantly felt cold. It was like a freezer —so cold you could see frost.

He brought her to a table and told her to sit.

She did as he told her, but her eyes never left him. She was captured by him, but she attempted to be cautious. There was something about him that made her uneasy.

Was it his power or seemingly affluence by the size and decor of his home that attracted her, she was unsure. She contemplated on if she was out of her league, but pushed it aside as he spoke. He took off his hat and set it down, and almost instantly, there was an appearance of a servant who grabbed his cane and other objects he had already removed before sitting down.

He didn't raise his voice; he whispered to them, and they instantly went away without a word or a sound. It would appear they floated away based on how light-footed they were. His eyes were mysterious; no light could be found in them. They glistened slightly from the moisture present in his eyes. His eyes were so dark, they looked black now that she could see him in the light.

"Tell me, Carol, what is it you desire?"

"What everyone wants. Freedom, power, presence."

"And?"

"Is there more?"

"There is always more, Carol."

"Do tell me something I don't know."

"Freedom, power, and presence come at a price. Nothing that lasts forever skips this test. It takes blood, and at times sweat, tears."

"I am familiar with loss," she replies.

"Are you?"

"Do you think you are the only one who has ever lost someone, Carol?"

She didn't speak immediately, but she thought, *how could he be in my head to know my past without me speaking it?*" She doesn't break her confidence by exposing her concern with her body language but remains affixed, calm, and collected as she replies. "No, loss is a part of life, and it comes with it. I am indifferent to loss and death."

"That is a virtue. To not overthink life and not to be so concerned with death. I do know what you really want, Carol. Or should I say, Effie and Digi."

She couldn't hold her peace; her face shifted to puzzlement as she replied, "Who are you?"

"The friend you want to make. The question is, do you have something that I want, because I know something you want? Immortality."

"And?"

"I want a worthy heir to rid myself of this body and have a more becoming one. I am not bad off, but I could be better, younger, stronger, faster. Do you catch my drift?"

"Sorry, I don't."

"I want to switch my existence for the one you carry. I was never able to have children."

"Sorry, you are mistaken. I am not pregnant."

"–But you are. And the baby grows strong within your belly. Give me your baby, and I will give you eternal life."

Her emotions are rattled. She thought, "I am pregnant? But how? How did we miss it, not feel it, or not show it?" She is searching for her thoughts and feelings and is uncertain of her response.

"Did you not just speak so confidently on not regarding death? Why do you hesitate now? Surely, a baby is not more important to you than your deepest desire? Your mothers or grandmothers? Don't all three flow in your vessel?"

"What do you mean, take my baby?"

"I mean, when the baby is born, his body and essence will be mine. He will become me, and I will become he. You will raise me and watch over me until I am old enough to fend for myself. I will teach you everything I know, and you will be free to go."

"Free to go?"

"Many who make deals with me can never be free or rid of me. But this is a bargain I am given that does not come often. It would be wise for you to take it," his lips slither out.

"What will I have in return?" The baby she feels flutter inside her womb for the first time. Her heart attempts to warm.

"I will give you what no baby or man could ever do. I will give you unthinkable power, presence, money, and yes, you can manage to never grow old. Now, does this sound like the deal of the century?"

"Or a deal with the devil," she remarks.

"What difference does it make? Do you want it or don't you?" he hisses.

The room grows hot, and within her womb she feels the flutters, and she can't help but think what life David's son would have with her? She never deserved him, and surely she didn't deserve to birth anything like him.

"Answer me. I will not ask again, Carol. Do you want all you have ever dreamed about, or don't you?" he says to break Carol's train of thought. "Do you want a graveling baby, calling your name, stealing your time, energy, beauty? Or do you want to be free to live life how you want to? To get what you have always deserved, freedom?"

She hesitates to answer, only staring into his black eyes.

"I can give you what you want, Carol. All I need is a baby you don't deserve. You don't want. And you don't need. Death is trivial. He won't miss it, and neither will you. David is gone. Let dead bones lie where they are. What will it be, or you will need to leave now because I am busy?"

"Alright, I will do it." In that moment, the baby stops moving, and she wonders if it could have died. She is handed a cup to drink by a figure who again felt like they walked in and skipped using the doorway.

"Don't worry, from here on out, drink it. I will be part of you, and you are part of me. Come with me." The two of them rise from the table and enter a dark room that only has lit candles to give light. There is a star on the ground, and at the center a circle. He tells Carol, "Go and sit within the circle." His voice was commanding and deeper than before. This room seems to be heavier on her shoulders. The magic in this room was deeper, richer, stronger than she had ever experienced.

With each step she took, the weight of her feet became like weights growing in pounds with every inch. She nearly had to drag herself to the center as she plopped down. Instantly, the room went aglow with a blue light that seemed to be welcomed through windows she had no idea were there, or if they were there. The man began to chant ancient words that rippled through the room.

The words were clear and distinct, and she memorized them. She watched his face, his body,

328

and she tried her best to absorb all she could. Then it hit her, it was a pain deep within her belly that nothing could describe. She gasped as the wind was knocked out of her. The deeper the pain she felt, the faster his eyelids seemed to flutter, revealing all white eyes. Was he here or somewhere else?

He spoke again, but this time with a voice unlike what she heard in the alley; it was deep and applied pressure to her body, pressing her down as he spoke, "Carol, you are no longer your own. You belong to me. By giving yourself to me and sacrificing your son to become one with me, I will command your every move. You will do nothing apart from me."

"Wait, that is not what you said," she replied

"A deal is a deal."

"I never agreed."

"But you did. I am Diablo, and I deal only in lies. You gave yourself willingly, and there is no redemption for you. Your soul is damned, and you will be with me always. We are now tethered together and will always be to your dying day."

She felt bamboozled as she lay there on the floor, but she was not convinced she would always be owned by anyone. She told him she wanted freedom, and this was the exact opposite. He lied, cheated her, and stole the only good thing that could have come from her. She was furious, and this fire is what the baby could feed off of and would push her to birth and raise a son she utterly hated.

She never coddled him, told him she loved him, or otherwise recognized him. He bore the appearance of her late love, but he was nothing like him. He was cruel, mean, and violent. He was never patient and demanded what he wanted from a young age. Her powers increased as she carried him, and more power surged in her bones, but she was suppressed, controlled. She knew the baby, the son, was the key to her transformation.

She had money, power, and presence by inheriting all she had to be reduced to a glorified nanny of a bugger child spoiled beyond reproach. She loathed his cries, and she hated having to wait on him hand and foot. If only she knew how to do what she must. She remembered the vessel her mother gave her long ago.

She told her that when the time came for her to use it, she would know what to do. Could now be the time? Should she risk it? What if her timing is too early? After several years of dealing with a growing boy who didn't seem like he would ever give her relief. The money lost its savor with her freedom suspended for nearly another fifteen years. She didn't want to do it, and now she realized her word meant nothing, and she, too, could lie if he could.

All is fair for freedom and power. I will do what I want, and what I want is what I will have, she professed. She drank the blood contained in the vessel, and her eyes were reopened. Her blood rushed faster, her body seemed lighter. She knew more, could feel more, and was hungry to do more.

She started to hear voices that were nearly silent, but they grew in volume as the days passed. She had motor skills that had memories she knew nothing about. Her mind could think of spells she had not learned. She started to test spells, read up on magic, and channel spirits she never knew.

Then it happened. She heard the voices that rang in her ears as a child. She heard her grand-mother's voice after nearly twenty years of her being under the ground. Her mother, six years departed, spoke again, and they both replied, "Good job, daughter. We are nearly there."

Carol replies, "Near what?"

"Near immortality, Carol," replies Digi.

"You are making our dreams come true. With each age we have advanced, and soon you will be able to bring us all back," replies Effie.

"How are you certain that I can?"

"The child, you need to combine his blood with ours. He needs to be part of us," replied Digi.

"And then what?"

"You need to drain some of his blood and drink it, then mix our blood with his blood. We will extract everything he knows. We will take our power back and get what we want."

Carol heard the instructions and knew what to do. She had to find a convenient way to get the blood where it would not be obvious. He was young but no fool. He had the consciousness of Diablo, and she knew he would sense her. The accident had to be child-related, something unavoidable. She was determined to teach him to ride a bike.

As she put him on the seat, he asked, "So is this really safe?"

"As safe as any kid would have," replied Carol.

"Shouldn't I have a helmet?"

"We are not on a motorbike. Relax and stop being a wuss," she replied.

The kid grinned and gritted his teeth. He was plotting against her, same as she was plotting for him. They both didn't trust each other, and what they didn't know was what kept them working in tandem. As she helped him to paddle, he started to learn quickly. She suggested removing the training wheels since he clearly had some recollection of biking from his previous life.

The kid agreed, "I told you, I could do this. I guess your wish for me to fail will come to an unhappy end. I am better than you, Carol, even as a child."

"You little, shit. You think you know everything, don't you?"

"It's hard not to when I am nearly 125 years old. Don't let the body fool you. I knew what you hoped to learn for decades before meeting you. I never wanted to be born this young; this is a first. Maybe I will empower you to be my forever nanny, maybe my wife?" He says as he laughs while riding the bike. He is doing great as he goes down the street. Up to this point, Carol's powers were controlled by the boy. He had a hold on her that only worked one way.

But with her mothers pumping in her veins, she knew how to summon spirits that were long-time friends of her grandmother. As the boy approached the road, his brakes didn't work, and he kept rolling. Carol, seeing the struggle the boy was having to break, called out to him, "Danny? Put your foot back!" She tried to sound concerned, but she was suppressing her smile as she saw the boy roll into the street.

As he looked up and to his left, there was a truck that couldn't stop soon enough. The little boy's body was hit and thrown across the street. She reached her hand into her pocket and sliced it on the blade she had put there in case the occasion arose. She ran to him with blood running down her right hand. He lay in the street bleeding from his head and other wounds around his body. As she kneels down at his side, she speaks to him as her hands move to capture the blood she needs.

She places the precut hand against the open wound on his leg and then to his forehead. As the little boy in him cries in pain, his pain dulls the consciousness of the old spirit that dwells within. There are onlookers who call for a paramedic, and as the siren swirls in the background, she puts the vile back in her pocket and travels with the boy to the hospital.

Seeing the little squirt come out of the ambulance on a stretcher was gratifying to Carol. She couldn't stand the smartalic shit he had become. She watched him be whisked off and couldn't wait to tap into the thoughts eagerly waiting to speak. She watched the young boy who had been given a sedative to calm his nerves and keep him from moving to aggravate his injuries, resting.

For a moment, she saw the man she fell in love with once. The boy didn't have the vile face of her newly formed enemy. He wasn't cursing at her or trying to find ways to harm her; he was just sleeping. He looked like the man she found dead when she awoke some six years ago. She was hurt in a new way because this boy represented the life she should have been able to live. Still, she is chasing the dreams of her mom and grandmother. When will she have the freedom to do what she wants?

"Girls, we did it. We are in. Carol, good job. When he wakes, he won't know what hit him," replies Digi. The three laugh as they relish in the thought of getting even with the one who had taken advantage of them. Carol had to think, now that she had everything she needed, why should she not get all that she wanted? What would make her want to bring back the two women who only meant suffocation for her? Her grandmother was a grumpy hag, and her mom killed the love of her life.

If anyone would live for eternity, it should be her. She determined then that she would not bring them back but use what she could to preserve herself for eternity. Her legacy would continue from her and go on because of her. She would absorb all of their powers into her, and she would rule alone with the resources of Diablo to reinvent herself according to her wishes.

He made promises she had every intention of him honoring, even if he never did. There will be only one queen, and that queen will be her. She never spoke her thoughts nor wrote them down.

She did, however, write down everything her mothers whispered and spoke. As the boy gained consciousness, the women worked to search his thoughts and relinquish that power to Carol. They told her secrets, spells, connections, and all that she needed to become him and even more. She had it all, and she wanted to keep it.

When the time came, she didn't hesitate to silence the voice of the boy, drain all of his powers into her, and place him in the same state she stood some six years ago. He was the first soul she absorbed to gain more power, but would not be the last. This was one of the tricks she learned from Diablo. After absorbing the boy's power, she learned even more. All the essence of him was now flowing through her veins.

It is with that power that her mothers thought their return was imminent. They grew with excitement and started to lose their patience. The book of knowledge she began to compile became more valuable as she planned to sever her ties with all three voices in her head, which seemed to war with her own mind. She wanted to be free; it was always about her freedom.

Her final spell was two-fold; it took her a year to learn and master, but she did it. She transferred her consciousness and swapped bodies with an unknown woman of a different bloodline. She was a woman who had come to her town, lost, and in need of help. She befriended the quiet girl and drugged her. As she dragged the unknowing girl to the circle, she was able to switch, but something was different. She didn't hear the voices anymore. She was more beautiful than any of the women before her.

This woman reminded her of a life she wanted and thought she would have. She was calm, and her eyes were sweet and trusting. She felt that with her body, she could gain more power, influence, and rise to the top. Beauty doesn't account for everything, but it will get you far. She needed more than she had, and she needed a body that was nothing like her own, but what she felt David would have deserved.

But there was still a voice she could not shake that spoke to her in the night. As she went to sleep, she heard it, and it felt like a rushing wind. It was bright like lightning and powerful. It said to her in a voice like thunder, "Carol. You do not know me, but you will learn me. The woman you have stolen from me, you will surely pay for. This is the day you have become my enemy, and I will not stop until I utterly destroy you."

The voice dripped with fear, keeping her up for hours. Who was the voice, and why did she hear it? Was it her mothers who put him up to this? Was it Diablo? She questioned the voice she could never forget. No matter how many years passed, no matter what spell she did, she could not forget it. She grew to understand that the voice was not of darkness, or she would have identified him; this voice had to be of the light. She thought, "What kind of power is this?"

To be continued…

About the Author

"God blesses those who work for peace, for they will be called the children of Yah (God)." Matthew 5:9

Dr. Lee has authored over fifty-one books across more than twelve genres: adult, children, youth fiction, self-help, spiritual growth, novels, business, empowerment, etc. to help people in their most profound times of need.

She is also passionate about coaching programs and web courses she created for WAE (Write Anything Easily) Process, Embrace Your Crown, Turn Key Solution for Small and New Businesses, Transform Go Beyond Change (Personal Development), and The Lesson for youth and teenagers.

She is a proud mother and wife.

Connect and Shop my books:

AuthorKLee.com

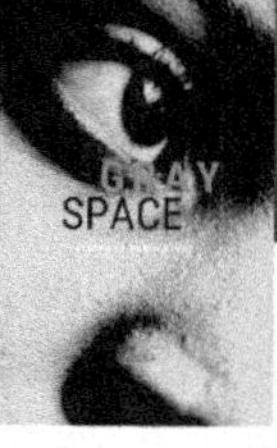

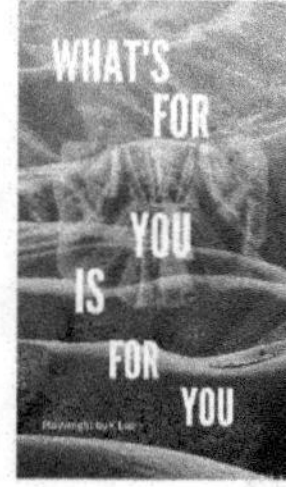

AuthorKLee.com Creator of *WAE Proce*

Explore over seven different book genres, and find something suitable for every member of the family.

Explore and learn more about published authors affiliated with KLE.

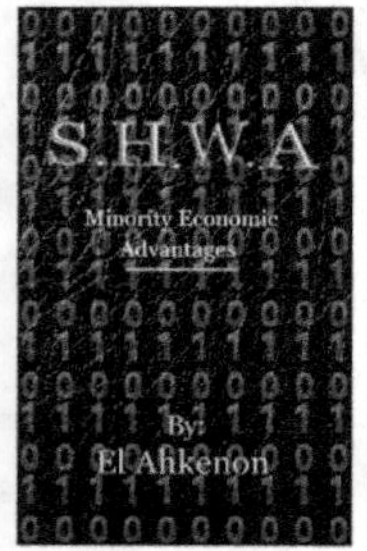

KLEPub.com

SCAN ME

Call or Text:
770-240-0089 Press Extension 1
Web: KLEpub.com
Email Services@klepub.com

It's time to start and finish   **YOUR Story!**

KLE Publishing specializes in helping people become authors. In as little as 15 to 90 days, we can help you develop your books and e-books and publish to 39,000 outlets! We also offer audiobook services.

Write, Edit, Format, Publish
We can help from
Start to Finish.

9 798899 879074